THE CEMETERY

Wyoming Clark

ISBN: 0615989004
ISBN 13: 9780615989006
Library of Congress Control Number: 2014905029
Wyoming Clark, Westmont, IL

It was a dark and foggy night as I drove north on Highway 101 toward Mapletown.

Mapletown was a small, quaint town, with a square in the middle of Main Street at Maple Drive where residents strolled on warm weather evenings. Everybody seemed to know everybody, and everything was within walking distance: Maggie's Diner, the town cinema, a barbershop, and the town doctor.

As I got closer, my mind was busy thinking about what lay ahead: the funeral arrangements for Aunt Millie. She had lived all her life in Mapletown; she never married and had no close kin but me.

Memories of my childhood raced through my mind. I used to visit on spring break every year. I had foggy memories of a man who called on Aunt Millie. Who was he? Why did she never marry him? What was his name? Oh well…I had too much to do to be thinking about the past.

The town looked ghostly, shrouded in dense fog; the old Victorian houses on Main Street were unwelcoming. I felt as if I was entering a terrifying nightmare; the idea made me shudder.

Everything looked surreal: the streetlights, the deserted streets, even the neon sign at the "as station" looked ominous with the *g* burned out. It felt like a warning, telling me to go back. I was very apprehensive.

With no idea where to start, I thought I should contact Aunt Millie's attorney first—a Mr. Angelloni. Or should I go make the necessary arrangements at the Smith Funeral Parlor? There was nothing to do at that moment, though; it was almost midnight—and I was tired and uneasy as I anticipated the next few days.

I would go straight to bed on my arrival at Aunt Millie's.

~

I got up early and went for breakfast at Maggie's Diner. Everything at the diner was the same as when I used to visit—except that Maggie had died a couple of years before and her son was now running the diner. I wasn't hungry; black coffee was good enough while I tried to straighten my thoughts. But they were far away. When I looked outside the diner's window, it seemed as if I had gone back in time.

In fact, nothing had changed at all in Mapletown. Traffic lights still hung on heavy electric cables. The large Victorian houses still gave a feeling of affluence and charm to the small town—except that last night, when I arrived, the moonlit shadows had made the houses look grotesque and cold. What was the population here? *Whatever it was, deduct one now—my aunt Millie.*

~

After leaving Maggie's Diner, I went to the funeral home to make the arrangements, then came back to Aunt Millie's house and started to take inventory of her possessions.

The place was heavy with a musty odor—same furniture, same drapes, area rugs completely worn to bare threads. I was also a perfect fit for the town: my clothes were rumpled and disheveled, my hair long and unkempt; I had no concern about my appearance.

As I went through an old armoire, I found some old newspaper clippings that, to my surprise, gave me the answer to why Aunt Millie had never married her suitor: he had been murdered in Chicago. He had worked for the notorious Ciprianno family in Chicago, the news clippings said; he was a gangster and had been murdered execution-style. Since his family lived in Mapletown, he was buried at Mapletown's old cemetery, where Aunt Millie would be laid to rest.

As I continued to go through her papers, my eyes caught something stashed at the bottom of one of the drawers. It looked like a map—an old map—marking a spot with the well known X.

Intrigued, I carefully studied the map. But unable to make sense of it, I set it aside and continued with my boring chore of sorting out journals, newspaper clippings, photographs, documents, letters, and all the things left behind when someone passes away.

I had to take a break from being absorbed in my thoughts—going for a breath of fresh air sounded good. I was the kind of guy who internalized feelings and thoughts and on the outside appeared cool, distant, collected, and with nothing to lose except time. The cool fresh air felt good and it started to clear my head suddenly it hit me! *The mysterious map was of Mapletown! Oh, yes! My gut feeling, that old gut feeling that had never been right before, now was telling me it was MAPLETOWN! Had nothing to lose...*

Mapletown? Why did Aunt Millie have an old map from the small town she had lived in all her life, had she? With an X marking the spot?

2

Mildred Ciprianno Wilmot was my aunt's legal name, according to the birth certificate I found. I had always known her as Mildred C. Wilmot—well! But I wasn't looking for her birth certificate; I was searching for the map, which I seemed to have misplaced. Where had I put it? Papers, papers everywhere! What do you do with such garbage?

I was getting more and more frustrated by the minute. *Keep calm*, I reminded myself; I had run out of pills for ASD; Acute Stress Disorder why we were so enamored with acronyms? I thought about torching the place and, like most twisted minds, make it look like an accident, cash the property insurance, and presto!—no more problems. But what about the map? The old hag had something valuable hidden somewhere; I was mad at her for leaving this mess Unexpectedly, I had made the connection with her middle name and the infamous Ciprianno family. Could that be possible?

The infamous Ciprianno family business ranged from racketeering, prostitution, and trafficking to murder; the family was the encyclopedia of crimes—and I was one of them? That explained the sinister emotions of cruelty I'd had to wrestle with during my youth, my weekly visits to the shrink forced by my mother, spending time in detention at the principal's office.

That must be where the compulsive gambling came from. My mind raced as memories engulfed me.

I felt ashamed of the things I had done.

When the old clock chimed midnight, I decided to call it a night and go to bed. I fell asleep thinking about the wake set for the following day—how eerie—and my sleep was visited by nightmares of my past that I had been so desperately trying to bury.

~

I woke up when I heard whispering voices. I was drenched in sweat; the settling noises of the old house seemed sinister and foreboding.

The Ciprianno family came to mind, as I was getting ready for the day's activities.

The evil associated with that name—now I understood why my aunt never used that part of her name. All my life, I'd felt an evil presence lurking inside me, voices within telling me there was no escape.

Putting my thoughts aside now, I hurried to the funeral parlor to check that everything was as Aunt Millie had specified—as if it mattered; I just wanted to get it over with.

"The viewing is set for five o'clock," Mr. Smith informed me coldly.

"What kind of viewing?" I foolishly asked.

"A closed casket."

"Oh?"

"You see, it was impossible to work with the remains after the terrible accident that poor woman suffered," Mr. Smith said, clearly showing his uneasiness.

"I thought she died a natural death," I said hesitantly.

He offered his sympathies…again.

"Where can I get a copy of her death certificate?" I asked.

He suggested that I see Mr. Angelloni, my aunt's attorney.

When I called Mr. Angelloni to make an appointment, a recorded voice announced, "The office is closed, please leave your name, and telephone number." I determined to walk to his office, only five blocks away. I had a headache—it felt like a freight train was going through my head. However, now I needed to know what had happened to Aunt Millie. Was Angelloni's secretary the one who had called me to give me the bad news about my auntie?

As I walked to Mr. Angelloni's office, I noticed that the leaves were turning; autumn was almost here.

I remembered most of the town residents and their homes, but I just couldn't remember a Mr. Angelloni. I wondered what had happened to my aunt's old attorney, Mr. Steinberg.

~

My mind was spinning. I'd decided to go to the police station, since Mr. Angelloni's office was closed, to get a copy of the "terrible accident" report. It was still in the same old building; it hadn't changed at all. As I walked inside, a heavy stench of sweat and cigarettes greeted me.

"Can I help you?" asked a voice through a speakerphone.

"Yes, I need an accident report," I said.

"Just a moment, please."

A burly albino man opened a door and guided me to a waiting room.

"I am Sergeant Miller. What can I do for you?" he asked formally.

"I need an accident report for Mildred C. Wilmot," I answered.

"Who are you?" he asked.

"I am Sam W. Stone."

"No, are you related to the victim?"

"She was my aunt," I replied.

"Do you have an ID?"

I glanced at my watch, a gift from Aunt Millie the last time I was in Mapletown, fifteen years ago. The visitation at the funeral parlor was about to start.

"Who notified you?" the policeman asked as he took the ID from my hand.

"Miss Harris, Angelloni's secretary, I believe," I answered.

"Leave your phone number. I will call you when the report is ready," he ordered.

I nodded.

Abruptly, he asked, "Do you know if she had enemies?"

I shrugged and left without looking back.

~

Back at the funeral parlor, I approached Mr. Angelloni and his good-looking secretary, Miss Elsa Harris, as they arrived. He was dressed like a boss, and all his polished demure announced that he was "the man in charge": hair slicked back, perfect teeth, shaven face. He wore a pinky signet ring and a gold, thick-chained bracelet, and a tea rose was impeccably pinned to his black Italian jacket.

"How come I was not informed that my aunt died as a result of an accident?" I asked him.

They exchanged looks. Mr. Angelloni shrugged his shoulders. He grabbed me by an arm and pulled me away from the mourners.

"Please come to my office tomorrow at ten o'clock," he said.

I nodded.

I had never been to a closed-casket service before. Strange thoughts were galloping through my head. *Maybe the casket was empty, or maybe someone else was inside the casket. Should I inspect the casket to see that every-thing was in order? Or demand that the casket be opened immediately and put a stop to the nonsense inside my head?*

I was really bothered by the sobbing and curiosity among the visi-tors, whoever they were. They seemed to have more curiosity than sorrow.

~

I was sipping my cup of coffee the next morning—without it, my day would be upside-down—when a soft rap at the kitchen back door startled me. I automatically looked at the kitchen's old clock; who could it be at such an early hour?

"Good morning," said an old man, who stood aside when I opened the door.

"Good morning," I replied hesitantly, looking for the other Jehovah Witness ready to gang-save me.

"I am Victor Parker, your aunt's butler," he said.

"Oh yeah, I saw you yesterday at the funeral parlor," I said.

"We need to talk," he said gravely.

"Come in."

Anybody could have smelled the fear all over him. With raspy voice, he narrated the strange events from two weeks before my aunt's demise. "Miss Millie stopped receiving all those `Cosa Nostra` char-acters, she and Angelloni were fighting. He yelled at her "you are dead!"that she refused to see him anymore. She moved some stuff out of the house, I offered to help, she said that she didn't want to cause me more trouble. She was asking me all the time "who is parked outside?"

"I thought that she was losing her marbels."

When he ended his narrative, he was drenched in sweat.

"She gave me an envelope," he said.

"Where is it?" I immediately asked.

"Her instructions were if something were to happen to her, to take it to the police." He sounded apologetic.

How did I know I could trust this guy? He'd just appeared unexpectedly with an envelope for me. Besides this guy did not look very friendly and didn't make eye contact; he was very fidgety.

"Did you?" I asked.

"No, I don't trust them," he said with disgust.

Victor explained that when my aunt was attacked, he had called 911. Yet, when the police showed up, it was too late.

"Why didn't you help her?"

"I was very scared."

"So…you just hid like a rat while she was killed?'

He just looked at the floor, unable to lift his eyes, the coward that he was.

"Do you know the killers?" I asked.

~

I was to meet Victor after the funeral at the cabin by the lake, where he had been hiding since my aunt's brutal attack. *Stupid old man*, I thought. The cabin belonged to my aunt. Besides, who was the man hiding from?

I was preparing to visit the town's clothing store to get something suitable for the memorial service when I remembered my appointment with Mr. Angelloni at ten o'clock. I found him impatiently waiting for me. I could feel his anger.

"You need to sign these papers," he said as he put a file on his desk. "As you know, your aunt named me her estate administrator."

"Exactly what am I signing?" I asked, feeling distrustful.

"Look, there's no time for questions! Sign the damn papers and leave town!" he barked.

But I yelled back, "Not without finding who killed my aunt and why!"

3

left Angelloni's office without signing the documents. I needed answers about my aunt's death; and would not sign until I got them. Unhurriedly, I walked toward the funeral parlor; maybe the chill in the air would help clear my mind. The memorial service was set for 1:00 p.m.

I stopped at Maggie's Diner for lunch. The place was busy. The banging of dishes and the chatter of the patrons stopped as I walked in; everybody's eyes were fixed on me.

Sergeant Miller entered the diner and came straight to my table. Without waiting for an invitation to sit down, he pulled up a chair and sat down.

"Do you have the report?" I inquired.

"No," he answered.

"Why are you here, then?" I asked.

"Can a guy have some coffee?" he said.

"There are plenty of other tables. I want to be alone."

"This is my regular table," he said calmly.

Quickly I moved to another table.

"Leave your address, and I'll send you a copy of the report," he said.

"Thanks, but I'll wait for it here."

"Sorry, you can't. You have twenty-four hours to leave town." His voice sounded menacing now.

"What if I don't?"

"I will charge you with the murder of Mildred C. Wilmot." The veins in his temples were bulging. I could almost hear his rage. Even little kids stopped fussing and whining. I could've heard a pin drop.

"So, she *was* murdered?"

"You had motive and time," he said.

"How's that so?" I was curious.

"Simple. You are the only heir."

"And how's that a motive to murder her?" I asked.

"In our investigation, it came up that you're broke and need cash to pay a betting debt. And that, Sam, makes you a person of interest."

"I lost my appetite." I got up.

"Twenty-four hours!" he yelled as I left.

~

Three days in Mapletown and I had two invitations to leave town. Why? What was going on?

Well, I had news for everybody: I had no place to go; I had lost everything gambling. I was in deep shit; I owed money to loan sharks, and leaving was not an option. I thought of better times, when I was a decent member of society, devoted to my wife and work, living in a posh suburb of San Francisco.

I went back to Aunt Millie's home to freshen up and change for the memorial service. "I have twenty-four hours," I said to myself as I was dressing. The new shirt felt very good and didn't come from Good Willie Fashions. I couldn't remember the last time I bought a new shirt. I looked in the mirror. I had a different look—I hardly recognized myself. Nevertheless, I felt a shiver run down my back.

~

The funeral parlor looked somber and dark. Maybe it was just my state of mind.

Mr. Smith was at the door, wryly welcoming the mourners. "Please sign the registry," he said, directing people with his droning voice, emotionless and cold.

I scanned the room, looking for Victor. Well, I just had to wait for the interment to conclude, and then I could go to the cabin. I felt anxious about meeting with him.

As I sat through the monotonous service, the funeral director approached Angelloni and gave him a large manila envelope. I felt a forewarning churn at my guts. Sergeant Miller's eyes caught mine.

Could he really charge me with a murder I did not commit? Not if I could find the killers first!

But what was in the manila envelope?

The priest finished his service with Psalm 23. The mourners got up and went to their vehicles to start the procession to the old town cemetery, while the pallbearers—I only recognized two, Miller and Angelloni—got situated to carry the casket to the hearse.

A light rain started to fall as we reached the old cemetery. We entered through the main gate. Suddenly I got a revelation about the map I'd found at Aunt Millie's house. The cemetery was where the X was. I needed to go back to the house and get the map before I went to meet Victor. Maybe he would be able to tell me what it was all about. I grew very impatient as the casket was lowered.

~

When I arrived back at Aunt Millie's house, I looked at my watch. "Twenty-four hours to leave town" echoed in my mind. The fucking train was going through my head again full force. "Don't think about it," I kept telling myself. "The train will disappear like it always does."

I entered the house through the back door and started undressing from my formal funeral attire. What would happen after the twenty-four hours ran out? Would I be in jail or far away from Mapletown?

~

I checked, and the map was folded inside my jacket pocket. The rain was coming down hard, and the wind was blowing—very cold, I thought as I closed the door behind me. A shadowy figure approached me from behind.

"Come with me." The male voice was hoarse.

"Sorry, I have an appointment."

"Your appointment has been canceled. I am taking you to sign some papers."

"You must be Mr. Angelloni's assistant."

"Are you coming, or do I have to drag you?" He sounded serious.

I was able to get away from the goon using the self-defense Krav Maga techniques I had learned when I took lessons a few years ago; I never thought I would use it, but tonight the tactics worked!

I got in my car and raced to the cabin, only to find the place engulfed in flames. Fire Department trucks, ambulances, and the police were already there.

I got out of my car to take a closer look when a hand grabbed my arm. It was Sergeant Miller. How did he get here so fast? I'd just seen him at the cemetery.

"What are you doing here?" he asked.

"It's my aunt's property," I replied defensively.

"Why did you set it on fire?" he asked accusingly.

"You got to be fucking kidding me," I said angrily as he grabbed the handcuffs from his utility belt.

"You are under arrest. You have the right…" As he placed the handcuffs on me, he finished reciting the Miranda rights. Then he said, "We are going to the station."

"What are the charges?" I asked incredulously.

"Arson." Then he pushed me inside his cruiser.

I felt like I was in a dream that I couldn't wake up from.

4

I was driving south on Highway 101, sore and in bad shape after the "workout" I'd received the night of my arrest. I had been forced to signed declarations confessing to arson. Mr. Angelloni paid for my release, but he made sure I signed the documents related to my aunt's estate, giving him general power of attorney.

Luckily, they did not search my car; the map was in the glove compartment. They had, however, searched every orifice of my body.

Where was Victor? Did he die in the fire? Had the envelope gone up in smoke, too?

I couldn't make sense of any of the actions that had occurred since my arrival in Mapletown.

I needed to talk to someone about the dealings that took place during the short week I spent in that town—who would be able to understand and help me? I had signed many papers under duress; but did it matter? What would be the outcome, and how would I be affected? My stomach was in knots, sensing the predicament I was in. I needed to stop and get aspirin and clear my head. I was very confused.

I felt alone. It was not the first time, but this time was different. I had been a loner and outsider most part of my life; I never made friends who were significant. I was a misfit. I had learned that it was better when you distanced yourself from everybody.

There had to be someone I could talk to, someone who could understand me. Feelings of anger began to boil inside. The more I thought about the situation, the angrier I got. Finally, I saw a truck stop a couple of miles away and decided to stop to get aspirin and a

Coke. I wondered how long I had been driving. I had completely lost a sense of time. I needed gas, too.

~

"Twenty-six dollars," announced the attendant, still heavy with sleep.

"How far is San Francisco?" I asked as I scrambled for money.

"Hundred and twenty miles," he answered, rubbing his eyes, unable to keep them open.

I would arrive at 2:00 a.m., I thought, looking at the clock on the wall.

I noticed that I was always looking at my watch and clocks, appearing to be mindful of time. It only meant I wanted to be left alone. Even when alone, I was always glancing at my watch and clocks.

"Where are you coming from?"

"Mapletown."

"What's new in that hellhole?"

"You know Mapletown?"

"Yep, not pleasant memories."

"Sorry, but how so?"

"The whole town is corrupt, especially the town's finest," he said.

"The cops?"

"Couple of days ago, an old man stopped here; he was from Mapletown." The attendant scratched his forehead. "I remembered because he looked scared."

"Did he say where he was going, do you remember?"

The attendant shook his head, and I left.

I wondered how many old men stopped at the gas station looking scared.

~

My eyes were heavy with fatigue. Everything looked distorted. I didn't recognize the highway I was on. Did I take the wrong exit? I glanced at the lighted dashboard clock. It was 2:50 a.m. I pulled to the side of the road for a quick snooze.

I finally made it to my tiny apartment, only to find an eviction notice taped to my door. I started to pack, thinking I had no place to go but my aunt's house in Mapletown.

A knock at the door startled me. *The* landlord, I thought.

"Sam, open up!" a raspy voice said.

"Victor?"

"Yes, it's me, hurry!"

"How did you find me?"

"Your aunt gave me your address."

"Do you have the envelope?"

~

We ran into the landlord going downstairs. "Sam, where is the fucking rent money?"

"Sorry, I don't have it."

"You have twenty-four hours to get me my money!"

"Do you know Sergeant Miller?" I asked.

"Who in the hell is that asshole?"

"Never mind, you can keep whatever you want from my belongings."

"I am not a trash collector. I want my money!"

"I'll catch you later, boss."

"Fucking loser!" he said, his face as red as a tomato, his dirty robe flying as he ran. He looked like a ridiculous superhero patrolling San Fran Arms. Giving him the finger, I left that dump of a place.

~

I pulled into a hamburger joint on our way out of town. Victor nervously sat still. He offered to pick up the tab—he had ten dollars available. We ordered hamburgers, fries, and Cokes. Boy, I was hungry and wolfed down my food without talking.

Victor was doing all the talking—however, looking over his shoulder.

"There were three men at your aunt's that night."

"Who were they?"

"I couldn't see their faces."

"How do you know then that they were men?"

"I was afraid."

"Did they see you?"

"I don't know."

"What about the fire?"

"They were the same voices I heard at your aunt's the night she was killed."

"The fire was intentional?"

"I think so."

"How did you escape?"

"When I heard the voices, I ran through the back door."

"The envelope burned?"

"No, it's safe!"

"Where is it?"

"It is safe."

"We need to get it as soon as we get to Mapletown." I stopped. "It is in Mapletown, right?"

~

It was dark and foggy as I drove back on Highway 101 toward Mapletown—*déjà vu*, I thought.

Victor had refused to come along; he gave me the key for a locker at the Greyhound Bus Depot. He also gave me a phone number for his sister in case I needed to contact him. I felt as if I was entering a lion's den; my gut was tense not knowing what was waiting in that damn town. I just wanted to turn around and forget the whole thing, but something inside me was much stronger. The anxiety grew, as I got closer, but so did the anticipation of finding out what was going on and who had killed Aunt Millie.

I decided to stop at a rest area and catch a wink or two. The rest area was deserted. I parked in the farthest space. The place looked eerie, but I was too tired and had no money for a room in a motel.

I needed to rest; maybe I could think of a plan of what I needed to do once I reached Mapletown. I knew that I needed to fulfill three objectives: retrieve the envelope, get the death certificate, and find out what I had signed. Nevertheless, what about the map? Plus, the police report. Maybe everything would tie together.

~

I must have slept awhile; I felt all twisted when I woke up. Five thirty. I still had two more hours of driving before I reached Mapletown. I washed up at the rest area before I drove off.

I made another stop at a roadside café to get a cup of coffee and muster the nerve to face the day. I checked my pockets to make sure I had the locker key. I was preparing mentally for the first stop: the Greyhound Depot.

Sergeant Miller and Mr. Angelloni came to mind, and my body shook violently.

I decided to eat a hearty country breakfast to help gather my strength after making such a stupid decision to come back. It wasn't the first time I had made a dumb decision, I knew as I thought about borrowing money from loan sharks to continue with my gambling addiction. I'd known I needed help, but I kept thinking I would be a winner the next time. That next time never came. I still longed for the rush—would the temptation of it ever go away?

I needed to get going and, for the first time, do what was right, no matter the consequences.

5

I pulled my Army-green Jeep into the driveway of Aunt Millie's house. This was going to be my residence for now. I didn't have much to unload, just a bag and a pillowcase with my clothes in it.

I would stay away from the main house—it was still a crime scene or not—Now I would make my accommodations in the garden cottage at the back of the property just in case.

This time, I would not be intimidated by anybody and would find out what happened to Aunt Millie and why.

In the cottage, I glanced at the mirror, slowly taking inventory of my appearance. The beard had to go; actually, the homeless look had to go. I pulled out the outfit I bought for the funeral—not the best quality, but it would do for now.

~

The mountain of papers scattered throughout the main house could offer clues and information to start forming a vantage point. What had happened here? Would I ever find out? I needed to get busy and start piecing it together. I didn't know why I thought I could do it, but I'd be damned if I didn't try. I was deep into shit, and it stank.

First, I started for the bus depot. Where was it? Oh yeah, I remembered: Maple and Second Street. Close to the police station—great! I remembered Aunt Millie picking me up there many summers ago. Maybe—just maybe—with my "new look," Sergeant Miller's henchman wouldn't recognized me.

~

I put money into a parking meter close to the depot; I didn't want to attract attention. I mingled with the boisterous travelers and their screaming children—how much I detested screaming children. I then went directly to the locker area, but there were no lockers as Victor had said there would be. He *had* said the Greyhound Depot.

It was not going to be as easy as I thought. I located the depot manager because nobody else knew anything.

"Where are the fucking lockers?" I demanded irritably.

"Ugh, they were taken away."

"Who took them?"

"They were bought by a scrap-metal company."

"When were they taken?"

"It must have been today, early in the morning."

~

I left the fucking bus depot with a name and address for the scrap-metal company. A parking ticket was on my Jeep; the meter had run out of time. Fuck. I'd take care of that later; for now, I had to rush to the salvage yard in the next town, twenty-five miles away.

When I got there, I could see the mountains of metals and cranes moving around. Gardel Metal Company.

I went to the small office where the smell of old coffee and sweat permeated the air. I rang the bell for service. A huge man came from behind the office; his overalls had seen better days. How long since he'd bathed? Did he own a toothbrush?

"What can I do you for?" he asked.

"I'm looking for a locker."

"A locker?"

"Yes, a bus depot locker."

"Look, pal, a locker is a locker, don't waste my time."

"I'm looking for the Mapletown Greyhound Bus Depot lockers that your driver picked up this morning."

"Let me check the driver's route," he grumbled as he looked through a pile of papers hung on a nail on the wall. "No, the driver isn't here yet."

"What time will he be back?"

The man glanced at a greasy clock on the wall. "If the son of a bitch doesn't stop for a pro, if you know what I mean, he will be back in three more hours."

"I'll wait."

"Sorry, you can't wait in here."

"I'll wait in my car."

~

I must have dozed off. I glanced at my watch: one thirty. That wasn't possible. I turned on the radio just as the radio announcer blared, "Three thirty is quitting time." My watch was old and not working; I needed to fix it. Aunt Millie had given it to me on one of my birthdays the last time I visited..

As I got out of the Jeep to stretch my legs, a falling-apart truck pulled into the yard. The huge man came out from the office. Clipboard in hand, he took inventory and had the driver sign.

"Is this the Mapletown driver?" I asked the huge man.

"No, this is the Riverdale one—see?" he snapped, showing me the manifest.

"How much longer you think?"

"I don't know."

"What time do you close?"

"We are closed now."

"Listen, buddy, I really need to get the locker," I said boldly, though I didn't want to mess with this guy. "What time do you open tomorrow?"

"Six."

"I'll see you tomorrow."

"Bring money—that baby won't be cheap."

I started to walk toward my car when I heard someone calling me. "Hey, mister! Where are you going?"

I looked toward the voice. It came from a woman dressed in dingy overalls and steel-toed boots. "Are you talking to me?" I asked.

"Yes!"

"I'm going to Mapletown."

"Can you give me a lift?"

"Sure." I needed some company.

"My name is Eva." Her fiery-red hair was in a ponytail.

"Do you work here? Seriously?" I shook my head, somewhat incredulous that someone with her looks worked in this place.

"I needed a job," she said as she started to slip off her overalls. "Are you looking for a job too?" she asked.

~

The trip back to Mapletown was pleasant. We stopped and grabbed a couple of burgers. I watched in amusement as she devoured the food. She asked if I would be finishing mine. I shook my head. Immediately, she grabbed it and wolfed it down.

"How long have you been living in Mapletown?" I asked.

"About six months," Eva replied, still chewing her food.

"Why?" I asked.

"Is a long story…and you?" she asked.

"A recent death in the family," I answered.

"Who?" she immediately asked.

"My aunt."

"How did she die?"

"Don't know…I'm here to find out," I said.

"Are you a detective?" she asked, trying to hide the panic in her voice.

"No."

"What were you doing at the scrap place?" she asked with a lot of curiosity.

"Looking for a locker."

"Oh yeah, the lockers from the bus depot."

"I need to get locker one-thirty," I told her.

"What's so special about one-thirty?" she asked.

"I need to know the same thing," I said.

"I'm afraid it's too late…they've been sold. That kind of locker is so popular that as soon as they are tweeted, they are sold," she replied.

We made plans to ride together to Gardel's the following day.

~

It was 5:30 a.m. when I picked Eva up. We stopped at the convenience store for coffee and Danish rolls. It was still dark and overcast; the day looked depressing and not very promising.

I was brooding and quiet. "I didn't sleep last night," I muttered.

"Sorry. The locker kept you awake?"

"I don't know."

"It must be really important for you to be up early on such a fucking morning."

"I don't know. I feel like I'm chasing a ghost."

"Come on, don't be so grim," she said.

"How am I supposed to feel?" Then I told her my situation since I'd arrived at Mapletown for my aunt's funeral.

6

Eva offered to help. She suggested I give her the locker key and she would find it, in exchange for a ride back to town at quitting time.

"I thought you said the lockers had been sold." I had to control myself to keep from yelling.

"I said the lockers were sold, but they have to be checked for stuff left behind. Besides, Rick is hard to deal with," she said with disgust.

"Who is Rick?"

"The bastard you were talking to yesterday."

"Does he ever bathe?"

"You can smell him a mile away, man!" she exclaimed, grabbing her nostrils with her thumb and index.

"How come you're working there?"

"Like I said, I needed a job."

"There are other places, like the bank, stores, attorneys…"

"I needed a job in an out-of-the-way place."

"Are you hiding?"

"That transparent, huh?"

"We're here," I said, announcing our arrival at Gardel's.

"The key?" She extended her hand.

I hesitated for an instant. What did I have to lose? My heart was pounding as I handed her the key.

"See you at three-thirty," she said and took the key.

~

I went straight to Aunt Millie's house. I really needed to get busy and look for clues among Aunt Millie's possessions. I wondered how Eva was doing at the salvage yard.

I decided to start in my aunt's bedroom, but strangely, her bedroom door was locked. I ran to the kitchen and grabbed a knife to pick the door open. Who locked the door?

The house was Victorian, with heavy doors, and the knife wasn't good enough for the task. I went to the basement to look for tools better suited for the job. I had a feeling of despair looking at the disarray around me.

I was losing precious time trying to find solutions for problems popping up all over the place. I was overwhelmed. It was past noon, and I had not accomplished much.

The basement was humid. I remembered a secret place I used to hide when I was a kid. Was it still there?

Junk had accumulated through the years—boxes of old toys, books, clothes, and furniture. I couldn't see the walls; it was as if they had disappeared behind the boxes stacked upon boxes. Where were the tools? I desperately needed a plan of attack.

Since the day was already wasted in futility—I didn't have tools, I didn't know exactly whether the property was still a crime scene, I didn't have the map or, for that matter, my aunt's death certificate and police report—I decided to continue in the basement for a couple of more hours.

I was enthralled. I shifted boxes in an attempt to find my hiding place. I remembered there was a lever to open the door to the secret chamber, which I had found while trying to hide a dog from my aunt. The chamber had to be here!

As I touched the coldness of the concrete wall, I remembered: Eva! Shit! I'd forgotten to go to pick her up!

I raced to the salvage yard. I told myself *to slow down; I didn't need to be pulled over by a fucking cop.*

It was three-thirty when I pulled into Gardel's. Eva was coming out of the office with Rick in tow; it seemed they were arguing. I lowered the volume of the radio just as he called her a "fucking bitch!" and grabbed her by the arm.

She turned around and kicked him in the groin. "Dirty bastard!"

"Paco, let the dogs out!" Rick yelled to another dirty guy working among the scrap.

Eva signaled me to stay put as she ran to the car.

"Let's go!" she said, out of breath.

"What was that all about?"

"Your fucking envelope, bastard!"

"Did you get it?"

"Yeah. Rick was accusing me of stealing company property."

"Let's go back and pay for it."

"No, fuck him!"

"What about your job?"

"Let's get out of here!"

~

We drove in silence back to Mapletown. How ironic—Victor thought the envelope my aunt had given him would be safe in a locker at the bus depot.

"Where is the envelope?" I finally asked Eva.

"Here," she said.

I extended my arm and grabbed for it.

"Not so fast," she said, pulling it back.

"Oh?"

"What's in it for me? I just lost my job, you know."

"What do you want?" I said, exasperated.

"I don't know…what about partners?"

"Partners?" I repeated.

"It's a deal."

"No! I don't even know you."

"I don't know you, either."

I explained that she would be crazy to get involved with me. I didn't even know what I was up against. "A couple of loan sharks, a crazy police sergeant, attorneys, and an angry landlord. Besides, I got no money," I said.

She shrugged her shoulders. "Seems to me that you need someone's help," she said.

"Just give me the fucking envelope!"

"Partners?"

"Who are you running away from?" I asked.

"I'm the one with the envelope," she said, threatening to throw it out the window.

"If we are going to be partners, I need to know what kind of trouble you're in."

"What do you mean? On a scale of zero to ten? Zero being the least trouble?" she said jokingly.

"Stop! You know what I mean." Now I needed to add Eva to my list of problems.

"Lots of trouble," she said in a whisper.

~

It was going to be an "as Eva needed to know" partnership. Of course, I didn't tell her that. However, for sure she *would* give me the envelope!

At Aunt Millie's house, she gasped as she saw the amount of stuff all over the place. After she examined the house and nosed around, I wondered if I could trust her.

"The first thing I need is a hot shower," she announced as she started to remove her overalls.

While she was in the shower, I frantically looked for the envelope. Where in hell…?

~

She came out of the shower wrapped in a towel. She was statuesque, strong, shapely, with long legs—very, very sexy.

She stopped me in the middle of my thoughts. "We are business partners *only*!" she snapped.

"Is it time to hand the envelope over, partner?" I said, putting my hand out.

"Here." She placed it on my hand, and as she came close, I caught a whiff of her. She smelled fresh and inviting.

Over a glass of wine, she told me she was running away from her husband; she had seen him killing a man. She knew he was involved with some wise guys in New York. Now she was a witness. Knowing the violence her husband was capable of, she knew she was in danger and ran away.

~

Our immediate plan was for Eva to go to City Hall and find out about Aunt Millie's house, using the excuse that she was interested in buying it.

"By the way, the red hair has to go," I said firmly.

"Blond?" she asked.

"No, brunette."

"How boring is that!"

"You need to keep a low profile as long as you're in hiding."

I needed to get her out of the house so I could examine the envelope and find the hiding place in the basement.

But where had I left the envelope? How could I be so stupid and forget the important things? "Fuck!" Whenever I saw a beautiful woman, my mind turned to Jell-O and stopped working. I really was in trouble.

Maybe with brunette hair, Eva would look plain, just like Sophia did. My feelings for Sophia were warm at best, but she was daddy's girl, and daddy was the CEO of Security Partners, a multimillion-dollar software corporation. I'd met Sophia in college, and we got married right after graduation. I went to work for Security Partners. In other words, I married her for a job.

Shit! I had to stop thinking about all this crap and concentrate. I had to wait for Eva to set the rules.

~

Eva was to leave the store with a dull pantsuit, black pumps, and a black purse. She went to the drugstore to pick her new hair color; I knew that she loved her fiery red hair, but she knew that I was right—she needed a low profile.

Chestnut-brown? *Yuk!* I could hear her on the back of my mind; I also knew what she thought of other hair colors. She loved to look trashy and vulgar with the worn-holey jeans, the constant and annoying chewing and cracking of gum; for someone trying to hide, she was a sore thumb.

It wasn't clear to me whether she and I had truly become partners or what she felt was really in it for her. Obviously, she didn't need more trouble. She had enough to think about, keeping one step ahead of her husband and the FBI, which wanted her for questioning. *Oops! I forgot to tell Eva that I knew about the FBI!* Had Rick called the cops on her?

~

I was in a bad mood when Eva walked in.

"Where is the fucking envelope?" I barked as soon as I saw her.

"Whoa." She stopped in her tracks and looked at me with disdain.

"If you think this is a fucking game…," I said, exasperated by the time I'd lost looking for the damn thing.

"What's your fucking problem?"

"The envelope," I said, extending my hand.

"Didn't I give it to you already?"

"I don't remember you giving it to me."

"There's nothing in it that interests me."

"How do you know what's in it?"

"Didn't I tell you that it was open when I found it?"

"You opened it? Fucking bitch!" I said as I walked menacingly toward her.

"No, I swear it was open!"

"How? I had the only key."

"Each locker has double keys in case the person with the key doesn't come back, didn't you know?"

"I don't care about the damned locker! You can have it. I just want the envelope that was i-n-s-i-d-e-." I just looked at her in complete disbelief.

"Didn't you place it on top of the fireplace mantel?" she asked, pointing at it.

There was so much stuff stirred up around the place that it was hard to find things. I didn't remember my aunt living in squalor; she was always neat and clean.

"Thanks," I said sheepishly.

"I'm hungry."

~

Dinner was very simple—steak and potatoes at a nearby chop-house. Eva looked like a completely different person with her brunette hair; yet there was nothing plain about her. She was very nervous and had asked me not to check the envelope yet.

"There are a couple of guys staring—don't look!" she whispered. "Just act normal."

After a while, the two guys got up and left. We stayed for coffee.

"Do you think your husband has any idea where you are?" I asked bluntly.

"I'm also worried about the FBI," she said.

"FBI?" I acted as if I didn't know. How did I know? Let's say a birdie told me.

"They want me as a witness against my husband."

"There are laws about husbands and wives testifying against each other, aren't there?"

~

As Eva and I were leaving the chophouse, Sergeant Miller walked in with another man. I was relieved that Miller didn't seem to recognize me. But he couldn't hide if he wanted to, the whiteness of his hair and his red eyes were like another sore thumb.

"Feels like we have to look over our shoulders," Eva said.

"Let's go home."

Our trip back home was in silence; we both were tired. Who was the man with Miller? I had seen him before—was he one of the pallbearers? No. I just could not place him. I was too tired to think right now.

"Eva, could we spend the night at your place?"

"You would have to sleep on the floor."

"That's OK."

"Why do you want to do that?"

"I have a feeling."

"Bad?"

7

Her place was tiny, but I felt safe—at least for tonight. As much as I wanted to check the contents of the envelope, I decided to wait until tomorrow.

The floor was hard on my ribs, and I was cold. I could see the rain falling on the tiny windowpane. Eva was sound asleep. How someone in much trouble could sleep…I got pissed.

I tossed and turned all night, trying to find a comfortable position. What time was it? I needed to buy an inexpensive watch and take my old watch to be repaired. Add it to the "to-do list." It was ironic to be in this situation when I used to sleep on expensive therapeutic beds with flannel sheets. Sophia liked flannel sheets. Anyway, that was ancient history.

~

When Eva got up and took a shower, I moved to her bed. The soft bed felt good; it was still warm, and her soft scent had permeated the pillow and blankets. I could lay there forever. I dozed off awhile; the smell of fresh coffee woke me up.

Eva was cooking eggs. "Did you sleep well?" she asked.

"No."

"Sorry."

"It's not your fault."

"I'll get ready to go to City Hall."

"Drop me at Aunt Millie's," I said before sipping the brew. The coffee was hot and strong.

I could hardly wait to be alone to open the envelope and examine its contents.

"Open it!" Eva commanded.

Holding my breath and with trembling hands, I opened the envelope. It looked like a letter. That was it. I didn't know what I was expecting, but a letter?

Disappointed, I put it back in the envelope without reading it.

"Read it!" Eva said.

"Later," I replied.

~

I opened the envelope as soon as I got to Aunt Millie's and read the letter:

November 16, 2004

Mapletown, CA Dear Few,

I grinned—"Few" was her short name for nephew.

If you are reading this letter, it is because I am dead.

The information that you need is in a safety deposit box at First National Bank under your name. See Mr. Bennett.

Watch your back and keep an eye on Mr. Angelloni; he is no good. He has several people in City Hall on his payroll.

Victor is very trustworthy and dedicated. You can trust him.

Also, do not forget the hiding place. You were a good kid and I had a great time when you came to visit.

Love,

Auntie M

PS: Bring an ID to First National.

The grandfather clock chimed ten o'clock. I'd better hurry up. Should I go to the bank first, or to the basement? I opted to stay and continue with the basement. I had to find the hiding place now that I still had the chance. Later, the house may belong to someone else.

I rushed downstairs and went directly to pull the lever—wow, I remembered! I choked on all the dust, and then before I could reach the lever, the light bulb burned out. Shit! I wasn't surprised; maybe it was the same bulb as when I was a kid, but...what else would go wrong?

Was there a flashlight? It was so dark; the basement door had closed behind me.

Where was the fucking lever? I told *myself not to panic.* The fucking train was running inside my head, full force.

~

There was no flashlight in the house, but again I wasn't ready for the tasks I had to do. A feeling of despair started to engulf me. I had no idea what I was doing or what I had to do next. I could hear Sophia saying, "You are good for nothing, darling." I had lived with the humiliation from her and her family the entire ten years we were married. I was more of a servant than a husband.

Thank God that there were no children. I was a loser, and I did not need to pass down such traits to the future generation, according to her family.

Gambling was my way out.

~

I thought about waiting for Eva to come back with the Jeep. Instead, I put on a jacket and walked toward the small hardware store only a few blocks away. The fresh air seemed to calm my senses. I checked my pockets for money and found a worn-out bill, my last twenty dollars.

In the distance, I noticed my Jeep parked in a corner by Angelloni's office. Eva was dropping someone.I stretch my gaze to see who it was, it seemed to be a man. What the hell…? I saw red. I whistled to get her attention, but she just sped away. I turned around and headed back to Aunt Millie's, running all the way there.

~

I entered the house as mad as a hornet and exhausted and panting from running. I had not run in years, and I wasn't a kid anymore.

Eva was very calm, drinking a cup of coffee. "Wait till you hear what I found out," she said nonchalantly.

I was boiling with anger and confronted her immediately. "What were you doing at Angelloni's?"

"Are you spying on me?"

"Who was the man you dropped off?" I demanded.

"I'm not your wife!" she said defensively.

"Thank God for that," I retorted.

"I was only doing what you sent me to do!"

"I don't recall sending you to Angelloni's!"

"I don't think this partnership is working," she declared.

"I didn't ask for this fucking partnership."

"Do you want to know or not?"

"Never mind!" I stormed out of the house, taking the car keys on my way out.

A voice inside my head was telling me not to trust Eva. How did I know she wasn't on Angelloni's payroll?

~

I sat in the car awhile. I couldn't bear the idea of leaving her alone in the house—she was a nosy bitch—but how could I get rid of her? Should I call the FBI and snitch about her whereabouts? I had options too, I thought.

I went back inside the house to find her sleeping on the couch. I grabbed her new purse and took it into the bathroom, closing the door behind me. I placed a towel over the sink to mute the sounds as I emptied it. The color left my face when I found a little addresses book with names of people I knew, among them Victor Parker and Mildred C. Wilmot. Who was this bitch?

Back in the living room, I glared at her asleep on the couch. I shook her to awaken her.

"Look, you need to go to your place," I said sternly.

"I don't understand," she replied unemotionally.

"I need to think things over."

"Fuck you!"

"Exactly!"

"Jerk!"

"Out of my house, bitch!"

"Not your house yet, asshole!"

"I'll give you a ride."

The ride to her place was in silence; after dropping her off, I headed toward the First National. My spirits were low. I didn't know what to expect at the bank. *I'm not feeling lucky*, I thought.

~

I made a mental list of the things I needed to do, glancing at my watch—force of habit. First thing was to buy a cheap watch, then go to the First National Bank and, lastly, the hardware store. After buying my brand-new watch, I set the time: four fifty. Where did time go? I hurried to the bank. The security guard was closing the door.

"Sorry, we are closed," he said courteously.

"Can I see the manager, please?"

"You have to come back tomorrow; we open at nine."

I went to my car disheartened. Couldn't I ever win one? Will the hardware store be open? This damn town!

I drove the couple of blocks to the Tools Emporium. It was open. Inside I politely asked the cashier, "Do I have time to pick up a few things?"

"Help yourself."

It was raining when I came out of the Tools Emporium.

From the corner of my eye, I noticed a black sedan parked behind my car. Shit, it was Miller. I didn't need a confrontation right now. But he exited his vehicle and crossed the street. That was too close for comfort.

I checked my mental list once more, making sure I got everything I needed; I couldn't afford any more delays. I went through my list: light bulbs, batteries, and a screwdriver set. But some things were missing: oh yeah, a flashlight and matches.

I went back to the store.

~

When I was paying for the additional items, Sergeant Miller walked into the store. *Shit!* I tried to act normal.

"Good evening," he said seriously "Hello, Sergeant Miller!" the cashier replied.

"Have you seen this woman?" he asked the cashier as he showed him a picture.

"No."

"And you?" He turned to me and showed me the picture.

"No," I replied without looking at him, hoping he couldn't read my nervousness.

"Who is she?" the cashier asked "Her name is Helen Prescott."

She is Eva! I felt like saying, but I bit my tongue.

"What did she do?" the curious cashier asked.

"I can't say, but she is involved in a murder back East." He pulled out a business card and gave it to the clerk.

Then he directed his defiant red stare at me.

"Have I ever seen you before?" he asked.

"Just passing by," I lied, almost pissing in my underwear. I couldn't believe that he didn't recognized me! Maybe he had an eyesight problem,,,the strange eye color. I didn't know if I was more scared stiff or furious at such an idiot who was unable to find out who murdered my aunt…and why.

~

I tried to keep my cool as I exited the store. My temples were pounding wildly as I tried to look behind me and see if he was going to stop me. Luckily, Eva had changed her hair color.

It was just past six when I made it home, ready to start working.

"Did you get everything you needed?" called a voice from the dark room.

"Eva! How in the hell did you get in?"

"The back door was unlocked."

"Do you know that the police are looking for you?" I cautiously asked.

"I thought I told you so."

"Sergeant Miller is showing your picture around."

"It doesn't surprise me." I could hear her fear.

"He said that you're connected to a murder back East."

"I see you burned the letter in the envelope," she said, changing subjects.

"Like, you didn't read it." Admit nothing.

"Look, I better get out of here…"

I wasn't about to trust Eva. She still seated in a chair she had placed by the front window. Like a sentinel, she watched my every movement, making me very uncomfortable.

Finally, she spoke. "Take me to Gardel's to pick up my check."

"Now?"

"My rent is due."

"My debt to the loan sharks is due at midnight," I said.

"We are fucked!" she said with such finality that it made me shiver.

8

I really needed a Xanax. Instead, I stopped at the liquor store and bought a case of beer; that had to do for now. My spirits were dampened; a dark misery was making its way toward me. Everything looked gloomy and eerie. Where was it going to end? Moreover, how? When? *Not tonight,* I thought sarcastically.

No, not tonight. Tonight, I was getting shit-faced. I needed to calm my mind down and stop the spinning around and around with the same questions about why Aunt Millie. In addition, there was Victor. And Eva? Yes, Eva! How did she fit into all this drama?

The scene at the scrap-metal yard had not been pleasant. Rick had refused to pay her. He threw her a handful of dollars and threatened to call the cops. Eva picked up the money, and we left while the sack of shit laughed.

Needless to say, Eva—or should I say Helen?—had cried all the way to her place.

~

I woke up the next day with a nasty headache, picked up the empty bottles, and drank black coffee. Enough of feeling sorry for myself. I got ready and went to the bank.

At the bank, I asked to see Mr. Bennett. *Ouch!* I felt like shit and wasn't taking it any more.

"May I have your name, please?" a teller asked.

"Sam W. Stone."

"Follow me, please."

I was led to a private area.

"Wait here, please."

I waited more than twenty minutes until at last a man entered the small waiting area. He was still shaking the crumbs from his ugly blue-and-yellow tie.

"I'm Ron Bennett," the banker said.

"Are you the manager?" I asked.

"Sorry about your aunt; she was a nice lady. It was a tragedy what happened to her."

"Thank you."

"What can I do for you?"

"I am Sam W. Stone, and I want my security box."

"I have to inform you that I have to call Mr. Angelloni and—"

"No! It won't happen!"

"Please wait."

"My aunt requested that Mr. Angelloni be present when I opened the box?" I asked indignantly.

"No, Mr. Angelloni did."

"Do you have a legal affidavit to confirm that?"

"Do you have an ID?"

I informed Mr. Bennett if he were to call Mr. Angelloni, I would press charges for violation of my privacy.

"I'll let you know when I'm finished here," I said when I had the safe-deposit box.

My heart was pounding—I could hear it! My breathing was shallow. With trembling hands, I inserted the key. I had a collapsible duffel bag with me, and I quickly emptied the contents of the security box into it. I felt exposed and vulnerable here, as if I were doing something wrong. The box held money, plenty of money!

I decided to rent a motel room on the outskirts of town where I could go through the contents inside the duffel bag without worrying that someone would watch me.

Since I had money now, I stopped at a phone store, and purchased a prepaid cellular phone—I'd heard they were not traceable. I also needed to locate another bank to rent a safe-deposit box—I couldn't carry this huge bag around all the time. Besides, it was heavy.

Nearby was the Orchard Motel. I stopped there and rented a room for a week. Then I couldn't wait any longer; in the room, I dumped the contents of the duffel bag onto the bed.

I couldn't believe my eyes: money, several envelopes, jewelry, and pictures. I started counting the money. *Wow!* I had never seen so much money in the same place—in my hands. That felt good.

My aunt's last will and testament was inside one of the envelopes.

LAST WILL AND TESTAMENT of Mildred C. Wilmot BE IT KNOWN that I, Mildred C. Wilmot, of 316 Primrose Lane, Mapletown, in the State of California, being of sound mind, do make and declare this is to be my Last Will and Testament expressly revoking all prior Wills and Codicils at any time made.

I. PERSONAL REPRESENTATIVE:

I appoint my nephew Samuel W. Stone of San Francisco, California, as my Personal Representative and General Administrator. In case he is not available to execute as my Personal Representative and General Power of Attorney, Marco Angelloni, my attorney, shall execute the appointed position.

II. BEQUESTS:

I direct that after payment of all my debt, my personal property and assets be bequeathed in the manner following:

Red Cross, the sum of $50,000.

Victor Parker, for his dedicated and loyal service, I bequeath him the Real Estate property and all belongings in the house located at 3211 Poplar St., Mapletown, CA, and a check in the sum of $50.000.

Samuel W. Stone, my nephew, I bequeath him all my assets, including the house on 316 Primrose Lane, Mapletown, CA, and all the house's belongings, furniture and fixtures included.

Mr. Angelloni will provide Samuel W. Stone with all legal documentation for deeds, bank accounts, and personal belongings. I am leaving copies available in case Mr. Angelloni is not available.

III. REMAINS DEPOSITION:

I have long been a resident of my beloved Mapletown, California. MY LAST WISHES ARE 1. A simple memorial to be held at Smith Funeral. THE *LORD IS MY SHEPHERD*. Shall be read by the minister in charge of the service.

My burial shall proceed with the reading of *THE LORD'S PRAYER* and the *AVE MARIA*.

It was midnight when I decided to set the will aside, and go to bed; I would have no problem sleeping tonight. The documents and the rest of the information in the envelopes would have to wait until tomorrow.

I felt elated knowing that my problems were about to be over—I had money now. That made all the difference in the world. Little did I know that my problems were about to start.

9

The next day I opened a bank account and rented a safe-deposit box at Capitol Bank in Riverdale. As I started putting the documents in the box, a picture fell out. I picked it up and glanced at it. I couldn't believe my eyes—it was of Eva, Victor, and Aunt Millie.

Once again, Eva came back to cause inquisitiveness and doubt in my mind: how did she know my aunt? How was she involved in my aunt's life? Or, for that matter even, her death? After all, I had seen her at Angelloni's office.

I took the picture with me. It was time to find out.

~

I drove back to Mapletown with the intention of stopping at Eva's place and confronting her. She'd better not fuck with me; she'd better come clean. This was the last chance I'd give her.

I arrived at her place at two p.m. I knocked on her door, but there was no answer. I turned the doorknob, and the door opened. *Strange.* I thought she was on the lookout and never left her door unlocked.

I went inside—curiosity killed the cat. The tiny apartment was in shambles: overthrown furniture, cupboards and drawers emptied, the tiny closet ransacked. Tiny droplets of blood were on the floor.

"Eva! Eva!" I called, but there was no answer.

"Do not touch anything," I told myself, "and get the hell out of here!" But I couldn't move.

I felt someone standing behind me, so I turned to see who it was. As I turned, I felt a sharp pain in the back of my head, and then everything went black.

~

The room was completely dark and cold. I had a terrible headache and couldn't see where I was. What was that smell? What time was it? My eyes began to adjust to the darkness, and I noticed a faint light coming through the bottom of the door. I got up and looked for the light switch, but damn, I couldn't see a fucking thing. *No! Do not turn on the light! The smell is gas!* I stumbled over something on the floor— overthrown furniture. When I finally reached the door and opened it, I was gasping for air.

Terror overcame me when I saw Eva's body on the floor. Was she dead? I felt for a pulse. Thank God! There was a faint one. She had the pallor of death. I wanted to run.

~

Dr. Thompson at the ER was very concerned not only for Eva's condition but also about the lack of information on her.

"It looks like suicide," he said.

"How is she?" I asked.

"You got here just in time."

"Will she be OK?"

"She is stable for now."

"I guess I'll be leaving then."

"Leave your name and phone number in case the police need it."

"I already told you that I don't know her."

"You don't look too good, either."

"I'm OK."

"There's blood on your head."

"Take care of her."

"The police are on the way."

"Good! They can ask her for the necessary information."

I left the hospital still dizzy and confused.

I thought about going to Aunt Millie's house, but immediately changed my mind and went to my motel room instead. I needed to rest.

~

Rest I didn't get. I got up with the train in my head. I didn't know if it was because of the impact on my head the night before or because of all the problems piling up around me.

I took a couple of aspirins and a cup of black coffee on my way to the bank to pick up Aunt Millie's last will and testament.

Shit! I realized that after I left the bank, I'd been in such a hurry that I forgot to make a copy of the will. I had to find a copy center in Mapletown.

I stopped at the local printing shop. "I need copies."

"Oh, Millie's testament," the clerk said.

"Did you know her?" I asked.

"Yes, nice lady. Come back in two hours," the clerk said.

"I'll wait." I didn't trust him. He wouldn't be able to nose through the will with me here, I thought.

"Suit yourself." He shrugged.

~

When I arrived at Mr. Angelloni's office, he was waiting for me.

"Do you have a copy for me?" he asked sarcastically.

"News travel fast in this fucking town," I replied with disdain.

"There's nothing that happens here that I don't know about," he said arrogantly.

"Then you must know what happened at Eva's."

"No, I know what happened to Helen."

"Sorry to inform you that your plan did not work," I said sardonically.

"For now," he replied.

"Also, I'm sorry to inform you that the papers I was forced to sign mean nothing."

He was livid by now; the arrogant grin had disappeared from his clean-shaven face.

"As you know, I've got the originals," I concluded disdainfully.

Menacingly, I told him I was on my way to the courthouse to have him removed completely from my aunt's estate.

10

It was starting to rain when I left Angelloni's office, so I didn't notice at first when two guys approached me.

"Come with us," one of the guys said as he grabbed me by the arm.

"The boss wants to see you," the other said, pushing me inside their car.

Will this ever end?

There was one more guy inside the car, the driver.

"Hello, Sam, do you remember me?" a voice with a heavy accent said.

"Joe Florentine. Or should I say, Moe, Larry, and Curly?" I was trying to be funny. Nevertheless, I felt the blood leaving my face.

"Where is my money, motherfucker?" Without giving me a chance to reply, Florentine started beating on me. "Let's go for a ride."

"Where, boss?" Larry, the driver, asked.

"To the fucking cemetery," Joe said in a raspy voice.

The menacing ride took forever. I knew what would happen; once we arrived, there would be a bloody nose or maybe a couple of broken ribs. I wasn't even going to ask how they found me.

"Joe, there's no need for this," I said desperately.

"You insulted my intelligence thinking you could hide," he said loudly.

"No, I had a family emergency," I said.

"So, where is my seventy-five K?" he asked.

"I have it," I promptly replied.

"Make it eighty-five Ks; I have to pay the finder's fee."

"C'mon, give me a break."

"You'll get your break as soon as we reach the damn cemetery."
They all laughed.

There was no way to placate these goons. They made a living giving
people these kinds of breaks. An ill feeling lodged at the bottom of my
stomach as I became nauseated and short of breath.

"We're here, boss," the driver announced.

"So, Sam, show me the money," Joe said.

"I don't have it with me," I said fretfully.

"So then you don't have it?" He spoke with impatience.

"Give me twenty-four hours," I begged. Now I was asking for the
satirical twenty-four hours.

"You really think I'm crazy, don't you?" Joe said.

~

I don't remember how long they punched me.

"You got twelve hours! Next time we won't be so gentle, *comprende,
amigo?*"

"*Si.*"

"Sal, stay with him, or he'll do a Houdini on us."

"What, boss, drown?" Sal asked.

"You idiot!"

"But, boss," Sal objected.

"You're responsible for him," Joe barked.

Sal and I were dropped off near my Jeep.

"I'll do the driving," Sal said, taking the keys from my hand.

I didn't object. I was still in pain.

"Where to?" he asked.

"To the…" I trailed off. "Give me a sec." *Come on, Sam, think! If we
go to the bank…*No, I didn't want Sal to know what bank. "To my motel,
but stop at the liquor store first," I ordered.

I bought beer and already-made sandwiches for the two of us. Sal
wasn't the sharpest knife in the drawer; maybe if I got him drunk, I
could get rid of him—at least while I went the bank.

~

Back at the motel room, Sal did not waste time; he immediately grabbed a beer and a sandwich. *Maybe I can pick his brain…and he'll tell me who gave them information on my whereabouts*, I thought.

"So, Sal Pasquale, how long you been in this line of work?" I asked.

"Awhile," he replied.

"Is the pay good?"

"Is easy work," he answered. As I had anticipated, he didn't have a clue that I was picking his brain.

"Any heavy lifting included?" I asked sarcastically.

"Sometimes," the moron answered.

I went for it, asking him what I wanted as we drank chilled beers and ate the sandwiches. "Do you get a cut of the finder's fee?"

"Depends," he answered.

"Here, another beer," I offered.

"Depends on who does the finding," he continued.

"Did you find me?" I asked, curious.

"No, the boss got a call from someone in this fucking town."

"Can I ask you a question?" I said.

"Shoot!"

"Excuse me?" I asked.

"Ask!" he said.

"Can I hire you as a finder?" I asked.

"What?" He sounded incredulous.

"Yeah, man, you have the right to make money too!" I said.

Sal didn't bite. After a few more beers, he was asleep. I didn't wait; I took the keys from his jacket pocket and took off.

11

I t was raining hard as I drove to Riverdale. I parked and waited for the bank to open around eight o'clock. I glanced at my watch—it was only one a.m. It was going to be a long night.

I must have fallen asleep because a loud rap on my window startled me.

"Are you OK?" the shadow at the window asked.

"Yes," I answered as I rolled the window down.

"You cannot camp here." It was a bank security officer.

"I'm waiting for the bank to open," I told him.

"The bank opens at eight; you'll have to move," he ordered.

"C'mon, man!" I said.

"There's a truck stop on Highway One-Eleven; you can wait there, friend."

~

I was getting very tired; maybe I'd just get the money from the safe-deposit box and take off to South America, leave everything behind. The idea sounded terrific, but finding out who killed Aunt Millie and who assaulted Eva sounded more thrilling. I had been running for too long, and it was time to stop. *I need to have my head examined*, I thought.

I couldn't sleep at all; the coming and going of vehicles at the truck stop was too noisy. I thought of better times when everything was much easier, when I didn't have to hide or run from anybody—only from Sophia and her father. How I longed for those easier times. I had vivid memories of soft beds, never having to sleep in the car, warm blankets, and soft pillows in the most expensive hotels and at home.

~

Sal was still sleeping when I came back. What a moron. I was sore all over; I felt like I had been run over by a truck.

Sal woke up and asked, "What are you up to?"

"I just came back from the bank, moron," I nonchalantly replied.

The color left his face when he realized he had failed to follow the orders given by his boss.

"Call Joe and tell him I got the money." I could smell his fear.

"If you tell Joe that you went alone, I'll kill you," he said.

"I think that you're in no position to make threats."

"Look, I'll do whatever if you don't tell Joe," he implored.

"Whatever?" I asked.

"Yes, I don't want to go to Box City," he answered.

"What?" I asked.

"Bumped off, erased, liquidated, you know?" He pointed at his right temple with his index finger.

"The cuckoo house?"

"No. Dead!"

Finally, Sal had bitten. Everybody wanted to cling to life, no matter how bad it got, and that's a fact.

I needed to get rid of Sal to continue with my work. I needed to go to the courthouse and start a motion against Angelloni, and then go to Aunt Millie's house to go back to the basement—now that I knew that I was the heir, I could come and go as needed.

Should I leave Sal at the motel room waiting for me? He said he would do whatever, didn't he? I saw the panic in his eyes when I told him what I was thinking.

"Call Joe," I told Sal.

"Now?" he asked, vexed.

"Yes, and remember you owe me big time, and I'm collecting," I said.

"You got me by the balls," he said indignantly.

"I know, asshole, and this is what I want from you," I said with contempt.

"Just ask."

"I need to know who gave Joe my location."

"I don't know," he answered nervously.

"You're going to find out for me!" I said.

"Either way, I'm a dead man! Gimme a break." Sal sounded hopeless.

"You'll get your break as soon as we reach the damn cemetery." It felt good to be in the driver's seat for once.

~

I was walking tall on my way to the courthouse information desk. From the corner of my eye, I saw Sergeant Miller walking in front of me. I wasn't ready for him yet—his time was coming. I found the information desk.

"Where is the estate court?" I asked.

"You mean probate court?" the clerk said dryly.

Fucking government workers. "Yes." I answered in like manner.

"Is this for you or somebody else?" she asked impatiently.

"My aunt died a few weeks ago and—"

She interrupted me. "What is your aunt's name?"

"Mildred C. Wilmot."

"Just a moment, let me look it up," she said, glancing at her computer.

"I need to remove her attorney from the estate," I said.

"Who are you?" she asked.

"Her nephew."

"Are you an attorney?"

"No," I replied.

"Do you have an attorney?"

"No."

"I suggest you get one," she said.

"Can you recommend one?" I asked.

"Sorry, we are not a referral service," she said flatly.

"Where can I find one?" I asked.

"Try the Bar Association."

"Thanks," I said tongue-in-cheek. *Bitch!*

I felt discouraged, but I was not giving up. At least I had taken care of Joe and his goons. Sal was to call me within twelve hours with the information I had requested in exchange for my discretion. I was in charge now.

Focus, Sam, focus, I told myself. *Don't go off on a tangent—remember what's important here.*

Yeah, I remembered. I was one of those "go off on a tangent" kind of guys. My college years were full of incidents that depressed me continuously to the point of insanity. I wasn't good enough...I would never amount to anything, yet I could have any girl I wanted...but I didn't want to have more pain. Dark thoughts and moods swings were my daily companions until I met Sophia. I think now that I was her charity case.

"Don't go off on a tangent, dear," she used to tell me.

I always ended up feeling that I was the "bad guy" in our relationship.

Sophia was the kind of woman who controlled her emotions with grace. She never made judgment calls about anybody—except me. She was right most of the time. I had nobody to blame but my unstable childhood and my cold mother.

To my consolation, that was then, and this was now.

~

Mapletown: anyone can lose their sense of time here. I couldn't remember how long I had been here since my aunt passed away. Was it two weeks? I wasn't sure—maybe two months.

The trees were completely naked by now; the breeze had turned into wind and the rain into ice. The streets and houses were gaily decorated with colorful lights, but inside me was a feeling of despair. This time of year left me feeling despondent and sad. I remembered the towering Christmas tree adorning our living room, elegantly decorated with gold and red, and exchanging lavish gifts with Sophia. Now here I was, sitting alone in the dark in Aunt Millie's musty house.

Stop feeling sorry for yourself, asshole, and finish this mess! I told myself.

I got dressed and headed for Maggie's Diner to eat dinner. I could use the noise.

~

I was finishing Maggie's specialty of meatloaf and mashed potatoes when a scruffy man approached my table.

"Sorry, I give to the homeless shelter," I said coldly.

"Excuse me?" he replied. "My name is Jacob Sinclair, attorney at law. Rita, the court clerk, told me that you needed an attorney to handle some legal issues related to probate law." He handed me his business card.

"Oh yeah, sit down. Would you like a cup of coffee?" Didn't the clerk say that they didn't do referrals?

"To be honest with you, can I have a piece of pie too?" he asked.

"Of course, order whatever you like," I said.

"Thank you!"

"What kind of law you practice?" I asked curiously.

"Probate and criminal law."

"Do you practice here in Mapletown?" I needed someone who knew the law in this damn town.

Jacob J. Sinclair had the qualifications I was looking for in an attorney: he wasn't connected, and he was broke and hungry. So broke that he was facing eviction from his office, he said.

"What are your honoraria?" I asked.

"Excuse me?" he replied with pie crumbs hanging from his unshaven face.

"Your fees!"

"Oh yes...my fees!"

"You need money, don't you?"

"Yes, I also need a place to stay, you know. I'm sleeping in my office."

I liked this guy's honesty, without forgetting that he was an attorney.

"Do you know Mr. Angelloni?"

"The attorney?"

"Yes."

"Who doesn't know him?"

"Well, I'm glad, because he is the one I'm going after."

"Nobody goes after him, he goes after everybody."

"I'm serious. Are you still interested?"

"He has fucked lots of people."

"Are you interested?"

"I have nothing to lose."

"Where should we start?" I asked.

~

I invited Jacob to Aunt Millie's house to talk over the case and the possibilities of taking Angelloni on.

I explained the whole situation that had been developing since I'd arrived in Mapletown. Jacob listened intently.

"It would be my pleasure to go after that motherfucker," he said.

"I see that you share my sentiments about Angelloni."

"I have waited for a moment like this." Jacob's eyes were aglow with anger.

"Well then, Jacob, this is your chance. One more thing, however. We need to leave our emotions out—you think you can do it?"

We were both tired. I asked him to stay the night since he didn't have a place to go. We continued talking until midnight.

"So, I told you my story; would you mind telling me yours?" I asked.

"The asshole was fucking my wife," Jacob said bitterly. When he'd found out about the affair, he'd filed for a divorce, and of course, Angelloni was his wife's attorney. "They stripped me of my dignity and all I had, to the point that I am in the midst of losing my practice, too."

All this sounded like music to my ears. He wanted to demonstrate the value of his knowledge and experience to someone. The other attorneys in the area were too intimidated by Angelloni, but not Jacob; he was ready to go for Angelloni's jugular.

I offered Jacob that while he worked on my aunt's legal case, he could use one of the rooms at my house—yes, my house—as his office. He liked the idea.

"I'll draw up the contract," he said.

"The sooner, the better," I replied.

"How's Angelloni involved?" he asked.

"He made me sign a document that I had given him my rights."

"We have problems."

"Not really. I have the original testament."

"Good. I will need deeds, documents, bank accounts, and her will."

"I have all that."

"Great! I think we have a case."

"Well, my aunt left a letter where she says that everybody is in Angelloni's pocket."

"Do you have the letter?"

"No, I burned it."

"We still have problems."

"I have something better than that."

"Yeah, what?"

"I have a list where my aunt names people."

"Can't fucking believe how my luck is turning," he gleefully said.

"How well do you know Sergeant Miller?" I asked Jacob.

"I think he is a good cop," he said casually.

"I think he is dirty," I replied cautiously.

"No, not Miller."

"There are lots of details that indicate he is in Angelloni's pocket."

"Leave Hiram Miller to me!"

"He threatened to charge me with my aunt's murder."

"Let me move my stuff, and then we'll take a ride to the police station."

"You can't go looking like that," I said.

"Do I really look homeless?"

"I'll advance you three grand. Buy yourself something that looks professional, and please, get a haircut!"

"When can you have your aunt's documents for me?"

"As soon as you're installed."

"I'll need two rooms—one for my office and one to sleep."

"No problem."

12

Early the next morning, I went to Capitol Bank at Riverdale and took all the documents to the copy center. I'd just met Jacob, and no way was I going to trust him by giving him all the originals. I'd let Jacob take care of all the legal stuff. I felt good; after this, I could concentrate on the basement.

At the copy center, I realized I hadn't gone through the different envelopes in the safe-deposit box; I'd just set them aside for another day. I would not give them to Jacob until I went through them all. I opened one of the envelopes that contained pictures and started going through each one. One caught my attention: it was of Jacob posing with several other people, including two I knew: Angelloni and Eva. I'd have to ask Jacob about it.

It took me a couple of hours to complete the copies; I just couldn't bring myself to trust them to anybody. Then I returned to the bank and put the originals in the safe-deposit box.

~

Jacob was waiting for me at my house to help him unload his few belongings from the rental U-Haul. He had more boxes than furniture. We piled his things in the living room while we emptied Aunt Millie's old bedroom—that was going to be Jacob's temporary accommodations. The bedroom was adjacent to a large parlor that Jacob could use to set up his office.

This project was harder than I had anticipated. "What should I do with my aunt's belongings?" I asked Jacob.

"Everything has to be catalogued as part of her estate," he said.

"How?"

"I know estate auctioneers. For a fee, they help with such agonizing chores."

"Can you call them?" I asked him.

"I see that your aunt had lots of antiques and art—was she a dealer?"

I didn't know much about my aunt's activities; I'd never paid attention. It never crossed my mind to wonder how she supported herself and this huge house. Where was her money coming from? How did she pay for Victor's services? Or the huge estate maintenance costs?

"Watch your back; everybody is connected in Mapletown." Her words resonated in my mind. Was she connected?

Suddenly, I remembered the picture and decided to ask Jacob.

"What can you tell me about this picture?" I watched for sudden changes in his demeanor.

"Where did you get it, and what do you need to know?" he said.

"Who are the people in this picture?"

"You know your aunt, Mr. Angelloni, and me of course. The other two are Judges O'Hara and Matson."

"And the woman?" I asked, pointing at Eva.

"I really don't know who she is. I heard she was married to Angelloni's son."

"Do you know the son?" I kept prodding him with more questions.

"No."

"So, Jacob, were you connected?"

"No. If I had been connected, I wouldn't have ended up homeless," he replied.

"I notice a hint of resentment," I said.

"Well, maybe if you were in my position, you, too, would be resentful."

"So, what was the occasion for the picture?"

"I don't know who took the photo, but that was a charity benefit dinner."

"Did you know my aunt?"

"I used to be a senior partner at Fischer and Lamb. Your aunt hired us for her estate planning."

"How was Angelloni involved? I don't understand."

"Angelloni married into the Lamb family."

"Were you fired from Fischer and Lamb?"

"I was very jealous when I found out my wife's infidelity, and the rest is history," he said. "I went to work for the DA after that."

"Did you get fired from the DA's too?"

"No. I wanted to have my own practice."

~

It took the rest of the day for Jacob to finish settling in. I decided to get out of his way and go to the hospital. I didn't know a single thing about Eva.

In the hospital's parking lot, I got cold feet. If she was involved with Angelloni, I'd better put some distance between us. I decided to have Jacob call the hospital. When I called him, his phone rang several times, but he didn't answer.

When I returned to my place, Jacob was walking away. He didn't see me, so I decided to follow him. The evening was very cold, but he didn't seem to mind.

Jacob was about forty-five years old, tall, and slender. His hair was beginning to gray. He was elegant even with his disheveled appearance. When he went inside the barbershop, I felt a sense of relief. He was trustworthy after all. *Just keep your guard up*, I reminded myself.

It was dark when he came out of the barbershop. I continued to follow him. With his long-legged stride, he arrived quickly at his second stop, the clothing store. He came out looking elegant and casual. *OK, that's enough*, I thought. I felt a little ashamed.

13

When Jacob came back home, loaded with packages, I informed him of some rules he had to respect as long as he was a guest at *my* house.

"You are not allowed in other areas of the house except the kitchen, the laundry room, and the living room."

"Understood." He didn't seem to mind.

"The only bathroom you can use is the one in your room."

"Anything else?" he asked.

"Yes, you clean up after yourself."

"No problem!"

"And you will not use this address as your own."

"I'll rent a box at the post office."

"By the way, you're beginning to look like an attorney!" I said.

"Thank you for giving me your trust," he replied.

"Not yet!"

"I won't disappoint you."

"Talking about that, I need you to do me a favor."

"For you, anything."

"I need you to call the hospital and ask for Eva."

"Eva…what is her last name?"

I realized Eva had never given me her last name, but I vaguely remembered that when I had searched her purse, I saw "Lacek" on her driver's license. "Eva Lacek?" I said.

"Who is Eva Lacek?" Jacob asked as he grabbed his telephone.

"The woman in the picture I showed you earlier."

"What? The one married to Angelloni's son?"

"I guess…"

"Have you lost your marbles?"

"No, that's why I want you to make the call."

"How do you know her?"

"I met her at Gardel's salvage yard."

"I can't fucking believe that you're connected to Angelloni in a very sinister way!" he said.

"I just want to know how she is doing after her attack." I told him all the events I'd had with Eva, her involvement with me, and how I took her to the ER. "She told me that she was running from her husband."

"I believe that!"

"That she was the witness to a murder."

"I've heard that Mickey Angelloni is a real bastard!"

"It was pretty bad!"

"As your attorney, I advise you to keep away from her!" Jacob said.

"She seemed nice."

"Did you give your name at the hospital?" he asked.

"No."

Then: "Did you eat?"

I shook my head no.

"Dinner's on me."

We got in my Jeep and drove to the town's chophouse.

~

The night was still young, and the crowd at the restaurant was light. We finished our dinners with a tumbler of brandy; the taste of the smooth liquor felt exquisite going down my throat.

Against my will, I thought of Sophia. She always insisted on taking our brandy on the formidable terrace of our expensive home. We had often made plans to have children—"at least two," she'd say. At that time, I guessed, I wasn't feeling sorry for myself.

"Do you see your wife at all?" I asked Jacob, trying to find out more about him.

"No. Last I heard of her, she was Angelloni's mistress."

"What's her name?"

"Kate." He answered without emotion.

"Do you have any children?"

"No, thank God!"

We were waiting for the check when Jacob motioned me to look toward the door. Sergeant Miller was walking in with a couple of guys. I felt uneasy.

I was ready to leave, but Jacob had other ideas.

"Take it easy," he said. "I think things are beginning to fall in place." He got up and walked with long strides straight to Miller's table. They shook hands and talked very amiably for a moment.

Then Jacob motioned for me to come to Miller's table. What was he thinking of? He knew that Miller wanted to charge me with murder; he had already booked me for arson.

"Hiram, I want to introduce you to my new client," Jacob said as I approached.

"I think we already met," I said, glaring at Jacob.

"I don't remember," Miller said, stretching his hand out. "I'm Hiram Miller, Sergeant Hiram Miller."

"I know. I'm Sam Stone."

Miller went pale. "What in the hell are you doing here?"

"Taking care of business," I answered.

I knew Jacob could feel the animosity between Miller and me. He leaned toward Miller and very attentively said, "From now on, Hiram, whatever you need to say to Mr. Stone, you have to come through me."

"I'm glad that you're back," Miller said to Jacob while glaring at me.

"Thank you. I'm handling his aunt's case."

"Whatever you need, Jacob," Miller's replied.

"I'll need Mildred's police report. Will it be OK if I pick it up tomorrow?" Jacob said matter-of-factly.

"Oh yeah, you can come any time," Miller said.

"I'll see you tomorrow at ten."

I felt good. I could pat myself on the back for making the right choice with Jacob. I thanked him profusely on our way home.

"I will have the contract ready tomorrow," he said calmly.

For the first time in a long time, I was able to sleep peacefully; no nightmares or night sweats came to disturb me.

~

It was eleven o'clock when I woke up the following morning. I felt rested and ready to take the day on. I found a note on the kitchen table:

> Went to the courthouse to file as your attorney of record; there's fresh coffee, see you later,
>
> Jacob
>
> PS: please get me all the records that you have on your aunt's estate.

I was on my second cup of coffee when my phone rang.

"Sam, this is Jacob."

"Oh? What's up?"

"I'm at the police station picking up the report on your aunt's murder."

"Any luck? Don't forget her death certificate."

"Angelloni must have the death certificate."

"Is Miller giving you shit about it?"

"No, but I need you to come to the police station."

"Why?"

"Formalities."

I didn't like this. *Fuck.* However, for some reason Jacob thought it was necessary; after all, he was the attorney.

~

As soon as I arrived at the police station, I was conducted to the interrogation room. Jacob was there waiting for me with fucking Sergeant Miller.

"What in the fuck is going on?" I asked.

"We have to take a declaration," Miller said.

"It's only a formality," Jacob added.

"A declaration about what?" I asked angrily.

"Your aunt's attack," Miller said.

"Am I a suspect?" I asked.

"Everybody is a person of interest," Miller replied.

"I don't know anything about her attack! I was in San Francisco."

"Then how did you know she was attacked?"

"Mr. Smith at the funeral parlor told me!"

"What about the fire in the cabin?"

"Why should I burn my own property?" I asked incredulously.

This line of questioning continued until Jacob said, "Are you going to charge my client?"

"Not for now," said Miller. "We will call you if we have more questions to ask Mr. Stone."

~

I was livid, and my anger grew even more when Jacob informed me that my declaration had been recorded. I was very sullen, and the silence between us was heavy. Jacob was the first to break it.

"It was necessary to do this, you know."

I didn't answer.

"We know now where Miller stands."

"Now what?" I asked.

"He doesn't have any evidence involving you at all," he said.

"I'm telling you, the man is dirty," I said angrily.

"No, he is not. I know Miller real well."

"He and Angelloni are in cahoots," I told him.

"We will see," Jacob replied.

"Did you file?" I asked.

"No. I needed her death certificate."

"You didn't ask Miller for it?"

'No. He has the accident report."

"Who in the hell has it?"

"Angelloni has the death certificate, and Miller has the crime report."

"Which one do we need?"

"Both. Did you get the papers I asked you for?" Jacob asked in return.

"Yes," I answered dryly.

"Great! We can't lose time."

But I was still mad. I felt that Jacob and Miller had set me up. I had to keep my eyes and ears open, I told myself. "Is there anything else you need from me besides the docs?" I asked dryly.

~

Something bothered me about the camaraderie between Jacob and Miller. I decided to follow my hunch by paying a visit to the court clerk—what was her name? *Think, Sam, think!*

I looked to see if she was wearing an ID, but shit, her ID was backward. I tried to find her name at her desk, but there was only a calendar: Thursday, December 12, 2005.

Finally, I just asked casually, "Hi, do you remember me?"

"Oh yes. The estate case, right?" she said.

"Yes, I just wanted to…" I trailed off.

"Just a moment, let me finish with this," she said apologetically.

What's her name?

"OK. How can I help you?" she asked. At that moment, I overheard someone greeting her by name.

"Yes, Rita, I just came to thank you for sending Jacob Sinclair," I said sincerely.

"I beg your pardon? I didn't send anybody," she exclaimed.

"Jacob Sinclair said you sent him," I interjected.

"I told you that we do not do referrals," she said exasperatedly.

"Do you know Jacob Sinclair?" I asked.

"Of course I know him. He is, or was, an excellent attorney."

"I'm still confused," I said.

"If you hired him as your attorney, you made the right choice; there's not many like him left," she concluded.

14

Rita was a pleasant-looking woman in her mid-forties. She appeared to be knowledgeable and efficient at her desk. She didn't have a wedding band on her finger. I tried to make small talk to see if I could get any kind of useful information from her.

"Seems that you're very popular," I said, trying to make her feel important.

"Yes, I've been working here for fifteen years!" she said proudly.

"Fifteen years! Wow! You must have started when you were thirteen!" I said, trying to compliment her.

"Something like that," she said jokingly.

We both laughed.

"I'm new in this area, and I don't know anybody," I said. "What about we go for a cup of coffee?"

"Sure!" she said.

"When?" I asked.

"I get off in half an hour," she said, glancing at her watch.

"Where?"

"Around the block is a coffee shop, the Early Riser. I'll see you there in half an hour."

~

I couldn't believe my eyes when this gorgeous blonde approached my table.

"What are you drinking?" she asked in a seductive way.

Yes, it was Rita. Her long, silky, blond hair hung freely about her shoulders. She was wearing burgundy lipstick, which made her lips sumptuous and kissable, and her figure, yes, her figure, was svelte.

Her eyes were blue and full of kindness. This wasn't the same dull Rita who sat behind the court clerk's desk.

"I'm just drinking a cup of black coffee. Can I get you something?" I asked.

"Whatever you're drinking," she said.

That was easy, I thought.

I didn't want it to appear too obvious that the only reason I invited her for a cup of coffee was to pick her brain. I started some casual chitchat to break the ice. "How long you have lived in Mapletown?"

"I was born here," she said. "When I turned twenty-one, I left."

"Where did you go?" I asked, trying to keep the conversation going.

"I went to New York. And you?"

"I was born in San Francisco, and I came here when my aunt died."

"Mildred C. Wilmot…I'm so sorry!" she said.

I completely forgot the events of the day, though I did notice that my anger had dissipated entirely. We talked about our failed marriages, politics, and religion. I intentionally didn't ask questions related to her job. I was dying to ask her about Jacob, Angelloni, and Miller. *Some other time*, I told myself. For now, I just wanted to enjoy her company.

"I never introduced myself properly," I said a while later. "My name is Sam W. Stone." I extended my hand.

"Rita Malone. Nice to meet you!" she said in return.

It was very cold when we left the Early Riser Café, and I offered her a ride home. On the way to her place, we made plans to have dinner the following evening.

~

I had really enjoyed Rita's company and was looking forward to seeing her again. In addition, I was looking forward to asking her— tactfully though—what she knew about Jacob, Miller, and Angelloni.

When I got home, Jacob was nowhere to be found. Maybe that was good—I didn't know how I would react when I saw him to confront him. I detested liars. Which was why I detested myself so much—I had my share of shit, too; come to think about it, I had shit loads.

I went straight to bed. I could still smell her perfume and hear her gleeful laughter. I said her name out loud: "Rita Malone."

~

I woke up the next day feeling alive. I felt so darn good that I decided not to confront Jacob about Rita. I would leave that issue until I found out more about him from Rita's own words.

I heard Jacob moving around in his room and went up and knocked on his door. As soon as he opened the door, I handed him the copies of the documents he had requested. He immediately asked, "Is the list with the names here?"

"No, I don't see the need for that," I immediately answered.

"What about the pictures?" he asked.

"I don't see the need for that either," I replied.

"I think it is important that I have all the documentation pertaining to your aunt," he said defensively.

"If you give me an explanation of how is that so, I wouldn't have a problem making it available for you," I said indifferently.

Jacob seemed very uncomfortable with the way the conversation was going; he opted to change the conversation by apologizing about the declaration at the police station the day before.

"Where did you go after we finished with Miller?" he inquired.

"I was so angry at the ambush, plus I needed to cool down, so I went for a cup of coffee," I said, still bothered.

"I'm sorry about that, but I thought that if Sergeant Miller wanted to arrest you, he had his chance," Jacob said.

"But you didn't say a thing, Jacob," I complained.

"I knew he had nothing on you. Otherwise, believe me, I wouldn't let you incriminate yourself."

Jacob sounded sincere and I believed him.

"I need to ask you another question," he said.

"Go ahead."

"Is Miller on the list?"

I was embarrassed to admit that I hadn't gone over the list completely. "I don't remember—I'll check on that," I said carefully.

"Please do so, and let me know, Sam." His voice was barely audible.

Then he turned his attention to the envelopes I had handed him, earnestly opening one of them. Jacob was disciplined, organized, and very articulate; I hoped he had what it took for his new challenge: taking on Angelloni.

"I'll sort out these docs as soon as possible," he said matter-of-factly.

"Will it take long?" I asked.

"It depends."

"Depends on what?" I asked.

"First of all, I need to find out what kind of docs these are." He was peering into the envelopes.

"OK, let me know if you need me to help." I had to bite my lips. I was dying to confront him, but I reminded myself to wait.

"What are your plans for the rest of the day?" he asked casually.

"I have something I need to attend to. By the way, did you call the company that you told me about?" I asked. "The estate auctioneers?"

"Oh yeah, I'll dig up their number later," he said apologetically.

"OK, I guess I'll start at the basement and take an inventory of the stuff there," I said, trying to sound trite. I really wanted to go to the secret place. "If you need anything, I'll be in the basement."

15

I got the flashlight and light bulbs I had purchased. I couldn't recollect when I'd bought the stuff. Was that important? I didn't think so.

I glanced at my watch: eleven o'clock in the morning. I had plenty of time to concentrate on the basement project.

The basement was humid and stale. I felt suffocated, but I was glad I had moved the stack of boxes away from the wall. I proceeded to change the burned-out light bulbs. I wished I had purchased a space heater—but that would be crazy; with the cramped boxes and furniture, it would be like setting the house on fire. Still, I kinda liked the idea—setting the house on fire.

As I was really toying with the idea of setting the house on fire and watching some of my problems going up in smoke, I suddenly remembered the fire at the cabin. Miller would have a legitimate opportunity to arrest me if this house went up in smoke too. I would keep the idea at the back of my mind; it might come in handy.

I was so busy thinking about solving some of my problems that I didn't notice Jacob at the top of the stairs, intently watching my moves.

"Boy, you have your hands full!" he said with astonishment.

"What in the hell?" I spurted out.

"I'm sorry, I didn't mean to startle you." He laughed. "I have the telephone number for the auctioneers."

"Thanks. Leave it on top of the kitchen table for me." I still felt shocked, though I managed to answer calmly.

"Do you need any help?" he asked.

"No, I can take care of this; you take care of the legal stuff," I said abruptly. I knew I sounded bothered and impatient, so I added, "I really appreciate your offer."

I pretended to continue taking inventory, but at the same time, I watched Jacob from the corner of my eye. He seemed to have gotten the message and took off without saying another word. I really hated nosy people; if Jacob turned out to be like that, I would have to ask him to leave.

~

Trying to gain access to the secret door, I moved a box out of the way, but the bottom gave out, and its contents spilled at my feet. I shined the flashlight toward the floor, where a photo album lay open at my feet. Carefully, I picked it up and saw some old pictures. *It's not a photo album; it's a door to the past*, I thought. A past I didn't care to remember.

There were photos of Dorothy C. Wilmot, my mother. Thinking about her chilled the blood in my veins. She would tell me time after time that I had been the product of a rape. That it would be better for me to die, that she couldn't stand the sight of me. I remembered waiting for a caress from her, but all I got was her brutal emotional abuse. She had gloated over my pain. Whenever I was in trouble at school, she would say, "Why should you be different? You came from shit, you'll always be shit."

The memories were painful. In a fit of anger, I destroyed her pictures.

Jacob appeared at the top of the stairs again and called, "Is everything OK?"

"Y-yes," I answered.

"I heard loud noises and wondered if you were all right."

"Some boxes fell," I said.

"Be careful. If something were to happen to you, I would never be able to find you in there." He sounded disturbed.

"Don't worry," I said reassuringly. "How's everything going with the docs?" I tried to change subjects.

"Making waves."

"Back to work," I said. With that, Jacob was gone.

16

My mother was a very beautiful, tall woman with soft ivory skin, wavy auburn hair, and a shapely figure. She was three years younger than plain-looking Aunt Millie. I remembered her eyes, how they looked golden when hit by the sun.

I never met my father, but according to Aunt Millie, I was his spitting image. I never asked about him. I never knew his name. I never gathered the courage to ask Aunt Millie or my mother about him. Was he dead? I guessed I would never know.

The only two people who could give me information about him were dead. I had a very strange feeling as I tormented myself—like an excuse for my fuck-ups. Wasn't that what society said? I was a victim of my genes and my upbringing. That was a good argument for fuck-ups like me.

I decided to leave feeling sorry for myself for another day. I really needed to work on this damned mess for now.

I could hear Jacob rummaging around upstairs; the house was old, and the floorboards were constantly creaking. I didn't need to see him to know that at that moment he was staring out the window, smoking a cigarette.

It was amazing how I could remember the layout of what used to be Aunt Millie's quarters. I thought of summer nights when Aunt Millie would wait for me to come back from an escapade. I would come to her bedroom and talk for hours. But we never, ever talked about my mother or my father.

Millie was the only relative who had treated me with tenderness and respect. I swore to find her killer.

~

I finally got the burned-out light bulb changed. But when I turned the switch on, sparks flew all over the place, and the light bulb went out again. *Shit!* I was about to lose my wits over the fucking situation. I shined the flashlight all over the place, looking for an extinguisher just in case I needed one.

The idea of setting the house on fire came back to mind. I immediately shook it off, like shaking water from your head after a rain. I had never been a handyman; I had no idea where to start. It never occurred to me that maybe the wiring was faulty and old, like the rest of the house.

Glancing at my watch, I knew it was getting late. I was frustrated that I'd spent the whole day in the basement without accomplishing anything. I was furious at the wasted time. I had to quit this futile attempt to replace the light bulb. I needed an electrician.

~

I stopped at the hardware store on my way to pick up Rita for our dinner date.

"I'm having problems with a burned-out light bulb—what can I do?" I asked the clerk.

"What kind of a problem?" the clerk asked helpfully.

"I've changed the light bulb about three times, but every time I turn the switch on, it burns out again."

"Have you checked the wiring?" the clerk asked.

"No, how can I do that?" I asked, feeling dimwitted.

"You will need a tester, for starters," he said.

"I have never done anything like that!" I replied, alarmed.

"In that case, I suggest you call an electrician."

"Do you have a how-to book?" I asked idiotically.

"Don't spend your money; get an electrician."

That was as far as I would take it, at least for today. Tomorrow would be a new day.

I got in my Jeep and drove to Rita's place on Willow Avenue.

~

When I came to Rita's door, I noticed a black car driving away. I knocked, but there was no answer. The house was dark; there was no

71

light at all. I knocked again and still no answer. I called her name. "Rita, hello Rita!"

I went back to my Jeep and sat for a while. Maybe she was getting ready and couldn't hear the door. I went back and knocked once more. The house felt empty; there was no movement whatsoever.

Did she forget our dinner date? Disappointment took hold of me. She hadn't even had the courtesy to call it off. I pictured her laughing behind the curtains of her front window. A cold rain started to fall. Finally, I drove away. I felt stupid.

~

It was nine o'clock when I made it back home. I saw the light still on in Jacob's room. Jacob wasn't alone. The man was getting lucky. *I'm pretty sure he can handle it,* I thought and went straight to my room.

I lay awake for most of the night. Muffled voices came from Jacob's room. I strained my ears, trying to make out what they were arguing about; they sounded pissed. I got up and went to his door, where I stood quietly for a moment to see what I could catch. I heard Jacob's voice saying, "I told you it was a bad idea."

The woman's voice was almost a whisper, and I couldn't understand what she said. Sensing my presence on the other side of the door, they became silent. I decided to knock on his door.

"W-what?" came Jacob's angry response.

"Is everything OK in there?" I asked with concern.

"Y-yes, I have a friend over for a visit," he replied. "But everything is fine."

"In that case, have a good night."

As I went downstairs for a glass of cold water, I heard Jacob's voice behind me. "I'm sorry," he muttered.

"What for?" I asked.

"For having a friend over without clearing it with you first," he said.

"Who is she?" I was curious.

"An out-of-town friend," he said hesitantly.

I pretended to not notice his hesitation. "No problem. Is she going to spend the night?" I asked.

"No, she left."

"When will you have information for me about the documents?" I asked.

"Within a couple of days," he said.

"I'm going back to bed. I have some errands to run tomorrow," I said.

"Good night then. I'll let you know when the docs are ready."

I could smell Jacob's mystery friend's perfume still lingering in the air as I made my way upstairs. It smelled familiar.

I lay awake thinking of Rita.

was awakened by my telephone. The loud ringing penetrated my head like a drill.

"Sam?" a husky voice asked.

"Yes, this is Sam. Who is this?"

"Hi, Sam, this is Sal."

"Hi, Sal, I was beginning to think that you had disappeared," I said.

"No, I'm still here," Sal said.

"Do you have my information?" I asked him.

"No, not yet, that's why I'm calling you," he said apologetically.

"And when would you think you'd have it?" I asked.

"Look, cut me some slack. I cannot go around asking these guys," Sal said.

"I don't give a fuck! Get me my info!" I yelled.

"I'm waiting for Joe to go and pay the finder's fee, and then I'll know who found you," he said.

"There must be another way for you to find out, right?" I probed.

"I suppose," he replied.

"Listen, asshole, 'suppose' you get his phone-call record," I said angrily.

"If I get caught doing that, I'll get erased." He was nervous.

"Do you think I care?" I asked coldly.

"I'll get you the info as soon as I can, all right?" he assured me.

"Call me at the end of the day," I ordered him.

"Today?" he asked.

"Yes, moron, today!" I barked.

~

I thought of the day ahead, and I really didn't know where to start. I needed to get an electrician, but I didn't want to have someone nosing around in the basement.

What was the alternative? Shit. When things got complicated, they got really complicated.

I was very pessimistically drinking coffee when the idea came: *get extensions cords—that would solve the problem!*

The day was dreary, dark, and cold—maybe I should get a space heater, too, I thought. I anticipated the basement would be like the day: dreary, dark, and cold.

I left the house and drove once again to the hardware store. I felt like such an idiot trying to explain to the unimportant clerk that I needed about twenty electric-cord extensions.

The clerk's eyes opened big in surprise, and he tried to hold his laughter. He suggested a heavy-duty industrial electrical extension. "It's the safe way to tackle your project."

I glared at him.

"Can you show me where they are?" I asked disdainfully.

"Sure," he said.

"I will also need a space heater."

The unimportant clerk nodded as he walked with me in tow. "What kind of heater do you have in mind?" he asked.

"How many kinds are there?" I answered, irritated.

"Kerosene or electric?" he asked amused.

"What's the fucking difference?" I asked.

"Well, sir, you have to buy kerosene for the kerosene heater and need proper ventilation; the electric you just plug in," he said patronizingly.

"Show them to me," I barked.

"Do you want to see the extensions first, or the heaters?" he asked, holding his laughter.

The wise clerk suggested not to get either heater; the electric one wouldn't work because I was having problems with the electrical wiring, and the kerosene one wouldn't work because of the poor ventilation in the basement.

"You would be asking for trouble." He was condescending.

"I really appreciate it."

I could almost hear him say in his mind, *Mr. Idiot, what do you want the extension for?*

"I need to run light to the basement," I answered.

"Do you have a lamp to plug into the extension?" he asked.

"No, I didn't think about that," I said, feeling foolish.

"I thought so; do you want to get one?" the jerk said.

"I suppose," I answered.

This kid really made me feel like a moron; everybody made me feel like a moron. My self-worth had been deathly injured the past twenty-five years.

"I'll show you where they are—"

I interrupted him. I was beginning to appreciate his knowledge. "Go fetch one for me." I wanted to add, "fucking asshole," but I restrained myself. I guessed I was still resentful.

~

When I left the store, I drove to the courthouse. I wanted to see Rita and ask her what had happened yesterday. But when I arrived there, it seemed that everyone was leaving the place.

A guard stopped me at the door. "Sorry, you can't go in."

"Why?" I asked.

"We are evacuating the building," he said.

"Is there a threat?" I asked, intrigued.

"No, the heating system is malfunctioning," he informed me.

"I just need to find the clerk Rita Malone," I said.

"I haven't seen her."

"Can I go in quickly and see if I can find her?"

"Sorry, no one can go in."

People were leaving the building, bitching about the incident. I got back in my car and drove away.

The rain was heavy, and the wind was howling; the naked trees reaching toward the sky appeared to be grotesque ghosts dancing in the wind. A heavy darkness started to descend; everything looked eerie and menacing.

Enough of this Steven King shit, I told myself as I stopped at Rita's house.

I sat in the car awhile, wondering if I was doing the right thing. *What the fuck?* I thought. I got out and walked up to her door. I knocked and waited. The house was still and dark. Hesitant, I knocked again.

From the corner of my eye, I saw a neighbor peeping through the window of her house. By now, I was curious. I went next door and knocked at the neighbor's door.

Immediately the door opened.

"Who are you looking for?" an elderly woman asked, peeping through the door.

"Rita Malone," I answered.

"I haven't seen her," she replied.

~

I went back home after my failed attempt to locate Rita. Jacob was staring out the window again, smoking his cigarette. I didn't want him to see what I had purchased. I didn't want him to come and stick his nose in or ask me about my project in the basement.

I drove my Jeep to the back of the house and headed to the garage. Maybe I could haul the stuff through the kitchen door. I thought that having Jacob living at the house could become a problem, but I shrugged it off. Now it felt as if his eyes were always watching every move I made, to the point that I became quite uncomfortable; I felt that I had to give him explanations of my comings and goings.

He was at the kitchen door waiting for me. "What did you buy this time?" he asked.

None of your business, I felt like saying. Instead I answered as amiably as I could, "I needed this stuff to keep working in the basement."

"Have you advanced at all?" he asked.

"Not really. Every time I try to work there, something breaks," I replied.

"The house is old," he said.

"Yes. There's no light in the basement, among other things," I said hopelessly.

I had to give Jacob the impression that everything was in the open, so I acted very casual while I brought the stuff in.

"Sorry that I don't stop to chat," I said.

"I'd better leave you alone," Jacob said.

"What about you? Have you made any advances in the docs?" I asked.

"When you have a chance, I can show you where I'm at," he said.

"Sure, just give me an hour to finish taking this stuff to the basement," I said.

I continued to check the items I had purchased. I'd better get a padlock for the basement, I thought.

I had no idea whether the extension cord was going to do the job. I had no idea if it was long enough, either. The only idea I had was to confront Jacob about lying to me about Rita.

~

When I glanced at my watch, I saw that it was time to go upstairs to see Jacob.

I grabbed a bottle of scotch on my way up. I always felt more assertive with a couple of drinks in my system.

I offered him a drink, and he accepted with a nod. Then I would let him show me what he had accomplished with my aunt's docs. We sat comfortably, sipping our drinks without saying a word. We looked at each other, trying to read each other's mind.

"What do you have for me?" I asked at last.

"I wanted you to see the documents," Jacob said, pointing to his desk.

"What are they?" I asked.

"Deeds, stock certificates, insurance policies, bonds," he said.

"Are they worth anything?" I asked.

"You said that there were pictures and a list, right?"

"Yes," I answered.

"Do you still have them?" he asked.

"Yes, but I don't see that they are relevant to my aunt's estate," I replied.

"I would like to see them and make that determination," he said, lowering his voice.

"Jacob, I think we covered this before, didn't we?" I was intrigued. Why in hell did he need to see the pictures?

I got up to leave Jacob's room without reaching a determination on the pictures and the list. But I stopped before reaching the door and reminded him that we still hadn't signed a contract between him and me.

I noticed the color leaving Jacob's face as I closed the door behind me. Had I made a mistake by taking Jacob in? Who was he anyway? I needed to find out if he was who he said he was. How? How did someone find the background information on people?

I also needed to find Rita.

I could hear the train inside my head approaching. I retired to my room after taking a couple of aspirins; I didn't need to have a headache blurring my thinking.

18

I got up early the following day and went for breakfast at Maggie's Diner. I was ordering the early-bird special when a woman walked up next to the waiter and greeted me.

"Hello, Sam!" the weary voice said. It sounded familiar. I was expecting to see Rita. I lifted my head from the menu.

"Eva!" I couldn't believe my eyes.

"Surprised?" she asked.

"I thought I would never see you again!" I said earnestly.

"I thought I would never see me again too," she said with a weak smile.

"What happened—do you remember?" My voice quivered when I asked.

"No, I don't remember," she said, her voice sounding gravelly.

Unconvinced, I asked again, "Who did this to you? Did you see anyone?"

"I-I cannot remember. I lie awake at night trying to remember, but nothing!"

"When were you discharged?" I asked.

"Early today," she replied.

"I thought about you constantly. I wanted to call you," I said.

"I thought about you too. I thought about coming to your house looking for you," she said.

"You found me!" I said cheerfully.

"I want to ask you a question," Eva said, looking away.

"Go ahead, but first sit down," I said, pulling out a chair for her.

"Did you take me to the hospital?" she asked.

"Yes," I replied.

"Thanks. Did you see anybody at my place?"

"No. Someone hit my head from behind, and I lost consciousness."

"Thanks to you, Sam, I'm alive."

Eva looked disjointed and pale. She'd lost a lot of weight.

"How's your aunt's case going?" she asked, sounding curious.

"Not that well," I said, sounding disappointed.

"Where are you?" she asked.

"Well, I have an attorney working on the case," I informed her.

"Good! Who is he?" She tried to sound interested.

"Jacob Sinclair. He told me to keep away from you, that you were married to Angelloni's son. Is that so?"

She appeared to be uncomfortable with my question and avoided answering it. "Jacob Sinclair?" she said.

"Yes, do you know him?" I asked.

She got up, looked around her, and started to leave. "I-I really got to go," she said nervously.

"Eva, wait!" I called after her, but she was gone.

I felt disheartened. I had so many questions to ask her.

Well, I told myself, I had so many things and problems at hand that I didn't need to add her to the list—for now. I was sure I would run into her again. It was good, though, to see that she was alive and well, as far as I could tell.

I wondered where she was staying. Was she in danger? *The less you know…*, I told myself.

I thought of my own situation. My plate was full. I couldn't bring myself to trust anybody, and those thoughts were beginning to depress me. The bleak weather and the season weren't helping much, either. *Something has to give*, I thought desperately.

My appetite was gone. I pushed aside the warm breakfast; coffee would do for now.

I sat awhile, swirling my cup of coffee, silently watching the black and steaming ripples. My mind was blank, and it felt good.

~

It was about nine thirty when I left the diner. I drove by the court-house to see if it was back open. The parking lot was empty; only service trucks were parked on the lot. I assumed it was still closed and kept on driving.

I thought of taking another run to Rita's but decided against it. Maybe later.

On my way home, I drove by Angelloni's office. Through force of habit, I looked toward his office—maybe Eva had come this way. I was half a block past Angelloni's when I looked back through my rear-view mirror and saw a tall figure entering his office.

Not thinking much of it, I continued driving. Then my foot suddenly slammed on the brake. "Jacob!"

Tires screeched as I made a U-turn to go back by Angelloni's office.

I was acting irrational when I stumbled into Angelloni's and went past Miss Harris.

"Stop!" she yelled.

"Where is Angelloni?" I demanded.

"He is in a meeting. You can't go—" Too late. I was already inside his private office.

Angelloni and Jacob were drinking coffee.

"What in the hell?" Angelloni was furious.

"Sam, what are you doing here?" Jacob asked.

"What in the fuck are *you* doing here?" I asked Jacob angrily.

"Get out of my office!" Angelloni ordered.

"By the way, this is my building, asshole!" I informed Angelloni.

The pallor in Angelloni's face was noticeable.

"I hope you were discussing lease terms with Mr. Angelloni," I said to Jacob.

Both Angelloni and Jacob were without words, looking at each other.

"Don't mind me; continue with your meeting," I said very patronizingly as I sat down next to Jacob. "Seriously, guys, if you're discussing my aunt's estate, I need to be here." I was feeling tremendous.

Angelloni glared at me.

"By the way, can I have a cup of coffee?" I asked as if it were nothing.

"Sam, can I have a word with you?" Jacob asked.

"Yes, Jacob, shoot!" I said.

"In private," he muttered.

"Angelloni, can you give us a second?" I motioned for him to leave.

Angelloni stood up and started for the door.

"Please send Miss Harris in with my coffee," I told Angelloni.

"Fuck you!" he said as he exited.

"What in the fuck is wrong with you?" Jacob asked.

"Did I fart in your nest, Jacob?" I asked.

"What are you talking about?" he asked.

"Are you and Angelloni conspiring against me?" I retorted.

"No, since the court in not in session, I decided to meet him here," he said.

"Really?" I asked, unconvinced.

"Really. I wanted to see where he was standing in regard to your aunt's estate," he said.

"Now what?" I asked, feeling like a moron.

"I don't know. I hope that Angelloni is not pissed," he said.

"Afraid of him?" I asked.

"No, I was hoping to work in a professional manner," he said, glaring.

"Pigs don't have ethics!" I mumbled.

Angelloni came in carrying a hot, steaming cup of coffee.

"Look, Sam, we started off on the wrong foot," he said as he handed me the coffee.

"Talk to my attorney," I said as I got up and headed for the door.

~

I felt the urge to lose myself in nostalgic memories as I headed for home. Aunt Millie's gentle face was in my mind as if I'd seen her only yesterday. I could hear her voice resonating in my brain: "Sam, oh Sam, I'm so glad that you came to visit again." She never asked or talked about my mother—it was as if she didn't exist.

Aunt Millie treated me with love and respect. I felt bad that I had stopped visiting her, and I felt even worse that I wasn't making any progress on finding who murdered her.

I experienced a lot of turmoil as I took inventory of my standing with Aunt Millie's demise, Angelloni, the basement, and now Jacob. I had no idea how these played out. What about Eva and Rita? Not to mention the map that I'd found!

19

Rain was falling furiously when I arrived at the house. Lightning illuminated the dark and menacing sky; the thundering was deafening.

I parked the car in the driveway closest to the house. I was soaking wet by the time I got inside. I went directly to my room to remove the wet clothes.

I was heading toward the basement when my cell phone rang. "Hello," I answered.

Nothing—only static at the other end. I hung up.

My phone started to beep, letting me know there was a voice-mail message for me to retrieve.

"Sam, this is Sal. I have the info. I will see you at the cemetery tonight at eight."

It was still early, so I continued with the basement plan. Thinking about that plan sent shivers down my back; the lightning, thunder, and rain continued with no end in sight.

Anticipating the basement's coldness and dampness, I got the electrical extension ready to plug into the outlet. At that instant, the lamp connected to the extension cord went out. Shit! Where had I put the flashlight? I stumbled in the darkness to get to the door.

I flipped the light switch in the kitchen and—nothing. We were having a blackout.

Nothing I could do. In despair, I sat in the living room. It was creepy to see the optical illusions on the furniture and walls in the living room caused by the lightning. It seemed as if the furniture and objects had recovered lives of their own and were moving around.

I had seen many storms, but I had never paid attention to such a vivid optical display. The naked branch of the tree outside the front window looked like the arm of the Grim Reaper scratching the pane in its attempt to come inside and do its sinister duty.

I was abruptly pulled from my trance by the front door slamming with force. A silhouette appeared in the darkness. At first, it caught me by surprise, but within seconds, I was able to recognize the shadowy figure.

"Some storm," I said.

"You scared the shit out of me!" was Jacob's reply. "What in the hell are you doing sitting in the dark?"

"We have a blackout," I said pessimistically.

"Light some candles, for Pete's sake," he said.

"Do you have matches?" I asked.

"Have you seen a smoker without lights?" he said as he handed me a book of matches.

"I have no idea where the candles are either," I said, lighting a match.

"I thought you bought a couple of flashlights—didn't you?" he said.

"Yes, I did. They're in the basement," I said, feeling foolish.

Jacob had pulled another matchbook from his pocket and stroked it. "I thought I saw a candle by the dining room," he said, making his way past me.

"How did it go with Angelloni?" I asked him.

"I don't know. After your disruption I couldn't read his body language anymore," he said.

"How long were you there after I left?" I asked him.

"About two hours more," he replied.

"Did you reach an agreement?" I asked next.

"Kind of. I told him that I would discuss with you his intentions," he said.

"Intentions? What intentions?" I asked.

"As you know, he is your aunt's estate administrator of record, right?" Jacob said.

"Is he?"

"If it's OK with you, we should let him continue as such—"

I interrupted him. "Jacob, my aunt left me as the administrator."

"Yes, I know, but why delay the closing of the estate more by removing him?" he reasoned.

"What are the consequences if he continues?" I asked, concerned.

By this time, the candles had been burning, and their amber light made Jacob look ill omened. The rain kept falling unrelentingly, and the situation with Jacob was getting tense. I decided to confront him about Rita.

"Jacob, I don't know much about you," I casually told him.

"What's this all about?" he asked cautiously.

"What if you're not an attorney?" I said.

"What exactly do you mean?" he said defensively.

"Remember when we met?" I asked.

"Of course I do. What about it?" he said.

"You said that Rita Malone, the court clerk had sent you," I said accusingly.

"And?" he asked.

"I talked to Ms. Malone, and she said she never sent anybody."

His face looked more annoyed, as well as indignant at the insinuation that he had been caught in a lie. "So, you went checking on me?" He sounded angry.

"Of course. You don't think that I'm that naïve, do you?"

"I never implied you were," he said.

"So, Jacob, who are you?" I asked again.

"I'll show you my credentials tomorrow."

"First thing, please!" I said arrogantly.

"As your attorney I suggest—"

"As of now, you are not my attorney. Remember, we haven't signed an agreement yet. I'll decide tomorrow after I see your credentials whether you are my attorney or not," I concluded.

I could sense his state of mind at that very moment. He had tried to make me feel bad because I had never asked him before to show me any evidence of him being a licensed attorney at law.

"About Rita…she didn't send me," he said. "I overheard you asking her about a referral, and I took the chance. I'm sorry about that… why haven't you asked?"

"Jacob! It was not my obligation to ask you; it was your responsibility to tell me, don't you think?"

"Where do we go from here?" he asked.

"How am I supposed to trust you after this? Any suggestions?" I asked, disheartened.

"Sam, I'm a damn good attorney, I assure you!" he said smugly.

"You being a good attorney was never the question on my part, Jacob," I said earnestly.

We were silent awhile, staring at the candles' flickering flames. Occasional thunder still resonated in the distance; the rain softly washed down the windowpane. My stomach was still in knots as distrust started to settle into my mind—did I make the right choice with him? The moment and the place were uncanny.

The silence was broken by the telephone. Both Jacob and I checked our phones to see which one was ringing.

"Hello!" Jacob answered his phone.

"Jacob?" I could hear a female voice on the other end of Jacob's phone call.

"Yes, this is Jacob," he said.

"Is this Jacob?" The reply was another question.

"Yes, this is he. Who is this?" he asked impatiently.

Jacob's phone went dead.

20

I glanced at my watch; I still had to go meet Sal at the cemetery. "Jacob, I really want our association to work out. Have your credentials ready. For now, I have to get going to meet someone." I grabbed a candle and went to my room.

Jacob stayed behind trying to get the phone number for his lost call. I could hear him cussing angrily at his phone. "I'll see you tomorrow," he said.

I really didn't feel like going out tonight—especially to the cemetery on a night like this—but I really wanted to get the information from Sal.

I started to fantasize about getting my hands on the squealer and squeezing him until he sang "uncle" and begged to be spared from my wrath. I felt a sudden rush of adrenaline pumping inside me. It was the same feeling I experienced when I used to gamble. Could it be that I was addicted to the adrenaline rush and not to gambling?

I donned a raincoat and hat and looked for an umbrella. The rain was still coming down.

~

The streetlights were out all over town. My Jeep headlights were the only lights I could see in the town's darkness.

I made it to the cemetery at close to eight o'clock. I parked by the main gate and waited. The tombstones looked eerier enveloped in fog and lit by the retreating lightning in the sky. Where was Sal? I hoped close by.

Nine o'clock. Where in the hell was Sal? I would wait half an hour more. This was not the night to be out at the cemetery waiting for danger.

A car approached the cemetery; I could see the headlights coming. My heart started to thump faster with anticipation as the car got closer, but it zipped by fast without stopping.

I got my phone to dial Sal's phone number; the battery was low, and I didn't have a cord to recharge it. I was not a Boy Scout: I was never prepared.

The half hour ran out, and I drove away.

I'll call him when I get back home and give him an ultimatum, I thought with irritation.

I attempted to call Sal as soon as I walked into the house. The damn phones were dead; with the new phones, you needed electricity, I reminded myself. Where were the good old days? I became sullen and felt frustrated the rest of the night.

I went to bed thinking about how our ancestors had dealt with everyday life when they did everything by candlelight. Life was tough then, I thought; well it hadn't gotten any better.

I tossed and turned the whole night; I had chills and night sweats. As tired as I was, I just couldn't relax. Maybe a shot of scotch would help me relax. I got up and instinctively reached for the light on my night table. The electricity was still out. *Shit!* There was no use stumbling through the darkness to get to the scotch. Another thing I had to do without—the story of my life.

~

I stayed in bed late the following morning, trying to delay my meeting with Jacob. I felt bad about confronting him the night before. What's done was done. I shrugged. I had to face the consequences for my actions, the sooner the better.

As I went to clean myself up, I caught a glimpse of myself in the vanity mirror. I took a second, longer look. It came as a shock to see gray hair beginning to sprout on my head, and it didn't make me feel any better. It was hard to acknowledge that I was aging and didn't have any success I could be proud of. I'd be thirty-four years old next April. Resolutely, I plucked out the gray hairs I could see.

I smelled the fresh coffee coming from the kitchen. Pied Piper was luring me; but instead of a pipe, he was using coffee. I checked my cell phone to see if it was charged, though actually, it didn't matter; I could make my phone call as long as the phone was plugged in.

I pressed star-six-nine to block my number and then dialed Sal's number. The phone rang several times and then went to his voice mail.

"This is Sal, leave your number and I'll return your—" I stopped the call. I hoped he knew I wasn't playing games and would call me soon.

~

It was about ten thirty when I finally came downstairs. Jacob was in the kitchen, pouring a cup of steaming coffee for me.

"Good morning!" he said amiably.

"Thank you; good morning to you too," I replied morosely as I took the mug.

"Are you hungry?" he asked.

"Come to think of it, I'm starving!" I answered.

"I fixed eggs and ham. Would you like some?" he asked warmly.

"Sure!" I replied.

"I've been waiting for you since early," he said.

"Sorry, I overslept. I couldn't sleep last night."

"Yes, it was a tough night for the two of us."

"Two eggs, please."

"Did you get the info you went to get last night?" he asked affably.

"No," I said flatly.

"Well, I have the information you requested from me ready," he said.

I wolfed down the eggs and ham while Jacob looked at me in disbelief. "I just realized I haven't eaten a thing since yesterday," I said with my mouth full.

"I'm glad you like the food, Sam," Jacob said.

"Yeah, I didn't know that you knew how to cook," I said, thankful.

"I got up early this morning and started putting my credentials together," he said.

"OK, as soon as we are done with breakfast, I'll take a look," I said between sips of coffee.

"I also have the agreement to sign," he added.

"I hope you added client referrals as well," I said.

As soon as I swallowed my last piece of toast, we moved to Jacob's bedroom/studio.

~

He put a series of folders with different headings in front of me and said, "Start whenever you want."

I careful reviewed every one of his folders, starting with his university degrees and diploma. He had graduated from Loma Linda University in Los Angeles in 1985. He had passed his bar examination right after his graduation.

He had been a junior partner handling personal injury cases in a prestigious law firm in California for ten years. His dossier was extensive, and he had several merits and awards.

"This looks good, but I don't see names of clients," I said, disillusioned.

"I cannot show you that," he said.

"Why not?" I asked.

"Have you heard of client–attorney confidentiality?" he asked.

"Do you mind if I call these firms you worked for and see if they recommend you?" I asked him.

"I thought you wanted to see my credentials," he said.

I nodded.

Then he took a folder and pulled out a sheet of paper. "This is the agreement that I prepared for you," he said, handing me the document.

"I will review it and get back to you later," I said calmly.

"Do you have any idea when?" he asked, looking disconcerted.

"Relax, Jacob. As soon as I review it, we'll get together to discuss it, OK?" I said soothingly. I didn't tell him I was planning to go to the Bar Association and check his standing.

I thanked him for the breakfast and for his effort in putting his dossier together on such short notice.

grabbed my overcoat and left the house. With Rita on my mind, I drove past the courthouse to see if court was in session. A few cars were in the parking lot, besides the service vehicles. I parked my Jeep and walked toward the building.

A sign posted at the entrance read, "The Court will be back in session tomorrow, December 19, 2005."

The door was open.

"Sorry, sir, the court is not in session," a court officer said.

"What about all these people?" I asked the officer.

"They are inspectors and service personnel," he said.

"Do you know Rita Malone?"

The officer shook his head.

"She is the court clerk," I said.

"Come back tomorrow. Someone will be able to give you the information you need," he said.

"Do you know where the Bar Association is located?" I asked.

"Yes, in the Mapletown Professional Building across the street," he said pointing to a five-story redbrick building.

"Thank you!" I said earnestly and left.

The day was frigid. Heavy dark clouds hung menacingly in the horizon; they looked as if they could burst at any moment. I could hear wailing sirens in the distance, warning residents of incoming danger. People were alarmed, scurrying rapidly, commenting how a tornado had just hit a neighboring town.

I thought about Dorothy and the Wicked Witch of the West as I got in my car to drive the short distance to the Bar Association.

~

I felt a strange feeling in the pit of my stomach as I approached the building. Did the butterflies in my stomach mean I was nervous about finding out particulars about Jacob? Too late now; I was in front of the receptionist.

"May I help you?" a pleasant voice asked.

"What is the purpose of the bar?" I asked.

"The state requires membership in the Bar Association to practice law here," she said.

"And that means what?" I asked her.

"The Bar Association is responsible for the regulation of the legal profession," she said.

"I don't know where to start." I hesitated. "I'm hiring an attorney in the area, and I need to know if he is in good standing."

"Who is the attorney?" she asked.

"Sinclair, Jacob Sinclair," I said.

She entered the name into her computer, then stared at the screen, like an oracle staring at a crystal ball, in silence.

"I also want to know what the standard cost for a probate case is," I said.

"Usually the cost is three to seven percent of the total estate value," she said.

"What do the costs include?" I asked.

"Costs include appraisal costs, executor fees, court costs, surety bond, legal fees, and accounting fees." She recited the list without taking a breath.

Then she got up and went to a private office. I was impatient for her to reappear and give me the information on Jacob.

When she returned to her desk, she announced that a Mr. Blake would see me to give me the information I had requested.

An older man appeared and introduced himself. "Hello, my name is Steven Blake."

"Hi. I'm Sam W. Stone."

"I understand that you are inquiring about Jacob Sinclair?" he asked politely.

"Yes, I'm retaining him to represent me in an inheritance case," I said.

"The bar imposed a sanction for conduct indicating that Mr. Sinclair was not fit to practice law," he said.

"Why?" I asked.

"He was disbarred for dishonesty, deceit, and misrepresentation," he said.

"How long ago?" I asked, feeling pity for Jacob.

"Seven years ago."

"So he can't practice law?"

"Mr. Sinclair reapplied for membership five years ago."

"Has he been reinstated?"

"Yes. All charges were dropped, and he is a current member of the bar," he said.

"Anything else I should know?"

"You retain him under your own discretion. I'm doing my obligation to inform you." He sounded like I imagined Pontius Pilate must have sounded when he washed his hands to distance himself from Jesus Christ.

I thanked him, and he said, "Good luck!"

~

I was leaving the Bar Association building when I saw Angelloni walking to the entrance. It was too late to avoid him. I pretended to read the literature I got at the bar and act as if I didn't see him.

I was watching him from the corner of my eye; he was looking at me.

"Sam!" he said.

"Angelloni?" I lifted my eyes from the material I was pretending to read.

"How are you?" He tried to sound amiable.

"I have been better."

"I had been meaning to call you," he said.

"Me or Jacob?" I asked cautiously.

"You!" he said.

"You and I have nothing to discuss."

"Why don't you come by my office later on?" he said, dismissing what I said.

"I have nothing to say to you. You need to call Mr. Sinclair."

"I would like to talk to you without Mr. Sinclair—it is important!" He implied urgency.

What is he up to? "I'm sorry, I don't think that is ethical," I said, irritated.

"Ethics?" he repeated, laughing mordantly.

"Is that a funny word for you, Mr. Angelloni?" I said, also mordantly.

"What about lunch?" he said completely ignoring my question.

I was suspicious of Jacob, but Angelloni was beyond comprehension. I just didn't trust him.

"As I told you before, Mr. Angelloni, you need to talk to my attorney," I said firmly.

"Whenever you want the information you're looking for in here, come and see me," he said.

How did he know I was looking for information? I wanted to punch the haughtiness out of him. *One of these days.* His arrogance and conceit were appalling. With his characteristic demeanor, he ran his hands through his slicked-back hair.

I couldn't get away fast enough. I walked to the parking lot, while he, laughing, went into the building.

22

I hated small towns like Mapletown, where everybody knew your name and business. I really loved the aloofness of big-city dwellers; nobody minded others' business, only their own.

If I got out of the forest, maybe I would be able to see the trees. With that thought, going to San Fran for a few days sounded very appealing. But what about the basement? And Jacob? They would be here when I came back—I'm not that lucky, I thought.

Jacob would have free run of the house if I was gone. I had to make sure that the basement and my room would be locked up to stop him from wandering there.

A voice inside told me to resist the idea of a trip to San Fran, that the timing wasn't right. I decided to listen to my inner voice for once and stay put, at least for now.

I revisited my earlier encounter with Angelloni. What kind of information was he referring to? Was he talking about Eva? I doubted that. Maybe he was talking about Sal. I shook my head. Could he be talking about Jacob?

I detested the man! I wasn't about to fall for his vile trickery. But the idea of not knowing what he was talking about was very disturbing, to say the least.

The wheels in my mind kept churning, forcing me to analyze the three scenarios:

Eva: She was beyond my grasp. I didn't know enough about her to affect me at all.

Sal: I really didn't care to know who the snitcher was at all. I was just fucking with Sal and wanted him to know that one's situation could change without much notice.

Jacob: Everything about him could affect me in a very devastating way. What could Angelloni know about Jacob?

I knew that the animosity between Jacob and Angelloni was about a fucking woman—which, I reasoned, was always the source of problems between men. I was not going to allow them to use me. Was it worth it to hear what Angelloni had to say? Maybe the information he had was about Jacob, and would help me to determine if he was trustworthy.

I needed to clear my head, and get rid of the crazy ideas bombarding me relentlessly. I decided to stop at the diner for a piece of pumpkin pie and cup of coffee and some idle conversation with the diner's patrons.

~

I sat at what was becoming my regular table. I was determined to savor my slice of pie with a dollop of whipped cream. Its smell was very comforting, and as the delicious bite melted in my mouth, so did the ideas running through my mind.

Right at that very moment, I decided to live a day at a time. I would stop trying so hard. I would let events unfold unhurriedly before me.

The wind was blowing hard outside, and people were looking for a safe place to run to. Inside the diner, people were planning to go to the basement for safety.

I, on the other hand, was enjoying my coffee and pumpkin pie. I offered to buy pie for all the patrons at the diner in an effort to calm their nervousness. They looked at me as if I was crazy. I shrugged my shoulders and continued enjoying the pie and coffee.

The lights were flickering on-and-off. The diner's workers got some candles and oil lamps ready in case we had another power outage. The sirens started the warning wail, and the TV emergency broadcasting system was running the weather advisory for the Mapletown area.

After finishing my pie, I tried to examine the agreement Jacob had given me to sign. But the lights were flickering so much that the letters appeared and disappeared repeatedly. What's the hurry? I thought; one more day wasn't going to make a difference. Jacob just had to wait.

Besides, I really needed to think hard about the information from the Bar Association. Did I want to give Jacob a chance and have him represent me? I had to consider Jacob's standing at the bar. What Mr. Blake explained wasn't clear. He had said disbarment was a revocation of a lawyer's ability to practice law or argue cases, and sanctions were imposed for willfully disregarding the interests of clients or engaging in fraud. Had Jacob been disbarred or sanctioned? Was there a difference? Does it even matter now? He had to become a DA right after the sanctions were lifted; I felt sorry for him, but...we still didn't see eye to eye.

I thought about meeting Angelloni to find out what he wanted to tell me. But not today, that was for sure.

Everybody gasped when I decided to take a run for my Jeep. This weather wasn't going to intimidate me into being like the rest of the munchkins at the diner.

I sat in my Jeep awhile, the rain falling like cats and dogs by the moment. Visibility was not CAVU: ceiling and visibility unlimited. My mind went back to meeting with Angelloni. Was I crazy for doing such a thing? I considered him my enemy.

But someone once said that a good strategy was to "keep your friends close and your enemies closer."

23

I was startled out of my thoughts by the almost inaudible ring on my phone. Thunder muffled the sounds, but I managed to get to the phone in time.

"Hello, hello?" I asked anxiously. I heard nothing but static.

Could it have been Sal? I decided to give him a call later.

~

I felt that Jacob's future as an attorney was in my hands. The look on his face when I first met him told me he was destitute. I was the chance he was waiting for; he needed someone to trust him.

The problem I was having with him was his not coming clean. How could I trust him now? Everything he did was suspicious in my eyes.

Now, I had to go home, tell him of my visit to the Bar Association, and give him the chance to offer an explanation.

I could put myself in his shoes. Sophia offered me a chance to come clean about my gambling, and I didn't take it. I continued to lie until I was too deep in the hole and couldn't come back. I had lost everything because I wasn't able to trust Sophia.

I was feeling very distraught about this situation. I should have done my homework before. I was inexperienced and so eager and naïve to accept any kind of offer to bring Angelloni down.

I drove home, dragging my ass. I felt I was about to make a decision that would affect Jacob and me.

The streets were dark. We were experiencing another blackout; thunder and lightning illuminated the sky. I was feeling despondent. My aunt's Victorian house loomed on the horizon when lightning flashed in the sky. Its look made me shiver.

I walked inside the main vestibule of the house. I could smell the candles burning. As I entered the living room, I saw Jacob sitting in a chair, drinking. The amber flames of the lonely candle made him appear ethereal.

"Hello, Sam," he said matter-of-factly.

"Hello, Jacob," I replied.

"Another dark night," he said.

"Yeah, that's what it looks like," I said indifferently.

"Did you make a decision on the contract I gave you?" he asked.

"No, to be honest with you, I haven't looked at it yet," I said.

"Sam, it is very important!" he begged.

"I went to the Bar Association," I confessed.

He listened silently, looking very worried. He emptied the remains of his drink, got up, walked the few steps to the liquor cabinet, and poured another drink. He offered me one, but I declined.

"I talked to Mr. Blake," I said. "Do you know him?"

"Of course I know him! He and Angelloni cooked up some accusations against me!" he said.

"Jacob, you forced me to check on you!" I said defensively.

"You wouldn't have given me the time of day if I had come to you on my own," he said.

"Jacob, you lied to me!" I said accusingly.

"I'm sorry!" he said.

"You should have talked to me straight," I said.

"I was desperate—nobody trusted me!" he replied.

I was feeling sorry for the guy; it was tough when you were losing your last hope. This was the only shot he had to be reinstated in society and not be a pariah anymore, but I just couldn't put it out of my mind that I had been deceived. Deceit was one of the charges against him.

"Jacob, I gave you a fair chance," I honestly said.

Jacob got up from his seat and went to the liquor cabinet for another shot. "Do you want a drink, Sam?" he asked.

"Sure, why not," I said.

"Did Blake tell you about my disbarment?" he asked.

"He wasn't clear whether you were sanctioned or disbarred," I said.

"Did he tell you I had reapplied?" he asked.

"Yes, he said that," I answered.

"Look, Sam, I haven't been able to get cases at all. Even though I have been accepted at the bar and all charges had been cleared, I've been blackballed."

"Yes, I imagine—especially because of dishonesty, deceit, and misrepresentation," I said.

"Is that what Blake said?" he asked angrily.

"Yes," I said.

"Do you know that Blake and Angelloni are very close friends?" he asked.

"No, but I don't care," I said.

"Do you have any idea how many attorneys they have screwed?" he asked.

"No, and I don't care," I said impatiently.

"When honest attorneys refuse to play their game, they cook up accusations against them and ruin them," he said.

"Jacob, I haven't made a decision yet. I promise I will do so."

I could feel his pain, and again the memories were exposed raw and naked: first with Sophia and then with Joe.

"Sam, I've got plans to visit my sister for the Christmas season," Jacob said. "I hope you have an answer for me when I come back."

"You have a sister?" I asked with curiosity.

"And a brother," he answered.

"Where?" I asked, thinking that there were many things I didn't know about him.

"In the San Fernando Valley," he answered.

"When are you going?"

"On the twentieth."

It was music to my ears. I wouldn't have to go away for time alone to sort things out after all.

"I would like to lock my quarters, if it's OK with you," he said.

"By all means!"

"Look, Sam, I know I wasn't honest with you. When I come back, I will level with you," he said, looking straight into my cyes.

"I think we should do that, Jacob."

~

The house was dark, and I didn't feel like any more conversation that night. I went to my room to think. In two more days, with Jacob gone, I would be free to search the basement—hoping no more storms would interrupt the electrical power.

I kept pondering and came to the realization that I couldn't do a thing about my aunt's estate. I didn't have an attorney, and worst of all, I didn't know what Angelloni's intentions were.

It bothered me that Jacob had already declared his position about Angelloni: that he should be allowed to continue as estate administrator.

But I could wait; I wasn't in any hurry. The only two hurries I had were to find out about my aunt's killer and the secret that was hiding in the basement. I felt like a heavy burden had been removed from me, but how long would it last?

I wondered what I did to piss off Rita. I wondered if she even existed. I really didn't need to think about her. Tomorrow I would go to the courthouse to look for her for the last time.

For the second night I was able again to sleep without the tossing and turning.

24

I woke up refreshed and optimistic; my plans for the day were simple. The only item on my to-do list was to go to the courthouse and see Rita; the court was supposed to be back in session today.

The day was gray and cold; black clouds loomed on the horizon. Mapletown looked foreboding and sinister, but I wasn't going to let it disturb my optimism.

It was ten o'clock when I arrived at the courthouse. Immediately I went to the court clerk's office.

"Excuse me, is Rita Malone in?" I asked at the information desk.

"Just a minute, let me see if she is available."

Another clerk approached me as I waited. "How can I help you?" she said.

"I would like to see Rita Malone," I said.

"That's me. How can I help you?" she said.

It was not possible for this woman to be Rita. She looked close to sixty years old and was heavy. No way was she was the same Rita Malone, the one I'd had coffee with a few days ago!

This woman hair was short and gray-haired; of course, a wig would do the trick. This woman wore thick glasses with heavy rims. Yeah, contacts could do the trick there as well.

"Is there another Rita working here?" I felt stupid when I asked.

"No, I'm afraid I'm the only Rita here," she said matter-of-factly.

"What about in the whole court system?" I asked.

"I wouldn't know about that, sir."

"It's very important for me to find out," I said desperately.

I told her about having coffee with Rita and the plans we made for dinner the following evening; she said jokingly she was available for both. I concluded by telling her that I had gone to Rita's house to pick her up, but she wasn't there either.

"I was out of town," she said.

"Do you live at Ten Eleven Willow?" I asked.

"Yes, but I was out of town, as I told you." She looked puzzled.

"Do you have a daughter living with you?" I asked.

"No, I went to visit my daughter in Sacramento."

"I even asked your neighbor," I said.

"Are you sure that her name was Rita Malone?"

"Yes, that's why I'm here!" I said hotly.

"I suggest that you go to Human Resources and tell them what you just told me," she said.

"By the way," I said, turning back to her, "would you like to have a cup of coffee with me after work?" *What the heck!* I thought; maybe she could give me information as well.

"Sure, I would like to know more about this 'Rita,'" she said.

"I'll meet you at the Early Riser Café about five thirty?"

~

I went to the information clerk and asked for Human Resources. I was sent to the lower floor, where, I was told, the administrative offices were housed. I got in line to wait for the next available clerk.

"We have no openings," the next available clerk said.

"I'm not looking for a job," I said.

"Then what can I do for you?" she asked.

"I'm looking for one of your employees," I said.

"What department?" she asked.

"At the information desk?" I wasn't sure.

"You mean the court clerk?" she asked.

"I'm not sure," I replied.

"What's the name?" she asked, looking at her computer.

"It's a little complicated," I responded.

"Do you have a name?" she asked patiently.

"The name I have is Rita Malone. I just talked to a Rita Malone, but she is not the one I'm looking for," I said.

"What do you mean?" She seemed puzzled.

I gave her the "gorgeous Rita Malone" story; she was even more confused. "I might have mixed up her last name; do you have another Rita in your system?"

She looked in her computer files and then dialed a phone number. "Can you please come downstairs?" she said into the phone. Then she told me, "Please wait a minute."

I waited about twenty minutes, and then the Rita Malone I had just talked to came through the door.

"This gentleman is looking for you, and he told me a crazy story. Do you know him?" the clerk asked Rita.

"Yes, I sent him here," Rita said.

"There is no other Rita in the system," the clerk said.

"I thought so, but I wasn't sure," Rita said.

"Could someone have stolen your ID?" the clerk asked Rita.

"Should we call Homeland Security and report the incident?" Rita asked.

"Look, ladies, I may have confused the name," I said.

The two women went to the side and exchanged conversation. At that moment, I decided to take off.

The Human Resources clerk called after me, "You can't leave; please wait!"

I was already in the stairway. I didn't want to wait for the elevator; I needed to get out of there pronto!

"Leave your phone number in case we need you!"

~

Once again, I was waiting for Rita Malone at the Early Riser Café. I was very confused. Why would someone have taken someone else's ID? Who really was the Rita Malone I had enjoyed so much? Where was she? Nobody noticed this at the courthouse? Another piece missing from the puzzle.

I was running out of options and didn't know which way to turn. I felt as if I had dug a hole and couldn't get out of it.

I was lost in my thoughts when Rita approached the table. She was not alone.

"Hello, I never got your name," she said cordially.

"Hi, I'm Sam W. Stone." Déjà vu all over.

"This is my friend Margaret Cook," Rita said.

Margaret and I shook hands. Mine were clammy and shaky.

"Hello," Margaret said.

"Likewise," I said. *Fucking formalities*, I thought.

"Rita told me about the other Rita," Margaret said.

"Do you work in the same department?" I asked Margaret.

"Yes, that's why Rita invited me to meet you," she said.

"I hope you don't mind," Rita said apologetically.

"Can you describe her?" Margaret inquired.

"You could be her," I said.

Yes, this Margaret really could be "Rita": same body, same height; but her hair was a vibrant auburn, her eyes were green, and her voice was different.

"Do you remember what date it was?" she asked, ignoring my answer.

"Yes, it was December twelve," I replied.

"I was away on vacation. Were you there?" Rita asked Margaret.

"What day was it?" Margaret asked.

"It was Thursday," I replied.

There was silence for a while.

"Seven days ago," Rita said.

"I've got to check. I'm not sure, but I think I was home with a cold," Margaret said.

"We are supposed to wear IDs. Was she wearing one?" Rita asked.

"Yes, she was, but it was backward and up-side-down," I replied.

The women began to talk about how dangerous everything was since 9/11.

"You should run your credit report, Rita," Margaret said.

"Yeah, I was thinking about that; tomorrow I'll do it," Rita said.

I gave Rita my phone number to call me if she came across any information.

"I'll keep you posted," Rita said.

I offered to pay for the coffee and said good-bye.

~

It was around ten at night when I got back home. I sat in my Jeep awhile. I didn't want to see Jacob; I didn't have anything to say to him. On second thought, I needed to get the documents back.

I went to his room and knocked on his door. "Jacob! Open the door!" I demanded.

"OK, OK!" He held a glass of scotch when he opened the door. He was tipsy, and I wondered how long he had been drinking. His eyes were unfocused and cold.

"Are you leaving tomorrow?" I asked.

"Yes," he replied.

"What time?" I asked.

"Around seven."

"Do you have my aunt's documents handy?"

"You're not signing the agreement, are you?"

"You will have my answer when you return, I promise," I assured him.

"Then I will give you the docs when I come back," he said.

"Can I have them, please?"

"Please come in."

I followed him to his office. He pointed to a table. Had he worked on them at all?

"There are the papers."

The documents were neatly piled, and I was going to comment on that, but I bit my tongue and didn't ask if he'd had the chance to read them.

"The documents are staying here," Jacob said.

I would have time to think about Jacob while he was gone. I would also have to make plans to meet the real Rita Malone and pick her brain some other day.

Playing detective was exhausting, especially if you didn't know what you were doing.

Jacob's dark, suspicious eyes looked me up and down, trying to reach beyond my thoughts and anticipate what to expect upon his return.

I did the same thing. I stared directly into his dark eyes, trying to read his mind. I was looking for a hint of honesty.

Jacob offered me a glass of scotch, but I declined.

"Jacob, do you need a ride to the bus depot?" I asked him.

"As a matter of fact, I was going to ask you," he said.

"What time?" I asked.

"I have to take the eight o'clock bus," he said.

"Are you flying from San Francisco?" I asked.

Jacob shook his head no.

"Do you have your bus ticket?" I asked him.

He nodded.

"When are you coming back?" I inquired.

"January second," he replied.

"It's good to spend the holidays with family." I almost whispered, as if I were talking to myself.

"What are you doing?" he asked.

"I don't know yet." I was lying. I knew exactly what I was going to do. With Jacob gone, I would dedicate all the necessary time to go through the basement's secret place; it was time to finish that task.

"Jacob, who is in charge of calling the auctioneers?" I asked.

"We can talk about that as soon as you sign the agreement," he said curtly.

"That seems reasonable," I told him. "It has been about two months since my aunt—"

He interrupted me. "We'll get to it when I return."

I glanced at my watch just as the grandfather clock chimed midnight.

"That's it for me," I told Jacob.

"Likewise," he agreed.

~

The next morning came very quickly; I didn't remember if I was able to sleep. I heard Jacob in the bathroom taking a shower. I shifted my position and dozed off again.

I heard a soft rap at my door.

"Sam, it's seven o'clock!"

"I'll be right up!" I said.

"There's fresh coffee," he said through the door.

"Thank you," I said.

I put on a pair of jeans and tennis shoes—I would shower later.

Jacob was in the kitchen pouring a cup of coffee.

"All set to go?" I asked him.

"I'm as ready as I'll ever be," he answered.

"I'm ready too," I said.

"Sam, will I have a place to stay when I come back?" he asked suddenly.

"Whatever happens, I'll give you time." He'd caught me by surprise; I hadn't given any thought to the fact that he was living with me.

25

We rode in silence to the bus depot. It seemed a long time ago since I was here looking for the locker. *Time flies fast*, I thought.

"Jacob, I've been meaning to ask you if you ever got my aunt's death certificate from Miller." I looked at him seriously. I just couldn't remember who had what; Miller had the death certificate and Angelloni the crime report, or vice versa.

"No, I forgot about it," he said apologetically.

"Have a nice trip, Jacob," I said cordially.

"Thanks!' Jacob said.

Jacob was entering the building when I saw Eva getting out of a cab. I decided to catch her. She seemed in a hurry as she fumbled in her purse for change for the cabbie.

"Eva!" I yelled as I quickly got out of my Jeep.

She paid the cab driver, took her bag, and proceeded to the depot entrance.

"Eva! Wait!" I was almost behind her. She kept walking. She was unmindful of everyone around.

I reached her and grabbed her arm. She turned her head, and her smile froze when she saw me.

"Sam!" she said.

"Hello, Eva! Leaving town?" I asked.

"Yes, just for the holidays," she said.

"Where to?" I asked curiously.

"To visit my relatives," she said.

"In LA?" I asked.

Her face turned pale as she nodded. "How did you know?" She looked puzzled.

"Jacob is going, too. Do you know Jacob Sinclair? He is going to the San Fernando Valley. Close to LA, isn't?" I inquired.

"N-no, I don't know." She was hesitant.

I looked directly into her eyes; she was clearly uncomfortable.

"I better go now," she said.

I got back in my Jeep and drove off, thinking that at that moment my mind was made up about Jacob. I would make time to go see Angelloni. I had a whole lot of shit to do!

~

My cell phone rang; the caller ID showed "unavailable."

"Hello," I said.

"Sam?" The voice was raspy.

"Yes, this is Sam," I answered.

"Hi, this is Sal," the voice said.

I didn't recognize the voice; I had put Sal out of my mind and couldn't remember how his voice sounded. Something gave me a bad feeling.

"Yes, Sal, what can I do for you?" I asked politely.

"Can we meet?"

"I don't know—what is this about?" I asked tentatively.

"Can you make it at eight tonight?" he asked.

"No, I'll be very busy the next four days," I said.

"When can you make it?"

"Can you tell me what this is about?" I insisted.

"It's a delicate matter," the raspy voice said.

"I'm going to be at Maggie's Diner in another half hour," I said impatiently. "If it's as important as you say it is, meet me there."

"No, meet me by the cemetery at eight!" He spoke forcefully.

"Look, pal, I don't even know who you are, and you want me to meet you at the cemetery? Are you out of your fucking mind?" Deep in my gut, I knew this wasn't Sal. I pressed for some kind of indication of whom I was really talking to.

"I have the info you requested from Sal." He immediately tried to amend that, adding, "from me." It was too late; I'd caught the mistake. He waited for me to say something that indicated whether I'd caught his slip of tongue. I was curious, wondering if Sal had been caught trying to get the information I had demanded.

Following my gut feeling, I asked him, "Where do I know you from, Sal?"

Silence.

"Are you still there?"

I didn't get to find out who I was talking to, but for sure, it was not Sal.

I decided not to stop at the diner that night.

~

I was bothered by the idea that Eva and Jacob might be in cahoots. Maybe they were the ones who collected the finder's fee from Joe. *Who fucking cares anyway?* I thought as I sped away from the bus depot.

My mind kept turning. I tried to connect the dots and the coincidences since my aunt's death. There were too many.

Did Victor mention seeing the silhouettes of three *men* the night my aunt was murdered? It could have been two men and a woman, for all I knew.

Eva was in one of the pictures Aunt Millie had left in the safe-deposit box, as was Jacob. In addition, there was Jacob's insistence on getting a hold of the pictures.

I felt that the shroud of mystery was beginning to lift.

I decided not to get engulfed in guesswork. I was pretty sure the puzzle pieces were beginning to fit together. I had ten days to solve the basement mystery, and I didn't want to waste time. I went home and got ready to start.

~

The house felt strange and quiet without Jacob. In the short time he had lived here, his cigarettes, aftershave, and constant brewing of coffee had impregnated the air and made the house smell like him. It seemed like he knew the house too well; I had the feeling he'd been here before.

Instead of the basement, I found myself at the door of Jacob's quarters. I turned the doorknob, but it was locked. I felt the impulse to kick the door in. But I had ten days; I would have time to poke around, but not today.

I determined to proceed to the basement and continue with the task down there.

My phone rang the moment I started getting the equipment ready. "Hello?" I said.

"Sam?" It was the same raspy voice of the earlier caller.

"Yes!" I answered impatiently.

"I waited for you at the diner," he said angrily.

"Who is this?" I asked.

"This is S-Sal." His hesitation was perceptible.

"Look, moron, I told you earlier that I don't know you!"

"I have a message for you," he said.

"I have a message for you too: fuck off!" I pushed the button to disconnect the call.

If Sal wasn't the one calling, who was it?

I finished connecting the extension cords, and the bright light was shining in the basement.

The dampness in the basement was intolerable. I could see my breath billowing, and I started to shiver uncontrollably. Was I cold? Or simply excited that I was able to get to the secret place?

If I worked nonstop, I figured, it would take me the rest of the evening to accomplish my goal. I didn't want to overexert myself. It was seven thirty in the evening. I decided to force myself to work nonstop for three hours. I would stop at ten thirty and see how far I still needed to go.

I had worked for one hour when my phone rang again.

"Hello?" I answered coldly.

"May I speak with Mr. Stone?" a feminine voice asked.

"This is he," I said flatly.

"Hi, Mr. Stone, this is Sarah Cooper with Isaac Auctioneers," she said.

"What can I do for you? It's kinda late."

"We have been retained by Mr. Angelloni to come to your house and take an inventory of the personal property of Mildred C. Wilmot."

"Do you have to go through the whole house?" I asked.

"Yes, the garage, attic, and basement, plus every room in the house," she said solemnly.

"Can this wait until after the holidays?" I asked her.

"Yes, actually, that's why I'm calling," she said.

"OK."

"Sorry that I'm calling so late."

"Don't worry."

"When is good for you?" she asked.

"Do I have to be here?" I asked.

"No, not really," she said.

"OK."

"So, when is a good day for you?" she asked again.

"Well, any time after the fifth of January," I said.

"What about the seventh of January at ten in the morning?" she asked.

"Sounds good," I said.

"Great! See you then," she said.

I felt uneasy about having strangers come to my house and poke around. Besides, wasn't everything in the house left to me, according to my aunt's will?

~

I took a deep breath, so deep it felt as if my lungs were going to burst. Finally, I was at the door of the secret place. My legs and knees were shaking uncontrollably. I felt a cold sweat running down my back.

I reached for the door lever and pulled it. I remembered how anxiously I'd waited for the door to open when I was a kid, I thought that nobody else knew about this place and nobody would find me once I went in.

The door creaked. It was stuck. Frustrated, I yanked and pulled it, becoming very vociferous with profanity and the worst swear words known to humanity.

I checked the springs that activated the door; they needed lubrication. I had to make a trip to the hardware store once more.

At the store, I purchased the lubricant I needed but decided to stop for the day—after all, I had put several hours on the project until now. I was cold and hungry. A good steak would be so good, I thought.

I would get up early and finish the job tomorrow, I reasoned as I drove to the town's chophouse.

~

I was finishing my steak dinner when a familiar voice greeted me.

"Hello, Sam," Sergeant Miller said amiably.

I had not seen Miller since the afternoon Jacob called me to his office at the police station.

"Hello, Sergeant Miller," I replied.

"What's new?" he asked.

"Not much. By the way, did you ever get my aunt's report?" I saw the opportunity to ask him.

"I gave it to Jacob last time I saw him," he said.

"Are you sure?" I asked him.

"Yes!" he said, seeming bothered by my questioning.

"He didn't mention it to me, which was very strange," I said.

It bothered me that I'd had several conversations with Jacob and he'd never mentioned that he had a copy of the police report on my aunt's murder.

"Jacob is out of town for the holidays," I said. "Is it possible for you to get a copy for me?"

"I think so, but not until I go back to work," he said. "I'm on vacation."

"You think I can pick up a copy myself?" I asked hopefully.

"I'm in charge of that case, and it'd be better if I gave it to you," he said.

"Do you have suspects?" I asked cautiously. "That is, besides myself?"

He gave me a dirty look. "We have some leads."

"In other words, no, you don't have any suspects," I said tentatively.

"Good night, Mr. Stone!" he said sheepishly.

26

My mind couldn't stop thinking about Jacob. What reason did he have to hide such important information from me? I was driving myself crazy; my thoughts kept coming relentlessly, attacking my sanity.

I came home and headed to Jacob's room, determined to get inside. I needed to find answers.

It took me a while, but I pried the door open. I shined my flashlight into the room. It was in order; everything seemed to be in place. I went directly to his office area. I had a feeling at the pit of my stomach that I was breaking the law, even though it was my house.

I felt like a burglar as I worked my way in the dark with only my flashlight. The envelopes with the document copies were still neatly in order on the table. I opened one of his desk drawers only to find unimportant office stuff.

I was getting tired and was about to give up when I caught sight of an envelope in the bottom drawer. The envelope had a label, "MEDICAL CERTIFICATE OF DEATH." I nervously took it to my room.

~

I was shaking all over; my hands were trembling as I opened the envelope. I needed to get a drink. The chime of the grandfather clock startled me as it struck.

I recalled the time I first saw Jacob, with his tattered coat, the stale smell of cheap wine and booze coming from his dirty clothes, and his worn-out shoes—were they black? The more I thought about him, the angrier I got. I couldn't discern his malice—or was it ambition? Whatever it was, the son of a bitch was a cold and calculating bastard.

I had to muster psychological strength to take the certificate out of the envelope. I held it in my hands for a few moments. I did not know what to look for; I had never seen a death certificate before. On the top were the words "STATE OF CALIFORNIA," followed by "MEDICAL DEATH CERTIFICATE." I nervously saw that lines 1 through 17c were only my aunt's vitals. Line 18 was the one that indicated the cause of death. But it was not what I had expected. It read, "Pending until further laboratory tests be obtained."

This was not the crime report I had asked for, but I couldn't find that in Jacob's room. I couldn't do anything about it until Monday.

Now I understood why Jacob hadn't mentioned anything about the death certificate. However, I needed to see Sergeant Miller and ask him if this was the only information he'd provided to Jacob and why the cause of death was not recorded.

I couldn't believe that Jacob, not Angelloni, had been cleverer than me. I was convinced that either one of them was the murderer; if not, at least one of them gave the order. I remembered how Victor said he'd seen three silhouettes. Could they have been Jacob, Angelloni, and "Rita"?

What could have been the reason for such an eradication of a human being? Was it a vendetta? It could also have been ambition. From what I had seen, my aunt was loaded.

Where had the riches come from? The whole situation was of utmost intrigue.

I couldn't get answers fast enough.

~

It was a restless night; I was unable to sleep. I got up to get a shot of scotch. I wanted to put an end to the wheels churning in my mind with the craziest scenarios and plots.

I would work in the basement tomorrow for another four hours, and then I'd go to San Fran to see if I could find Victor.

When I had gotten shit-faced, I finally dozed off.

Aunt Millie's apparition visited my dreams. She was pointing her bony finger at me accusingly, saying repeatedly, "Find him…find him…" Her ghost appeared to be bloody and mangled. I kept seeing the shadows of the three murderers beating her without compassion. The three goons started chasing me. I ended up hiding in the cemetery.

I woke up drenched in sweat, my heart racing. I glanced at the clock. Shit! It was ten in the morning! I jumped out of bed, still feeling the stupor of my drinking. A cup of coffee would be nice.

All kinds of thoughts continued to attack without compassion. One of those was of the cabin by the lake. Was there any insurance on it? Was the insurance money supposed to be paid to Victor or me?

I needed to stop the incessant loads of questions. I needed to concentrate on the basement and forget everything else.

~

I was finishing my customary second cup of coffee when a loud knock on the door startled me. I opened the door and saw two brusque-looking men standing there. The older man had a clipboard in his hands.

"We ares Max and Clem," the older guy said. "We ares here to collect the goods."

"What goods?"

"We heard about the Big Aunt passin' away," he said, "and we haves our routine pickup for today."

"You must be the nephew," the younger man said.

"Yes, I was her nephew. What are you guys talking about?"

"The stuffs we needs to pick up would be in the basement," the older guy said.

"Are you guys from Good Willie?" I asked. Maybe they'd take some of the boxes from downstairs, I thought.

They looked at each other and laughed, the older guy with a toothless mouth, the other with teeth stained from tobacco chew.

"Whatever you say, just gives us the stuffs," the older guy said.

Disgusted, I said, "Get lost," and closed the door. But Max, the older guy, stuck his dirty boot into the door opening and stopped me from closing it. With a quick move, he pushed me aside and forced himself and Clem inside the house.

"To the basement," Max the toothless ordered.

I was nervous. These guys didn't have much for brains. But they had muscle, and that's what made me nervous. I tried to sound calm and said, "What exactly are we doing in the basement?"

"Gettin' the goods," the older guy barked.

"Look, I don't want any trouble," I said "If you know where my aunt kept the goods, let's get them."

The younger guy waited for the older to motion what their next step was to be. They were a dangerous "Dumb and Dumber."

"Shut up!" the older guy said. "Don't say more words." Then, directing his attention to the younger guy, he said, "You know what to do, Clem!"

The intimidating presence of these two guys was enough to frighten the holy shit out of anyone; these brutes were not kidding.

"We were told to get the goods and if anybody, uh…stops us, to waste them," Toothless Max said, "and we follows orders without questionin'."

I was in for some serious trouble. How was I going to get out of this? *Go with the flow*, I thought.

"Where does the stuff come from?" I nervously asked them.

"We don't know, we don't ask, and we don't care," the young guy answered.

"Shut up, Clem!" was the immediate order from the older guy.

They went straight to the secret place, as if they knew the house. I decided I had a better chance if I cooperated.

"Do you guys know what happened to my aunt?" I asked, trying to break the ice. "I'm offering a reward for information."

"That's not the side of the business that we ares involved with," Max announced.

These guys really gave me the willies. They stunk as if they had lived without soap and shaving for a long time. Their clothes were soiled and dingy. I looked for tattoos or specific characteristics for later reference—which was stupid of me, I realized; it was the dead of winter, and they were wearing heavy parkas and wool hats.

Good try, I told myself.

~

They went directly to the door of the secret place and pulled the lever.

"We saw the Big Aunt's doin' this whenever we did our rounds," said Toothless Max.

The door didn't open. He tried again...nothing. The look of his mouth was disgusting; the swearing was even worse.

"Open the fuckin' thing!" he ordered me menacingly.

"I don't know how," I retorted.

"Don't tell us you didn't know about this place," the younger riff-raff said.

I shook my head.

"Clem, go to the fuckin' truck and bring a crowbar," the toothless brute ordered his crony.

"Shit," Clem muttered. "Can I get a smoke?"

"Move your ass!" Max said. "We don't haves time to lose."

"Fuck you," Clem replied politely.

Once Clem was out of sight, I tried to tempt Max.

"Max? It's Max, right?" I said tentatively. "You're an intelligent guy—"

"Shut up!'' He cut me off.

"Look, I have money," I told him. "I'll give you one hundred big ones for the information on my aunt's death. You could retire—"

"How long you think I'd last if I did that?" he asked.

"You mean you're not the boss?" I asked in jest. "The way you boss Clem around?"

"He's just a kid that needs direction," he said very seriously.

Was he really serious? But I held my laughter and smart remarks. I weighed the possibilities of taking him on. Without the other guy, I stood a better chance, didn't I?

"Don't thinks anythin' stupid!" Toothless Max said as if reading my mind.

"You're a big man," I said. "Push the door down. I'm dying of curiosity to see what you're after."

At that, the door coming from the outside to the basement opened with a big slam.

"Clem, wheres in the fuck is the crowbar?"

Clem appeared at the door to the basement. He was bleeding profusely from an open gash on his forehead.

"Whats in the fuckin' hell?" Max said.

Standing behind Clem was a tall figure holding a gun. The light in the basement was dim, and I couldn't make out the person holding the gun.

"Hello, Max," the voice said. "You're still as hideous as ever."

The voice was profound and congealed the blood in my veins.

"You need help, Sam?" the shadow said, stepping into the light.

I felt the blood leaving my face. "Rita!" I exclaimed. "Or whoever you are!"

"Yes, I heard you were looking for me," she said unemotionally.

"What's going on?" I asked, alarmed.

"Well, darling, let's see. Your bitchy aunt screwed me," she said bitterly.

"You knew my aunt?" I asked.

"I worked for her, the fucking bitch!" she said angrily.

"Who are you?" I asked her.

"Louisa Malone. Not related to that fat-ass Rita Malone," she said.

"I can see that," I said.

"Your fucking aunt got what she deserved!" she said. "And I made sure she got it real good!" she added bitterly.

"Did you kill her?" I asked.

At that moment, I realized only one option was left. I had to think through my next step carefully. I would take the chance and play them against each other, which always seemed to work…in movies.

"Max, is this the worthless bitch working for Big Aunt that you were telling me about?" I asked ingenuously.

Max glared at me. "Look, man," he said, "I'm a dead man either way."

"You should have taken my offer," I said to him, "and Clem would have taken the blame, just as we were planning."

"I knew you would sell me out to save your ass!" Clem said to his partner.

"The three of you shut up!" Louisa ordered, waving her gun.

The next moment Clem was throwing a punch at Max. "Fucking asshole," he said.

The two of them got into a headlock and didn't care about the gun pointed at them.

Louisa shot a warning shot, but she lost footing with the force of the gun. Max jumped at the opportunity. He took the gun away from her, and in the struggle, he shot her in the chest. She fell like a heavy sack of potatoes, the wound squirting blood everywhere. Clearly, it was a fatal shot. Max was a pro at his job; there was no hesitation, no blinking of his eyes. Clem and Max high-fived as if they were at a stadium and their team had just scored.

I closed my eyes in horror, thinking that I was next. I was trembling, and words were stuck in my throat.

"Relax, we hads no orders to harms you," Max assured me.

"No dude, we just need to get the goods," Clem reassured me.

I had never seen a crime committed before my eyes. Was I now an accomplice to this murder? For all I knew about law, it was self-defense.

"We have to call nine-one-one!" I shouted hysterically.

"Ares you crazy?" said Max.

"No, it was fucking self-defense!" I said, thinking of the implications.

"Look, buddies, this is our business; we'll takes care of it," Max said impatiently.

Since I was now their buddy, I guess it was fucking OK to kill someone. "Look, I don't want to be implicated in your dirty work!" I yelled.

"After we gets the goods, we will take this bitch corpse with us and dump it far away from heres," he said without stopping to breathe. "All you hads to do is keep cool and clean this mess."

"And if I refuse?" I asked with some daring.

"Simple. You takes a rides with her!" he said without hesitation.

Both men laughed.

"Yeah, we are equal-opportunity killers," Clem said very childishly.

They high-fived again amused by their cleverness and wit.

"Do you have a medicine emergency kit?" Max asked me.

I nodded.

"While you patch Clem, I will open this damn door," butt-ugly Max said.

I felt cheated because I would never know who this woman was or get the clues I needed to know who murdered my aunt.

Since I was now Max and Clem's partner in crime, I decided to chance it with them.

"Who was the bitch?" I asked, pointing to Louisa.

"Don't know," the old man answered.

"Did you know her?" I asked the younger moron as I cleaned the gash on his forehead.

"I don't know who she was," he said, "until we saw her here at Big Aunt's."

"Yeah, I thoughts they were homos. You know…" Max said with a wink.

"She seemed to know you," Clem said. "Did she?"

I shook my head no. Then I asked, "Why do you call her 'the Big Aunt'?"

They looked at each other and shrugged their shoulders. Max said, "That's the ways she is known, I guess."

"Yeah, when we get orders to come here, we are told so," said "Dumber."

"How long have you been making this pickup?"

"Not sure…'bout six years?"

"Longer," Clem said. "I was seventeen when I started to work with you."

"You don't works *with* me, asshole, you works *for* me."

27

Max was all sweaty and frustrated; he hadn't been able to open the door.

"We needs dynamites."

"Is there a combination to open it?" the other moron asked.

Max pulled Louisa's gun and brandished it at me.

"Open it!" he ordered.

"Why don't you get a saw and cut the door open?" I suggested.

"Clem, get a saw!"

"Why do you always ask me to do the heavy work?"

"Is there a saw in this fuckin' place?" Max asked.

I shrugged my shoulders and said, "Maybe in the garage."

"We don'ts want to attracts no attentions," the older moron said.

One of the nicest things about Aunt Millie's house was its privacy. Surrounded by eight-foot-tall shrubbery thicker than a concrete wall—evergreens, I supposed—these shrubs served as a sound barrier as well.

"What are you guys driving?" I asked.

"We has a rental," said the boss. "As soons as we see the stuff, we will gets the truck."

"Is that your routine?"

"No, usually we get a truck to drop off the stuff," Clem said.

"I thought you were here to pick up the stuff," I said.

"We parks the truck in the other town's truck stop," Max said. "Like that, we don'ts attract no attentions."

"You mean you have stuff to drop off too?"

"That's how it works."

"Not this time," I said. "I have some people coming over related to my aunt's estate."

~

Max ended up going to the garage to check for the saw. "I don't needs to have mores surprise guests."

It was my time to mess with the younger goon's brain, or whatever he had.

"Clem, how's your head?"

"Still hurts a bit."

"No, I mean, why do you let that old fuck boss you around like that?"

"Eh?"

"You are the intelligent one," I told him. "Aren't you afraid that his mind is gone?"

"I don't ask questions."

"Look at the mess he put you in by killing that bitch!"

He was listening. I could feel his body becoming tense and upset.

"Look, you're young; you can begin a new life if you want," I continued.

"Shut up!"

"I can help you."

"And how can you help me?"

"I have some money to get you started."

"And why should you do that?"

"Because…I need your help to stay alive."

"How much are we talking?"

"Twenty Gs."

"No way man!" he said. "I make much more than that!"

"One hundred Gs?"

He was silent awhile. His mind was working the possibilities.

I got him! I thought.

"You should have seen Max's partner before I came in," he said. "He ended up suffering a gardening accident."

"Gardening accident?"

"Yeah, he fell into a wood chipper!" Horror was written all over his face.

We both became silent weighing the consequences. For me, if he told Max about my offer, I would be taking the ride with Louisa.

"I just wanted to help you because I have been in your situation," I said.

The silence that followed our interchange reminded me of the dialogues I had with Jacob, where each of us had our own agendas and expectations. Jacob and I knew that, as in all conflicts since Abel and Cain, there had to be a winner and a loser.

I was expecting the same outcome from this situation: the loser to be dead.

~

It took Max a couple of hours to come back. I didn't have my watch on, and I couldn't say how long I had been in this Mexican standoff.

"Where have you been?" Clem asked Max.

"Gettin' the fuckin' saw," he barked.

"I thought you left."

"I did. I had to go to the hardwares to gets it."

Clem was still carelessly holding the gun.

"Gimme the guns!" Max ordered him.

"What about, Max, if I give the orders now," Clem said, waving the gun at Max.

Max's face turned red, and he started to come at Clem like a fucking bull. Clem panicked and squeezed the trigger. A bullet flew from the gun and went directly to Max's chest.

"Fuckin' idiots!" Max said as he fell—and fell hard, with a frozen grin of disbelief.

Clem was paralyzed with fear, and I was in shock. I tried to seize the gun from Clem, but his hand was clamped on and I couldn't make him relax his hold.

The basement was a bloody mess.

~

There was something about blood that turned my stomach and made me vomit I was gagging at such a gory sight. The smell of blood was sickening; when you've been exposed to it, the feeling stays with you. Cleaning up was going to be tougher than disposing of the corpses, I thought.

A shot of whisky helped Clem regain composure, at least for a while.

"Clem, get a hold of yourself!"

"I didn't mean to kill Max!" He was shaking.

"I'll help you finish your job."

"How?"

"We have to come up with a scenario."

"I can't think straight," he said.

Could I? I thought.

I got a shot of whisky, too. I needed to think about a logical solution for this bloodshed.

"We have to clean up this mess!" I said.

I got rags, paper towels, buckets, and bleach. I had seen large garbage bags in the garage.

Louisa's blood was already coagulated, and caked on the concrete floor Max's was sticky, with the consistency of chocolate syrup and still warm. We needed rubber gloves.

I went up to the kitchen to look for the rubber gloves under the sink; the grandfather clock chimed: it was six o'clock. What a horrifying day. I anticipated that the cleaning was going to take the rest of the night.

When I returned to the basement, Clem was still incoherent and very scared.

"Clem, you need to pay attention. This is what I will help you do," I said.

I waited for his reaction. He slowly turned his face toward me.

"Are you listening?" I asked.

He nodded his head.

I told him that I would be his witness in case he needed one; therefore, we needed to agree to a story. "Do you understand?"

He nodded.

"Here we go." I started to describe scenario one: "Max and you were trying to open the storage area to get the stuff when Louisa appeared."

"And then?" Clem asked.

"She wanted to take the goods from you guys, and Max and she started fighting for the gun."

"There's only one gun. How can two people end up shot with the same gun?" he asked, starting to come around.

"The gun went off, shooting Max."

"How did the bitch end up dead then? I don't understand," Clem said.

"At the same moment Max got shot, he took the gun away from her and shot her as he took his last breath."

A long silence followed. I could see Clem's eyes beginning to shine with new hope.

"You take the stuff and the two bodies," I said.

Finally he said, "Let's get started."

28

We finished cleaning up the blood at eight o'clock the next morning. We both were tired. The bodies were tightly wrapped in garbage bags, as were the wasted rags. We had to wait until night-time for Clem to get the truck and load them.

I wanted to continue working, but I could hardly stand up.

"How are you holding up?" I asked Clem.

"I'm exhausted."

"Let's take a couple of hours to rest," I suggested.

"Thanks, man," he said.

"Are you hungry?"

"No. Who could think about food after cleaning such a disgusting mess."

I nodded. "There are a couple of lazy chairs upstairs," I offered.

"We need to start back at ten," he said.

"We'll open the door to the basement as soon as we are up."

~

The barely audible ringing of a phone woke me. *Shit—where did I leave it?* Anxiously, I looked for it, cussing the small object. How could that digital piece of crap get my attention as soon as it rang? Everything got pushed aside to answer it, just to get bad news or unimportant bullshit.

Clem grabbed the gun by instinct.

I glanced at the clock. "Careful. Remember, that's how you shot Max."

We could hear the muffled beep. "Someone left you a message," Clem said.

"Where in the fuck is the phone?"

Finally, I remembered I had left in my room. Yes, it was on my night table. I picked it up and saw that the damn thing was off.

"Did you find it?" Clem asked when I returned.

I nodded.

"Who was it?"

"My phone was off," I said. "Do you have a phone?"

He shook his head.

"Max had one?"

"Yeah, that's how we got our orders."

We both ran to the basement looking for Max's phone. It was nowhere to be found.

We could hear the muffled beeping. Where was it coming from? *Those fucking things*, I thought again.

We stopped and looked at each other. At that moment, we knew we had to unwrap Max and check his pockets. This was the kind of stuff that gave people unimaginable nightmares for the rest of their lives, even forcing them to look for a shrink. I wondered how it was going to affect me. Besides, I had thought I was done with this macabre chore.

We discussed the option of leaving the phone where it was; the answer was the same. Clem needed the contact information stored in Max's phone. Their boss could call, and he didn't know who the boss was. Not answering the call was worse than playing Russian roulette.

"Where do you need to make the drop?" I asked him.

"What drop?"

"You know…the stuff?"

"LA."

"Where in Los Angeles?"

"I don't have the address," he said shaking his head, "but I know how to get there."

We stood in silence, looking at Max's bag. We had no other option but to undo it.

I went to the garage to get more large garbage bags and a pair of scissors to cut the bundle open.

The silence was profound; the only sound was our own labored breathing. We both gasped in horror when we finally released Max's body.

He looked grotesque. His eyes and mouth were open. A streak of bloody water was oozing from his nostrils. His skin color was bluish with pinkish dots. Rigor mortis, I thought. I could feel the ice-cold temperature of his body. His hair was matted with dried blood. What a horrible sight!

The phone was inside his jacket pocket. Clem immediately tried to search for the lost call.

"Let's wrap him up first," I said. There was no emotion left in my voice. I couldn't believe I had spoken in such a way.

"Did Louisa have a telephone, too?" Clem asked.

"Does everybody have one?" I answered.

"Do we need to unwrap her?" His voice was trembling.

~

We retrieved Louisa's telephone too. It was important for me to see if I could find out who had sent her. Maybe Max and Clem were right and she was nothing more than a hurt lover done wrong by my aunt.

"Clem, were you able to get the message?" I asked him.

"No, I don't have the pass code," he said, discouraged.

"You have to wait to see if it rings again."

"He had no stored data, either," he said.

"Can you get the phone number of the last call that came in?"

"It was a blocked number," he said. "Not surprising."

"Are you ready to open this fucking door?" I asked him.

"Yeah, I don't want to spend another night here—it's too spooky!"

"Do you know what time is it?"

"It's about three."

"Boy, it was ten when we woke up."

I suggested that Clem go get the truck, but then I had a vision of him running away and not coming back. Shit! The idea was disturbing, to say the least.

"Clem, I changed my mind. We better go together, and we could grab a bite."

"Yeah, I haven't had anything to eat since yesterday."

~

We drove in silence to the truck stop in Riverdale. The traffic on the streets was jammed. Christmas shoppers, I thought.

"For Sunday, there's a lot of traffic," Clem observed.

"Three days until Christmas, man," I said. I started to feel nostalgic, remembering my last Christmas with Sophia.

Clem brought me back to reality. "Do you want a burger?" he asked.

"Ugh?"

"*Do you want a burger?*"

"You don't have to yell. Let's get the truck first."

We ordered hamburgers to go. We were so hungry, but when we bit into the burgers, bloody grease came out of the medium-rare meat. I immediately thought of Max when we were looking for his phone; it was so vivid I started to gag.

"Are you OK?" Clem asked.

I didn't want to ruin his appetite. The bloody grease was running down his hands. I got out of the vehicle and vomited.

"C'mon, man, we are running out of time—it's five o'clock!" Clem said.

~

The twelve-foot truck moved very slowly. The drive from Riverdale to Mapletown lasted forever.

Clem and I jumped when Max's phone started to ring; we just looked at each other.

"Answer the fucking thing!" I yelled.

"H-hello?"

I could hear a muffled voice asking for Max.

"He's not here," Clem said.

The muffled voice cussed.

"He's dead!" Clem said.

There was a moment of silence between Clem and the voice on the phone.

"Who is this?" Clem dared to ask.

"Fucking moron!" came out loud and clear from the other end.

Clem started to tell the story that we'd concocted with all the gory details. I couldn't hear the other guy's responses.

"Her name was Louisa Malone…This is Clem, Max's helper… We ran into problems with the pickup, but we are getting the goods tonight…The Big Aunt's nephew and me!…Yes, I know where the warehouse is to make the drop…Tuesday morning?"

I could sense Clem tension's from his quivering voice.

"Can I get your name and phone number in case I run into trouble?" Clem asked.

I heard the voice this time, muffled though it was: "If you are not here Tuesday morning, you are dead."

29

The phone call Clem received made the truck move faster. He was driving erratically and fast, determined to get to our destination in a hurry.

"What happened, man? Why the hurry all of a sudden?"

"I was delaying going to that damn house," he said. "You see, the hamburger reminded me of Max." He paused a long time before continuing. "Now, I have a deadline—a real 'DEAD' line, if you know what I mean."

"You mean that you'll be dead if you don't deliver by Tuesday?"

"Is your offer still good?" he asked.

"What offer?"

"The hundred grand."

I didn't answer him. I had forgotten about it.

"Well?" he prompted.

"The only thing I can offer right now is to help opening the door for you to get the stuff."

"Shit! I should have taken your offer."

"Did you recognize the guy on the phone?" I wanted to change the subject.

"I have never talked to these people before."

"Is this 'stuff' stolen goods?"

He shrugged. "I imagine so."

"What is it?"

He thought awhile and then said, "When we come for a pickup, we usually drop at the same time a shipment for a 'cooling period.'"

I tried to find a justification for my aunt, something that made sense, like maybe she was renting the space out to a repo company or something.

"Did you guys pay my aunt for the stuff?"

"I don't know much…I'm only the messenger."

"Park all the way in. Back up," I told Clem as soon as we arrived at my house.

Clem opened the gate on the back of the truck. "Give me a hand," he said.

I came to the back of the truck to see what he needed. The truck was half full of electronics of all sorts.

"Did you guys made a pickup somewhere else?"

"No, this is your drop—I mean the drop that was scheduled for the Big Aunt."

"No, no, no!" I said. "You can't leave that here!"

"C'mon, man, what do you want me to do with it?"

"Fuck, I don't know; take it back."

Clem looked scared; it was time to pay for his actions, I reasoned. I didn't need to feel responsible; I hadn't put him there.

We struggled for a couple of hours more with the basement door; it was almost eight o'clock when we finally managed to break it in.

The secret chamber was almost full of all kinds of computers, stereos, printers, digital cameras, even a few pieces of art.

I couldn't begin to imagine when my aunt got involved in this kind of business. I couldn't understand why.

"Clem, before we start loading this shit, we need to load the bodies."

He didn't move.

"Clem, did you hear me?"

"I don't know where Max was planning to dump the woman," he muttered.

"I thought that you and he did this kind of cleaning."

"I never did the dumping."

"Should we call the cops?"

"Let's get loading," he said.

"Let your employers deal with the load, man."

~

It was midnight when we finished loading. We were extremely drained, emotionally and physically. I went straight to bed, while Clem faced about eight more hours of driving, with pit stops and all. I wished him well and hoped never to see him again.

I felt anxious about the complications that could arise after my encounter with the thugs.

I was pleasantly surprised that I was able to sleep like a baby—no ghostly nightmares. I was relieved to know I had a load off my shoulders. I felt at peace and ready to start the next day, to tackle the other problems I still had pending.

With Monday being a day of commerce, I looked forward to taking care of business with a couple of guys in City Hall. I felt as if I had grown cajónes since my run-in with Max and Clem and was ready to take on anybody.

My next move was to see Sergeant Miller.

~

My body hurt when I woke up the next day; the heavy lifting had been brutal and nonstop. The worst feeling was when we'd moved the two stiffs; I swear that a lifeless body is much heavier than a living one.

I wondered if Clem made it to LA without problems. I also wondered if, and how, he disposed of the "extra baggage." But I had other, more important problems to focus on than thinking about Clem.

I was moving very slowly, and it became a real chore to walk to the kitchen for a cup of coffee and a couple of aspirins. I felt stiff and worn to shreds. I was groaning and moaning with every step I took. I heard a phone ringing, but I just couldn't budge fast enough to answer it. I glanced at the kitchen clock. I couldn't believe it was noon!

I suddenly remembered that I'd never turned my phone back on. Could Clem have forgotten Max's phone? No, I made sure he took it with him! Shit! I remembered that Clem and I had done the same disgusting job of searching the other body, too. I had forgotten about it. Louisa's phone was the one ringing.

Her cell phone was on the dining room table. I picked it up; the face showed "missed called." I tried to retrieve the last call that came in, but before I could do so, the phone's battery went dead. How rude of Louisa to not leave the charger.

Who really was Louisa Malone? What was she doing at the courthouse? Had she been my aunt's lover? I'd never know. What a cunning bitch!

I changed gears and decided that maybe the one I should pay a visit to was Angelloni. If someone could shed light on this puzzle, it would be him, I thought.

I looked at a calendar: December 22, 2005. I didn't have much time; Jacob was supposed to be back in January. At least the secret place in the basement was completed and finished. I went downstairs to double-check that the basement was thoroughly cleaned, that all incriminating evidence had been removed. The place looked spotless.

The thought of Louisa came back to mind. What had she been after? Maybe Victor knew who she was. I would call Victor's sister and find out more, if I could, about Louisa and my aunt.

Was Louisa taunting me when she said she watched when my aunt was wasted? Moreover, that my aunt deserved what happened to her?

Victor had said he saw three men the night my aunt was killed. Was it only two men and Louisa? I had thought Eva might have been the one present when my aunt was murdered.

I began to feel better after taking the aspirin.

30

I don't remember what I did on Monday. I just remember that my muscles were aching.

I remember that I made plans to see Angelloni, but I never made it to his office.

Sergeant Miller was in my plans, too, but I didn't see him, either.

I decided not to do anything about Angelloni and Miller; it would be better to go and try to find Victor in San Fran. I had lot of questions to ask him related to my aunt.

My mind was going fast and then slow; it was like a whirlpool of insane ideas. I couldn't decide what I was going to do next. I needed to get out of this place for a while to cool down and think clearly. I had many unanswered questions.

A loud knock on the front door interrupted my pondering. I peeked through the window and saw a delivery vehicle parked in front of my house.

Cautiously, I opened the door.

"I have a delivery for a Sam Stone. Is he here?" the messenger asked.

"That's me. Who sent it?"

"I don't know who sent it," he answered. "Please sign here."

I took the clipboard and pen from him and scrawled my name on the dotted line.

He took them back, then tore off a copy and handed it to me. *Small town*, I thought. Then he handed me an envelope.

With curiosity, I slit the envelope open with my aunt's silver-and-mother-of-pearl letter opener. I couldn't believe she still had it; I had given it to her for her fiftieth birthday.

The letter was from McGregor and Associates, an insurance company. Whoever they were, they were informing me that the investigation to determine whether the fire at the cabin was arson or accidental was still on course, and they would soon contact me to let me know the decision on the claim. In addition, whatever monies were dispersed would be to the estate of Mildred C. Wilmot. Finally, the letter said I needed to provide them with a copy of my aunt's death certificate as soon as possible.

Crap that was all I needed— other assholes putting the screws to me.

I tossed the letter onto my dresser, grabbed the small suitcase, and threw a few items in it.

~

I arrived in San Francisco at five o'clock and drove directly to the address that Victor's sister had given me over the phone.

I was very excited to see the beautiful city again. Coit Tower welcomed me with its shimmering lights. The Golden Gate Bridge looked like a dangling necklace suspended in air. I rolled the windows down so I could savor the salty evening breeze and hear the city sounds. Tonight I would dine at my favorite restaurant at Fisherman's Wharf.

I glanced at my watch; it was four thirty. Maybe Victor would like to dine with me. After a nice dinner, a few glasses of wine, and casual conversation, maybe he would be willing to tell me whatever he knew about Aunt Millie. I was sure that he had eavesdropped on my aunt's business and personal privacy. How long did he say he'd worked for my aunt?

I was convinced that he also knew about the stuff in the basement's secret room.

The closer I got to his sister's place, the more anxious I felt. Soon I was knocking at the door. I heard steps moving toward the door. I felt someone's eyes checking me out, and finally the chain of the safety latch slid back. The door opened slowly and cautiously.

A tall, bony, flat-chested woman appeared at the door. I could swear it was Victor in drag.

"Sam?" she asked in a dry voice.

"Yes," I answered.

"Are you alone?" she asked nervously.

"Yes."

"Come in," she said.

"Is Victor in?"

Then "she" removed the stiff-haired wig from Victor's head and said, "It's me, Sam."

I burst out laughing so hard that tears came to my eyes. He looked serious and embarrassed.

"I'm sorry. I didn't know that you were—"

"No, I'm not gay, nor a trans-dresser!" He sounded pissed.

"Are you going to a masquerade party?" He made such an ugly woman, I thought.

"No, I'm just being cautious."

I pleaded for him to put the wig on again; reluctantly, he did. I couldn't believe my eyes: he bore a resemblance to…Louisa Malone!

"Is your sister home?" I asked him.

"N-no."

"Look, Victor, I'm here because I need to find out some things about my aunt."

He looked at me intently, without blinking; there was no feeling in his eyes. After a prolonged silence, he said, "I don't know a thing."

"Look, Victor, don't try to fool me," I snarled. "You worked for her…how long?"

"Long enough to keep my mouth shut!" he sneered.

"Have you eaten dinner yet?" I changed pace.

"N-no."

"Let's go to Fisherman's Wharf."

"I'm ready," he said.

"Are you really going dressed like that?"

~

Nothing I said made him change his clothes. We arrived at my favorite restaurant at Ghirardelli Square. The patrons of the chic eatery stared at us with curiosity; we were seated immediately. I ordered a bottle of Chianti, and Victor started to relax after his second glass of wine.

"How long you been doing this?" I asked him.

"You mean dressing like a woman?"

"Who are you hiding from?"

"Your aunt was involved with all kinds of people."

"Are those clothes comfortable?" I asked teasingly.

"Are you crazy?" he replied.

"What do you know about the goods that she had in storage in the basement?" I asked.

He shifted in his seat and excused himself for a trip to the restroom. I wondered which one he'd use, the ladies' or the gents'?

Victor was a raw nerve, looking over his shoulder all the time. What had he seen that caused him to dress and act like this? I needed to extract whatever information I could from him. I would press harder as soon as he returned from his toilet excuse.

I took a fleeting look at him as he headed back to the table; as panicky as he was, he still looked like Rita...Louisa.

"Are you OK?" I asked him as he sat down.

"I just don't know what to tell you about your aunt," he replied, fidgeting.

"Just whatever I ask."

"It's not that simple."

"For starters, did you know Louisa Malone?" I said, looking intently at his facial expressions and body language.

His facial muscles gave him away; they started to tense up. And slight perspiration was forming on his upper lip. Was he going to excuse himself for another restroom trip?

He cleared his throat several times, then said, "How do you know of her?"

"Did you know her?" I persisted.

"She was your aunt's assistant," he muttered.

"Her assistant or her lover?" I asked him sarcastically.

"They were pretty close."

"What about Max and Clem?"

"Your aunt's delivery guys."

"Cut the shit, Victor!"

I realized he wasn't going to say anything that compromised him. He knew someone was keeping an eye on him. I couldn't stop contemplating the level of involvement he'd had in whatever my aunt's dealings were. How could he not know anything after all the years he'd worked for her? He knew who was coming to the house all the time.

"Did Clem and Max waste my aunt?"

He shook his head and looked away, avoiding eye contact with me.

"Victor, I understand how frightened you are," I coaxed. "Whatever you tell me is not to be mentioned again."

He continued with his indifferent silence.

"God damn it, Victor, I need your help!"

"Take me home" were the words that came out of his mouth, putting an end to the failed conversation.

"Victor, is someone paying you to keep tight-lipped?"

~

We rode in silence through the hilly streets. From the corner of my eye, I could see how twitchy Victor was; his lips remained hermetically sealed during the twenty-minute drive to his place. When I reached it, he looked at me, for an instant his face softer.

"Your aunt was very decent to me, and I tried to reciprocate," he said. "But she is dead, and whatever I say won't bring her back."

"I know...but at least it will bring the murderers to justice."

"I suggest you leave things as they are, Sam."

"You will have to come back to Mapletown," I said. "She included you in her will."

31

I drove away as soon as Victor slammed the Jeep's door shut. I was feeling tired and dejected; I didn't have a particular place to go.

I decided to get a motel room; it was almost ten o'clock, and I didn't feel like driving the three hours to Mapletown.

I turned the radio on to see if it would help keep the gloomy thoughts from running wild. I felt the train ready to start chugging through my head once again.

"Silver Bells" started to play on the radio. I tried to be unsusceptible to the Christmas season, but this carol took me back to Sophia and our Christmases together.

I took Highway 280 South toward San Mateo. I found myself driving on Middlefield Road. I couldn't remember how many times I'd traveled this road before. It used to be a very pleasant thirty-minute ride from my office in downtown San Francisco.

Sophia would be waiting for me to dine together. She was very proper and poised all the time—except when she had a fight with her mother, who never forgave her for not being beautiful.

She had attended the best prep schools but always felt like a misfit. Her mother pushed her to befriend the beautiful debutants in the Bay Area, but Sophia was shy and withdrawn.

I didn't notice when I parked in front of the gates of Fifty-One Oak Leaf Way. My heart was pounding so loudly that I was afraid Sophia would hear it. I sat there admiring the elegant Christmas decorations in the house.

Unexpectedly, I heard her voice. "Who is this?" She said. "And... do you know what time it is?"

I didn't realize that I had unconsciously pressed the intercom button at the front gate. I'd forgotten that an outside camera would be watching my every move.

"Oh God! It is you, Sam!"

The gate opened slowly, and I drove into the driveway toward the house.

~

I was shaking uncontrollably when Ida, the maid, opened the door. "Good evening, sir."

"I was in the neighborhood and dropped by to wish a merry Christmas," I said sheepishly.

"What are you doing here, really?" Sophia asked.

I couldn't believe my eyes—she looked stunning. Her hair was blond and cropped, stylishly and perfectly framing her young-looking face. She was wearing a slinky black dress that outlined her shapely figure.

"You look amazing!" I said.

"I just came home," she said.

"*The Nutcracker*?" I asked.

She nodded. "Really, what are you doing in San Francisco?"

"I came to see Victor; he used to be my aunt's butler."

"How's your aunt?"

"Dead."

I had taken Sophia to meet Aunt Millie before we got married; she had met Victor, too.

"What happened? Was she sick?"

"No."

"How did she die then?"

"She was murdered."

"What!" She was all shook up. "It's impossible."

I stood silently watching her reaction.

"When?"

"Over two months ago, more or less."

~

She offered me a drink and invited me to sit down. While we sipped our drinks, I told her the situation in Mapletown. Once again, she took pity on me.

"When are you going back?" she asked.

"Tomorrow evening."

"Where are you saying tonight?"

"Um…I have to find a motel."

"The guest room is available," she offered.

"I don't want to impose."

"Ida!"

The maid came immediately.

"Please turn down the bed in the guest room. Mr. Stone is spending the night."

The maid promptly disappeared in the hallway.

Sophia served another shot of brandy. "Did they catch the murderer?"

"No, I don't even have the crime report."

"The post-mortem report?"

I nodded.

"Three fucking intruders beat her to death," I said. "I'm sorry; I know how much you dislike profanity."

"How do you know there were three killers?"

"Victor."

"He saw the crime being committed?"

"He says he did."

"Sam, it is strange that he is alive, isn't it?"

"I don't understand," I said.

"Usually there are no eyewitnesses left alive."

We were silent for a moment.

"Anyway, why were you visiting him?"

"To see if I could get more information from him."

"He didn't give you any, right?"

"No, his lips were sealed."

"Isn't it strange?"

I nodded.

"He worked for your aunt for several years. Doesn't he have a duty to help?"

"He claims his life is in jeopardy if he talks."

"How's that?"

"He is keeping a low profile by dressing like a woman—do you believe it?"

"What do the police say?"

"I'm the prime suspect!"

"What? Do you have an attorney?"

I told her about Jacob and the way he'd approached me. I also told her about the murders of Louisa and Max and the truckload of goods.

"You're up to the gills, dear." Her mouth was hanging open. "You better get a real good attorney to represent you."

I opened my mouth, and the cascade of events kept spilling out. It felt good to speak in confidence to someone without fear that she was on the other side.

She gave me the name of an attorney, Steve Stavropoulos.

"Tomorrow we'll see him," she said.

"Sophia, tomorrow is Christmas Eve."

She said she had his private line and could get to him whenever she wanted. She also offered the name of a private eye, "the one I used to trail you," she muttered, turning red. "Sam, I have to confess that I was glad that it was gambling, and not another woman."

"I'm so sorry that I fucked up and hurt you."

"I always wondered what my reaction would be if I ever saw you again," she said very intently.

"I'm so sorry I put you through that."

"I'm glad that you are here."

"You were always very forgiving, darling."

"I thought about you all the time, especially on Christmas."

"So did I, Sophie."

"Steve respects me and wants to get married. Anybody in your life?" she asked cautiously.

I shook my head. "I'm glad you have Steve."

"He is a good guy." Her face turned red again.

"Who is he?" I asked her, curious.

"His name is Steve Stavropoulos."

"Steve…what?"

"S-T-A-V-R-O-P-O-L-O-U-S."

"I mean who is he? Where is he from?"

We both laughed. I used to like the way she threw her head back when she laughed. We were always comfortable with each other. *Fucking gambling.*

"You look gorgeous as a blonde."

We talked about the old college years, her lack of confidence. I came to be her savior.

We both remembered the first time she introduced me to her parents. I was very nervous when I saw where she lived. Her father, Frank, was a gregarious, self-made millionaire; her mother, Monica, a glamorous woman who wasted no time before belittling her plain-looking daughter.

"Sam, you know what time is it?"

"Good heavens! It's three o'clock in the morning."

"Let's go to bed, darling…," she said teasingly.

I would have done so easily. I would have given anything to go to bed with her and to feel her warmth once more. I had never felt like such a loser as I did right now.

She leaned close to me and kissed me on the cheek. I could smell her fragrance. Her perfume lingered for the rest of the night. She still wore Joy.

"Good night, Sam."

"Good night, Sophie, and thank you."

32

We got up early the next morning. Ida was waiting for us with a mouth-watering breakfast; it felt like the old days.

Sophia looked radiant and well rested. During breakfast, she informed me that she had talked to Steve about my situation and that he would join us for lunch.

"You didn't have to bother the man on my behalf," I told Sophia.

"We have a plane to catch at four thirty," she announced.

"Where are you going?"

"To meet his parents in Athens."

"Are you marrying him?" I didn't know what else to say.

"Don't know for sure."

"How long will you be gone?"

"Just for the holidays."

We finished our meal in silence. It was great while it lasted, I thought.

"Sam, please leave me your phone number. I'd like to know that you'll be OK."

"I would like to have yours too."

"It's the same."

"What about the PI?" I asked.

"He will join us for lunch too," she said.

"What's his name?"

"Andrew Daniels," she said. "He works with Steve."

~

Was I in a dream? I never imagined that I would be back in the Stone house after our divorce. I hadn't wanted to take any of the furnishings that were bought especially for the house. I took only my personal belongings. Sophia was very classy; even then, she had left the country so I could have the liberty of gathering the stuff I was taking with me.

My life became a mess after I left. I became disorganized to the point that I turned into a slob. I stopped shaving and bathing. I guess I stopped caring.

I took a tour of the residence now—for the last time.

The house was open and spacious. My former office was off the living room, enclosed by French doors. I tried to stay out of it; it brought back memories of using that privacy to hide my newfound gambling craving from Sophia.

"It's my office now," she said. It was like the rest of the house, elegantly decorated and very functional. I noticed a pleasing-to-the-eye portrait of her parents on the credenza that once held my decanters of liquor.

"How are your parents doing?" I asked politely.

"Mother died five years ago," she said, sounding despaired for a moment. "And Dad died last year."

"I'm sorry."

"I have to ask you a question, Sam." Her face became serious.

"I guess I owe you that…go ahead."

"Do you still gamble?"

"No." I told her about the loan sharks, how close they had come to taking my life.

"What are you doing for Christmas?" she asked.

It was a long time since I'd planned for Christmas; how can you make preparations when you don't have anybody to plan with? "I suppose I have to entertain myself."

Ida came into the room and whispered to Sophia; the two of them left the room.

"I'll be right back."

I continued exploring the house with curiosity to see what had changed since I left. I opened the French doors to the outside terrace adjacent to the office and stepped out. The morning was cool and breezy, the lawn perfectly manicured, and the bushes flawlessly trimmed. The view was tranquil and relaxing.

I saw a black, shining car enter the gate. Sophia waited close by. *It must be Steve.*

I felt a stab of jealousy as I gazed intently at the happenings in the driveway. Then I felt embarrassed at my lack of discretion and went inside. Ida came into the room once more and announced that Mrs. Stone would be back shortly.

~

I sat in the office for a long while. I was beginning to feel uncomfortable and bothered, but I waited patiently.

Ida appeared again, carrying a tray with a coffee decanter, creamer, bowl of sugar, and three cups and saucers. The napkins were embroidered with SSS. Everything in the house carried the same SSS. I couldn't believe she still used my aunt's wedding present to us: Sam, Sophia, Stone. Would she get rid of these mementos once she married Steve? What a coincidence that their monogram would be SSS as well!

I was deep in contemplation of the events that had taken place in my life and had put me here now when I heard footsteps and voices growing louder as they approached. Sophia was cheerful.

33

I stood facing the window; I didn't want them to see my nervousness. "Sam, this is Steve Stavropoulos."

"Hello!" he said, stretching his hand out.

"Hello!" I repeated, hesitant to shake his hand; my hand was clammy.

"Sophia gave me some details of your legal situation," he said. "There are always lots of complications. Why don't we make an appointment?"

His voice was deep and velvety, the kind women like; his dress was casual yet distinguished; and he looked collected and trustworthy. With dark hair, dark eyes, and an olive complexion, he was about six feet tall, the type women liked, and maybe fortyish.

From the corner of my eye, I caught Sophia watching him with adoration. I noticed a lipstick smudge on his lips. I had to admit, enviously, that they were a classy couple.

I felt the veins of my temples throbbing, excused myself, and went to the powder room. I splashed cold water on my face to wash away my visions of choking her for the humiliation I was suffering. I couldn't understand these feelings.

I came back to find them embracing. Sophia's face turned red.

"I live in Mapletown," I managed to say.

"No problem," he said. "We'll do a phone interview."

"A phone interview?" I asked.

"Yes, I'll determine if I can be of help to you," he continued. "And if I can help you, I will come to Mapletown to talk."

"Would you do that?" Sophia asked, enveloped in a trance-like reverence.

"Is Mapletown in Mendocino County?"

"By the way, Steve, where is Andrew?" Sophia asked, referring to the private detective.

"He had to take Little Andy Christmas shopping."

Ida interrupted to announce that lunch was served.

~

As always, everything looked delectable and elegant: finger sandwiches, veggies, fruit served in silver platters. Mini éclairs and other types of fancy desserts were served on crystal platters. Poinsettias and other floral arrangements adorned the dining room.

Steve and Sophia were whispering to each other in a familiar way, and I felt like a moron just sitting there feeding my face.

"I have to call it a day," I said, trying not to sound bitter. "The two of you need to get going too."

"Sam, I'll be calling you as soon as we are back," Steve said.

"What kind of law do you practice?" I asked him.

"You have your aunt's estate pending, right?"

I hated when people answered with a question. "Yes, I'm also a person of interest in her murder."

"Sophia, you didn't mention murder to me."

"Steve...like you said, this thing is complicated," I said.

"You handle murder too, don't you dear?" Sophia asked Steve.

"Upon your return, I will tell you the order of events as they took place," I told him.

Ida came into the room to ask if they wanted her to call the taxi to take them to the airport.

"I can take you," I volunteered.

They exchanged glances, the way couples do to see if each agreed.

Steve nodded slightly, imperceptibly giving her the green light.

"Are you sure?" Sophia asked.

"Of course," I replied.

"Great! I can ask you some questions on the way," Steve said.

"Shall I call Andrew?" I asked Steve.

"Do you think you have a need for a PI?" he asked.

"It will help," I said. "You see, that's why I'm here in San Fran. There's this guy that saw my aunt get murdered."

"Yes, Steve, and he is refusing to tell Sam who did it!"

"The man is scared out of his wits; he is even dressing like a woman to keep a low profile," I explained.

"Why?" Steve asked.

"I think that my aunt was dealing with stolen goods."

"This is hot!" Steve muttered.

"I can't follow the plot!" Sophia exclaimed.

~

I waited for them to get going. Finally, they grabbed carry-on luggage, one for each. Sophia disappeared briefly to give instructions to Ida. Then we headed for the door.

"Where are the rest of your suitcases?" I asked them.

"That's all we are taking," Sophia answered.

"We shipped our wardrobe ahead," Steve added.

"Is that something new?" I asked.

"It's not new, but it's becoming more popular," Sophia replied.

We continued with small talk until everyone was in the Jeep. Then Sophia said, "Steve, why don't you sit in the front so you and Sam can talk?"

A momentary silence followed. Steve checked to make sure he had his documentation handy. I reached for the volume of the radio to lower it as "The Drummer Boy" was blaring.

"Steve, do they play these carols in Greece?" Sophia asked, breaking the silence.

He just laughed. Then he turned to me, shaking his head in perplexity. "Sam, what's going on?"

"I don't know what is what." I was frustrated. "My aunt was murdered over two months ago."

Steve and Sophia listened attentively to every word I uttered, but I felt like I was alone, speaking to myself. The ride to the San Francisco International Airport lasted forty-five minutes, and I realized I had been talking nonstop the entire time.

"Sam, let me stop you for a minute," Steve finally said.

I was perspiring, and my breathing was labored. I felt my heart beating furiously against my chest.

'You need to catch your breath, Sam." I heard Sophia's voice in a dreamlike manner.

"What does the death certificate say?" Steve asked. "And have you seen the post-mortem report?"

"The cause of death was trauma and excessive force to the head. I'm not quite sure. The ME wrote that until the labs come back—"

"What do the police say?" he asked.

"I'm the prime suspect. According to them, I had time and motive."

"According to them, what was your motive?" he asked.

"I was the only heir." I moaned.

"Sam, promise me that you will leave this alone until I come back," he said.

"What should I do about Jacob?" I asked.

"Keep him waiting and don't tell him about me, but above all, do not sign anything."

"Please take care of yourself," Sophia warned.

"I'll help you solve this mess, Sam," Steve said, shaking my hand.

~

I became very anxious the moment they left the Jeep. A feeling of desolation was invading me, and I felt terribly alone. I waved them good-bye and took off. I felt sick to my stomach to see Sophia leave with another man. I watched Steve put his arm gently around her waist. *She deserves to be happy.*

Steve had given me the PI's telephone number. I decided to call this guy. I left a short message on his voice mail.

34

I stopped at a coffee shop close to the Bay Area, hoping the PI would return my call, and soon. The clock on the dingy wall read three o'clock. The voices of the café patrons were monotonous and loud, competing with the Christmas music coming from the cheap speakers in the place. I felt a train was ready to take off inside my head.

The server approached my table and offered a warm-up, pointing to my coffee. I complained to her about the music. She could do nothing about it, she said; she'd had enough of "Frosty the Snowman" too.

My cell started to ring. I caught it on the third ring.

"Hello?" I said anxiously. "This is Sam."

"Yes, I'm still in the area," I said.

The voice sounded muffled and there was lots of static. I was afraid of dropped calls so I moved toward the door to get a better reception.

"Yes, I know where Ghirardelli Square is."

"Three- thirty is fine."

I went to the restroom to check on my appearance. I looked dreary. I ran my fingers through my hair in an effort to look more presentable, but I looked old beyond my years; the past few months had made a mark on me.

I returned to my table to pick up the check and left a twenty to cover the coffee and tip.

I was getting into my Jeep when the young server came running after me. "Sir, your change!" she said, waving the handful of money.

I just waved good-bye.

~

I really loved the "City by the Bay." I contemplated the idea of moving back as soon as—no, now. I should leave my aunt's legal stuff in the hands of attorneys; her murder should be in the hands of the police. Now I had money and could afford a decent living.

My phone rang again. I didn't recognize the number on the caller ID. I wasn't expecting calls, but what the heck? I was curious.

"Hello?" I answered on the fifth ring.

"Sam?"

I couldn't believe it was Sophia. "Sophia!" I said, very excited.

Silence.

"Sophia, are you still there?"

"I just wanted to tell you that it was nice seeing you." She sounded nostalgic.

"Sophie, please be careful and don't trust anybody, and if you need me, call me, and I'll fly to wherever you are," I blurted out.

"Thank you, Sam."

"I'm on my way to meet Andrew Daniels, the PI you recommended."

"They are calling us to board our flight. I'll talk to you when I come back."

"Merry Christmas, Sophie!"

~

Twilights in San Francisco are spectacular; they are the nostalgic stuff poets and songwriters write about. Tonight's twilight was very pleasant for wintry weather; nevertheless, it was winter. The clouds seemed to hang lower on the horizon, and the golden hue of the sun reflecting over the Pacific Ocean looked magical. A golden flare-up was taking over the bay.

Why had I never noticed this beauty before? Why had I never appreciated Sophia before?

I parked my Jeep in a garage and glanced at my watch. It was still early, so I decided to take a cable car to Fisherman's Wharf. I tried to imagine what Andrew Daniels looked like. I pictured him to be overweight and bald. Kojak came to mind, a hard-boiled, thick-skinned detective, perhaps a heavy smoker, hot-tempered, with a dirty mouth and lots of street smarts.

I arrived at the Irish Pub on Beach Street at exactly three thirty.

A slender, blond man came to meet me—nothing like the hard-core PI I'd imagined. Mr. Daniels looked gangly and pale, as if he had just finished college.

"You must be Sam Stone," he said.

"Are you Andrew Daniels?" I was disillusioned.

"Yes, Steve told me about you and your problems."

"Did he tell you that he was one of my problems?"

"Yes, he is lots of people's problem."

"What can you tell me about him dating my ex-wife?"

"I thought that you needed our services." He gave me a puzzled look.

"What I need to know is what Steve wants from Sophia."

"It's not your damn business."

"The fucker is after her money."

"You think she is that ugly that the only attractiveness in her is her money?"

"That is not the case at all—she is naïve."

"Then you think she is stupid?"

"How come his parents didn't come to America instead?"

"I have a question for you," he said. "If you care so much for her, why did you divorce her?"

"Not your fucking business."

"I guess this meeting is over. Thank you for wasting my time."

Shit! At that moment I thought I had just lost the opportunity to learn about Steve. "I-I'm sorry, man," I said. "I guess I have watched too many programs on how men kill their lovers overseas."

He was sympathetic and extended his hand; we had a truce.

~

I told him I didn't have time to get information from Steve's law firm.

"What do you need to know?" he asked.

"How long you have been in business together?"

"We met right after he got his law degree." He was pensive. "I was a detective with the San Francisco Police Department."

"What happened?"

"Personal problems," he muttered as if talking to himself.

I deducted that he wasn't going to go into them. "What kind of law does Steve practice?"

"Criminal."

"Has he ever been married?"

"Yes. Nora died five years ago."

My skin crawled as soon as he said that. "How?"

"She died in an accident."

The place started to spin. I tried to focus on Andrew's words, but the words, "He killed her!" came effortlessly out of my mouth like poisoned darts.

"She died during one of their vacations."

Andrew and I just sat staring at each other; he was shaking his head faintly. I dialed Sophia's phone number.

"No, no, impossible! She died in a boating accident," Andrew whispered.

"Sophia's phone is off," I muttered.

"Steve is a decent person…he cares for her," Andrew said. "Besides, it's not the first time they've gone away together."

"He has kids?"

"Yes, he had a son with his first wife." He looked at me quizzically.

"You don't even know much about your own partner, Andrew. For heaven's sake!"

He was unable to utter anything. He intently watched the ice in his scotch as he swirled it around. I felt good inside, glowing with malice!

I gave him the information on Victor Parker and a check to cover his first week. I told him I needed reports on the target every other day. I wanted Victor tailed twenty-four/seven. I wanted to know who he was talking to, where he was going, and what he bought.

"By the way, I also want pictures," I said.

He took the check and stored my phone number on his BlackBerry.

"I would also like updates on Steve and Sophia."

He entered all my requests on his gizmo.

"Do you have a picture of Mr. Parker?" he asked. "Does he live in San Francisco?"

I felt like saying, *Yeah, I carry his picture in my wallet, asshole.* Instead I gave him Victor's address. I said I would fax a picture as soon as I got to Mapletown.

He took off then, and I went to the Buena Vista Café at the wharf for dinner before I started on my way home.

~

A dense fog made the trip home long and dreary. The bright headlights seemed to bounce off the fog. For a moment, I thought I was lost; I couldn't recognize the road I was on. I had to stop for a moment and clear my head. I couldn't tell whether I was going north or south on Highway 101. Shit! I couldn't see a thing. I decided to continue with the trip but reduce the speed.

It was white-knuckle driving, and at moments I found myself driving down the middle of the road. I was glad it was Christmas Eve and the road was deserted. I turned on the radio for company; I made an effort not to bitch about the nonstop Christmas music playing on most of the stations.

The music brought back memories of my bleak childhood at Christmastime. I remembered going to bed with silent fantasies of Santa Claus bringing me a bicycle, then waking up the next morning only to find out that I had been a "bad boy" and Santa hadn't stopped at our house. My mother justified herself by saying it was my fault. I would cry, and then resentment would build up inside me. I was very angry at Santa and my mother when I saw other kids with their shining new toys.

I was about eight years old when Aunt Millie got the bicycle for me. Once she entered my life, Christmas wasn't depressing anymore. Still, Christmas music always brought unpleasant memories of me being a "bad boy."

~

A loud, trumpet-like sound brought me out of my reverie. Shit! A huge semitruck was coming head-on toward my Jeep. I veered to my left and by a split second avoided the crash. I had been driving on the wrong side of the road. Fucking fog, I thought only after I'd regained control.

Appearing out of nowhere was a faint neon light from a coffee shop; the density of the fog made the sign looked like it was floating in the air. I had to stop for a cup of coffee. The parking lot was empty, and the place looked deserted. The red neon light by the door said "open," though, so I parked my car and got out. My legs were wobbly and achy.

The coffee shop was colorfully decorated with a Nativity scene and Christmas ornaments that had seen better times; the Christmas carols were loudly blaring. The waitress told me to sit wherever I wanted.

She came quickly with a cup in one hand and the coffee carafe in the other. "Freshly made," she offered.

"Thanks."

"Are you going far?" she asked.

"Mendocino County."

"I just heard a fog advisory on the radio," she said.

"How bad?"

"Until four o'clock," she said.

I glanced at my watch: good grief! I had been driving for only an hour and a half! It was nine forty-five; I should have been almost home by now.

She poured the coffee and left.

I hadn't accomplished much on my trip, but seeing Sophia made it worthwhile. The other possibility was the PI; I hoped he would be able to deliver the information on Victor that I had requested.

35

I was exhausted physically and mentally by the time I made it back to Mapletown.

I had left Fisherman's Wharf after dinner at Café Buena Vista around seven thirty; it took me five hours of driving, plus the two hours at the roadside coffee shop. Under normal circumstances, three hours was all I needed for the trip.

The house was dark and silent. I felt ill at ease when I remembered the events of a few days ago. The silence was deafening and evil; I could still feel the dead weight of the bodies being moved to the truck. I shivered with fear.

I heard muffled noises coming from the basement. I didn't dare check them out. I was experiencing fright so intense that my shirt was soaked with perspiration.

I decided my mind was in the final stage of deterioration and was playing wicked tricks on me. I would get a drink, a strong drink at that, something to put me out of my misery, at least for tonight. I poured a straight double scotch and pounded it down. I started to calm down immediately. I was almost asleep when my cell started to ring persistently.

"Hello," I said. I listened briefly—nothing—then hung up. I sat down on my bed and fumbled with the phone, trying to find out who had called. It was a private number. I put the phone on the dresser and started to undress, when it rang again.

"Hello."

"Sam?"

"Yes, this is Sam."

"It's Jacob, Sam. Sorry I am calling so late. I just wanted to wish you a merry Christmas."

I was surprised that Jacob was calling me at three thirty in the morning. I mumbled something blasphemous under my breath.

"Excuse me?" he said.

"I said merry Christmas to you too!" Tongue in cheek, I said, "Ho, ho, ho!"

"Are you drunk?" he asked.

"No, I'm relaxed…I had a long day."

"What've you been up to?"

As much as I disliked talking to Jacob, I was somewhat thankful for his call. Almost instantaneously, I went from being terror-stricken to being full of vexation. At this moment, I thought, I would much rather be angry than scared.

"How's Eva?" I asked brazenly.

"Eva?"

"Yes, the one you warned me to stay away from, remember?"

There was a prolonged silence. I thought Jacob had disconnected, so I hung up too.

The phone rang again. I got it at the first ring to see who was calling before I answered. It was the same number. I didn't answer. My phone started to beep unremittingly—he had left a message. I turned it off.

I drank another double shot and drifted off to sleep.

~

Next day I stayed in bed most of the day. I did a lot of pondering and soul searching.

It was yet another gift less Christmas Day—no special gift, no special dinner, just me. I had nobody to call with warm holiday wishes, nothing…just void and emptiness.

I had stopped blaming everybody for my failures, accepting that I was the only one responsible for my mistakes. I felt a sudden anger rising inside me for being such an irresponsible fool. I felt that this year would be the same as before. I couldn't escape this vicious cycle. If I could only solve my aunt's murder, I thought, that could change my life.

It was one-thirty in the afternoon when I finally got up. My shower was long and hot. I used extra soap in an effort to scrub my stench and failures away. I felt morose and heavily laden, unable to move. I stood naked and dripped for a long time. Nothing mattered. I was alone.

Finally, I changed into a sweatshirt and pants.

I dragged myself to the kitchen to make coffee—coffee was magic; it always helped me. I was self-absorbedly drinking my hot cup of coffee when I heard a loud tap at the kitchen door.

I got up to see who was knocking, then immediately changed my mind and continued drinking my coffee. I wasn't in the mood to entertain anybody today. I hadn't finished that thought when the door violently bolted open and a couple of angry guys tumbled in.

"Where is my stuff?" demanded the short, heavyset guy.

"Hi, I'm Sam. Merry Christmas and with whom I have the pleasure of speaking?" I was scornful.

There was no answer. One of the guys came menacingly toward me and grabbed me by the neck.

"You're the second set of guys that have come to my house for the 'stuff,'" I said.

"So, where is it?" Shorty asked.

"Dun no," I answered childishly and shrugged.

"Max and Clem never arrived," he said.

"You know what happened to Max, right?" I said.

"And that's exactly what's gonna happen to you if keep on fucking with me."

Shit, nothing matters. "Sorry, but I'm unable to help you. Clem left last Monday, and he took everything with him."

"Show me the basement!" the guy ordered.

Everybody seemed to know about what I thought was a "secret" place. I shuddered at the idea of going back to the basement, but the second guy pointed a gun behind my head.

"Would you guys like a cup of coffee before?" I couldn't believe I said that.

They looked at each other with astonishment. The second guy waved the damn gun toward the basement and barked, "Move it, clown."

"You guys chose a bad day to come here," I said.

"Any day is a bad day when my stuff is missing," Shorty said.

As soon as Shorty opened the door to the basement, the smell of death and blood came rushing to my nostrils. I started to gag violently. Shorty was in front and turned his head to see what was going on. I was vomiting. The second guy stepped on the slime, lost his balance, and fell down the stairs. Trying to regain balance, he let go of his gun. I quickly moved aside, and he brought Shorty along on his fall. It happened so fast it was comical.

I grabbed the gun from the step and started to laugh aloud. "I told you it was a bad day," I said with tears in my eyes.

The two assholes looked miserable. "I hope you brought a truck like Max and Clem," I said, still laughing uncontrollably.

When I finally stopped laughing, I waved the gun at them and ordered them to their feet.

The second guy had a broken ankle and couldn't get up. I shook my head and said, "You should have accepted the cup of coffee." I started to laugh again, enjoying how humiliated they looked.

"Just because it's Christmas, I'm going to do something nice," I said compassionately.

I ordered them to walk toward the not-so-secret place and open it.

"I said there's nothing here. Clem took it all."

They looked taken aback that I was telling them the truth about the stuff.

"If I let you go, do you promise that you won't come back to harass me?" I asked.

They looked at each other once again and nodded.

"I won't take your nodding for an answer. Speak up!"

"I swear on my mother's eyes that I'll never see you again," Shorty said.

I waved the gun in front of the second guy. "And you?"

"Th-the s-same," he said in excruciating pain.

"Sorry, that won't do. Crooks are crooks, and I won't fall for that shit," I said.

"I-I won't come here again, I swear."

"Just to be on the safe side, you'll put it in writing."

I left them in the basement while I went to Jacob's room to look for a legal pad. I came back with pen and paper.

"What is your full name?" I asked Shorty.

"Ray Incarnatti."

"And yours?"

"Anthony Giacomonti," he said.

I scribbled down the information and took off again, locking the basement door.

How cool was it? No violence, we were three gentlemen negotiating a win-win.

I returned to the basement with a written statement that evidence of their unlawful activities would go to the authorities if they came close to me. I hoped this would work with such hardened criminals.

I handed each the declaration and a pen. They read it.

"Is there a question?"

"No," Shorty said.

"N-no," the second man said.

They signed the papers and gave them to me. I escorted them upstairs and out the door.

"You should take your friend to a hospital," I advised Shorty.

Anthony, the second guy, screamed in pain at each step he took. "Shut up, already," the short guy grunted.

"Wait!" I called out. "Here's your gun…and…Merry Christmas!"

They got in their sedan and left. And I let out a sound of relief and went back to drinking coffee.

I couldn't help but laugh when I remembered those two idiots. Clem and Max were moronic. But Ray and Anthony were…pathetic! I felt better thinking that I wasn't the only loser out there. Those guys reminded me of Mel Brooks and his wacky movies. I wondered who their boss was.

I trembled to think what the outcome could have been if I hadn't puked. I started to feel hope.

I went back to my room to get my phone. I turned it on and saw that I had several messages. The first was from Jacob informing me that he was coming back on the second of January. Eight more days, I thought.

The next message was from Andrew the PI. He had some information. I was to call him back on the twenty-sixth. There was a wrong-number call and then a message from the auctioneers reminding me of our appointment.

The last message was from Sophia. "Sam, I got your message, thank you. I hope that you have a nice Christmas. I'll call you upon my return." I played it repeatedly. It was so nice to hear her voice on Christmas Day.

I guessed that with the stuff from the basement gone, it would be OK for the auctioneers to come and organize this disarray of boxes and objects. Maybe with all this shit out of the way, it would be easier for me to find clues leading me to my aunt's killers. I thought of the map I had found when I first came to her house.

The answer was right under my nose—I just couldn't see it for now.

I thought I'd make an effort to go see Angelloni the next day. After all, he had never read my aunt's will and testament to me. Maybe we would even go to lunch together, as he had suggested the last time I saw him.

For today, I would take it easy and lounge around.

36

I got up early the next morning, ready to take the day on. I showered and shaved, looking forward to having lunch with Angelloni. He didn't know it yet, and that made it more exciting.

It was raining when I left the house. The chill in the air felt brisk and invigorating. I zipped up to keep warm.

I walked the few blocks to Angelloni's office. I checked my watch when I entered the building: eleven twenty.

The front office was deserted. I heard noises coming from Angelloni's private office. I couldn't determine what sort of sounds they were…pain? Moaning perhaps? I opened the door. Angelloni had his secretary sprawled over his desk; his pants were down to his ankles. They stopped immediately when they heard the door being opened.

"Don't stop on my account," I said mockingly.

"What in the hell are you doing here?" Angelloni said, obviously not liking that he was caught with his pants down.

"Merry Christmas!" I said gleefully. "You invited me for lunch."

"Oh yes?" he said, trying to pull his pants up while his secretary excused herself.

"I'll go to the waiting area while you finish."

"Where is Jacob?"

"He won't be joining us today," I said nonchalantly. "By the way, how's Mrs. Angelloni?"

He glared at me irately.

I left his office and went to the waiting area. I sat down, grabbed a copy of *People* magazine, and casually opened it while I waited for Angelloni. He appeared at the door, his shirt tucked in and collected.

"OK, Sam, what is this all about?"

"It has been nearly three months since my aunt died, and you haven't read her testament."

"I thought Jacob was representing you."

"I have a copy of my aunt's testament, and I'm her only heir."

"Where did you get it?"

"My aunt left me a copy of her original will in her safe-deposit box."

His face turned white, as if he had seen a ghost. He was silent for a moment. I could sense his tension rising; he became fidgety and anxious.

"What else did she leave you in her deposit box?" he asked nervously.

"Several documents, and some photographs."

"Do you have them?"

I didn't answer. I just looked at him, studying his reactions in an effort to read his body language.

"Answer me, God damn it!" he demanded, losing his composure.

He was very uncomfortable by now. Tiny droplets of perspiration were forming on his upper lip. Miss Harris, his secretary, came running, concerned about the uproar. I just sat motionless.

He waited for my answer. I decided to play with his emotions, so I gave him a deliberate response. "No, I don't have them," I lied just to see his response.

"Where are they?" he shouted.

"Jacob has them," I said tentatively.

By now, his pallor was evident. His lips appeared parched. He muttered something to Miss Harris, and she darted toward the liquor cabinet, poured a shot of vodka, and handed it to him. He gulped it down and asked for another.

Miss Harris asked if I wanted one. I declined.

"Where's Jacob?" he asked, regaining composure.

"Out of town."

"Where did he go?"

"To visit his sister, I guess…"

"God damn it! Where?"

"He said to San Joaquin or San Fernando Valley."

"When is he coming back?"

"He said January second."

Angelloni was shooting his questions like a machine gun. Looking straight at my eyes, he shouted, "Did he take the documents with him?" He pounded his fist on the table for effect.

I hesitated for a moment, which was too long for him to bear.

"Answer me, God damn it!" He pounded his fist on the table again.

"Cut the swearing," I said, tired of hearing his cussing.

"Look, it's very important for me to know."

"Don't say," I retorted.

"Do you know where the documents are?"

"No."

"Do you know if a map was among the papers?" he asked nervously.

"I don't know."

"Did you check the documents before giving them to Jacob?"

"No, I don't know much about legal documents."

"How do you know then that you have your aunt's original testament?"

"One of the papers read 'Last Will and Testament of Mildred C. Wilmot.'"

I needed to go check the documents again. Something was staring me in my face. For now, I needed to carry on with my game.

"You mentioned a map…what kind of map?" I asked ingenuously to keep on with my charade.

He looked at me intently, trying to penetrate the depths of my mind and read my thoughts. His temples were throbbing. He kept tugging at his collar.

"Why did my aunt want a map?" I continued. "Was she planning a trip?"

The ringing of a telephone interrupted us; instinctively, we all pulled out and checked our own cells.

It was Angelloni's office telephone. Miss Harris answered. She handed the phone to Angelloni. "Your wife," she told him coldly.

"I guess it's time for me to leave," I announced.

Angelloni motioned to me to hang on. He covered the receiver with one hand and said, "Don't leave; we need to finish this." Then he said into the phone, "It's Sam Stone, dear, Mildred Wilmot's nephew."

Miss Harris left the room, slamming the door on her way out. I smirked and chuckled.

Angelloni talked to his wife for a few more minutes.

I pointed at my watch in an effort to hurry him.

Gently he hung up. "Fucking bitches."

"Does Mrs. Angelloni knows that you're screwing your secretary?" I asked.

"Son of a bitch!" he retorted furiously.

I winked at him. *I got you, motherfucker.* This time he read my thoughts without fault.

"I bet she would like to know, don't you?" I dared to say. "Just as I would like to know who killed my aunt," I added maliciously.

Silence engulfed us. He just sat there looking at me.

"Do you have any information for me, Angelloni?"

I guessed our lunch date was off. I was feeling great that I got the fucker in my pocket. My mind was working feverishly on several scenarios to keep this arrogant jerk on his toes from now on.

"Should we reschedule our lunch date?" I asked him mockingly.

He got up from the chair he was sitting in and walked trance-like toward the exit, then left.

I called after him, "I want to have the information by tomorrow."

He looked back. "This is not over," he said in a threatening voice.

"Say merry Christmas to Mrs. Angelloni for me; maybe I'll drop by to wish her a prosperous new year in person." I shrugged.

He glared at me wrathfully and pointed at me with his index finger in a gun-like manner.

I couldn't believe that I had struck a nerve with the pretentious and poised attorney at law whom everybody feared.

I found Miss Harris at her desk, crying. "Lock up when you leave, honey," I said.

I walked toward the exit, Miss Harris behind me. I turned around and asked her, "Would you like to have lunch with me?" She nodded, and we left together. We had to walk to my place to get my car.

She continued crying on the way to the same restaurant that, I'd overheard, Angelloni and his wife were going to. I offered my handkerchief and suggested she reapply fresh lipstick.

She was a pretty woman. Large boobs, leggy, and platinum blond. She dressed in a trashy way. Her blouse was cut low and revealing; she was wearing red stilettos.

I was anticipating seeing Angelloni's face when we entered the posh eatery together.

"How long have you been working with Angelloni?" I said, trying to break the ice with Miss Harris.

"Since high school." Her voice was hoarse.

"Last year?" I said, trying to flatter her.

"Don't be silly—almost ten years," she said, drying her tears.

I felt like asking her how long since he'd started screwing her, but instead I said, "How long have you been his mistress?"

"It's not your fucking business!"

"Yeah, you're right. I'm sorry I asked such a personal question."

"It's OK."

"Mrs. Angelloni knows?"

"She doesn't like me," she said. I nodded sympathetically, but I was thinking, *Of course she doesn't like you, slut.*

Her eyes looked red from crying. Her makeup was running all over her face. Black smudges around her eyes make her face look cartoon-like comical. I stopped at a service station and suggested she use the lavatory to refresh herself. She asked me to get her a pack of menthol cigarettes.

She came out of the lavatory all refreshed. She had applied a cheap fragrance that was making me gag. It was not Joy, I thought.

She lighted a cigarette and took a long puff. She offered me a smoke; I politely declined.

"You look nice," I said, trying to gain her trust.

"Thank you," she said as she breathed a cloud of smoke from her nostrils.

I thought about how classy and refined Sophia was. She never smoked, nor used vulgar words. Even her perfume was classy.

"Did you love your aunt?" she asked all of a sudden.

She caught me by surprise, and I didn't know what to say. I was hesitant to answer.

She patiently waited for my answer, lighting another cigarette. With pleasure, she sucked in the nicotine in a long drag. I could tell she was a heavy smoker from the lines around her plump mouth and the yellowish stains on her fingers. I cracked open the window to let fresh air in. Her cheap perfume and the tobacco were nauseating.

The cold air felt good on my face. She was starting to loosen up.

"She was my only family," I finally said.

"What?"

"Yes, I loved her," I said.

"She was a tough woman."

"Did you know her?"

She looked away and lighted another cigarette. The crying had stopped altogether.

"I can use a drink," she said flatly. I observed keenly the changes in her voice and her body language. "She had been Marco's client long before I started working for him." She spoke furtively between puffs. "I heard that her net worth was several million." She paused to collect her thoughts.

I was astounded that I'd never known where her money came from. "Do you know where her fortune came from?" I asked.

She shook her head. "Not at the beginning."

I looked at her going through those cigarettes fast—I should have gotten two packs, I thought. "Was my aunt fencing stolen goods?"

Miss Harris gave me a long look, accompanied by a long puff of smoke out of her mouth and nostrils, without saying a word.

37

We arrived at the Seagull restaurant, and I gave the keys to the valet. We walked inside. The place was jammed with people waiting for a table. I approached the hostess, flashed a fifty, and asked in a hush tone, away from Miss Harris, that she seat us close to Marco Angelloni's table. The hostess covertly took the money and checked the seating list. She took a couple of menus and motioned us to follow her, saying aloud as she walked in front of us, "Your reservation is ready, Mr…"

"Stone," I quickly said.

"Yes…Mr. Stone," she said casually. The waiting patrons glared at her. She coldly ignored their glares and, smiling, took us to our table. It was nice to have money readily available to purchase people, positions, and things, I thought.

Gentlemanly, I pulled out a chair for Miss Harris to sit on, hoping Marco would see us. As she placed the menus in front of us, the hostess said, "The table over there is for an important couple." She winked at me. I understood that Angelloni was to arrive soon. I thanked her.

I couldn't remember Miss Harris's first name. "Can I call you by your first name?" I asked her.

"If you buy me a martini, you can call me whatever you want," she said teasingly.

Darn it! Tell me your name, cheap slut! I wanted to shout. "So, what's your name?" I asked.

"Elsa, you guff," she said.

It couldn't work any better, I thought; she was playful. The waiter came to our table, and I ordered a martini and a scotch with water. Elsa checked the menu, seeming unsure of what she wanted to eat.

The place's ambience was for romance or for pickups. People were dancing, but my eyes were on the door. I wanted to see when Angelloni and his wife came to their table. Elsa was sucking on her second martini when I saw Angelloni following the hostess. She winked as she passed our table.

Angelloni didn't seem to notice us, and I pretended not to see him too. I got up as he was sitting down and, with Elsa on my arm, "accidentally" bumped into him. I started to apologize for my clumsiness when Mrs. Angelloni recognized Elsa and immediately shot a dirty look at her.

"Mr. Angelloni!" I said with delight. "What a nice surprise."

He stared with disgust at Elsa; I ignored the situation.

"Mr. Angelloni, I hope you don't mind that I took the liberty to ask your secretary out for lunch."

"Young man," his wife said, "why are you apologizing?"

I could see who was in charge in that relationship. Mr. Angelloni became sullen and despondent. He wasn't the same man who'd been banging his secretary early this morning. His wife reprimanded him about his manners.

"Honey, this is Sam Stone," he said.

"You're Millie's nephew?"

I took her polished hand and gave it a slight kiss.

She completely ignored Elsa.

"You know Elsa Harris—she is your husband's secretary."

Without deigning to look at her, she said, "Of course I know her."

Elsa hung from my arm and said, "C'mon, Sam, let's dance."

I excused myself and went to the dance floor with Elsa. She rubbed her body against mine in an attempt to make Angelloni jealous. I reciprocated; I rubbed my body against her hard body. She started biting my earlobe, and I kissed her neck. I could feel the stare of two sets of eyes.

When the music started playing again, I asked Mrs. Angelloni to dance.

"Are you attracted to Miss Harris?" she asked with disdain.

I could see Angelloni arguing with Miss Harris. "No, not exactly," I calmly said. "She was not feeling good when I left your husband's office earlier today."

"Tell me, Sam, did they ever catch your aunt's killers?" she asked.

"Not yet."

"I'm sorry. She was a dear lady."

"Do you know what happened?"

"Not really. I heard Marco talking to so many people about it that I don't know what to think."

We came back to the table laughing and kidding. "Marco," she said, "Sam and I are going to meet Saturday to introduce him to available ladies."

"Can Miss Harris accompany me?" I asked.

"I don't think it's a good idea," Mr. Angelloni said.

"Elsa, would you like to come with me to the dance Saturday?" I asked.

"Sam, don't forget to come to my house so we can talk," Mrs. Angelloni said.

"Elsa, why don't you dance with your boss?" I pushed the situation.

When Elsa finished her dance, she had been completely snubbed by Mrs. Angelloni.

Our meals arrived at the table. She had an order of lobster and filet mignon; I had ordered a delicate fifteen-ounce New York strip steak.

The two ladies excused themselves. Marco and I stayed talking, and in an arguing manner, he said, "You better leave Miss Harris alone."

"I don't think Mrs. Angelloni approves of your possessiveness toward your secretary."

When Mrs. Angelloni and Elsa returned, the two women's faces looked like masks with fake smiles painted on.

Mrs. Angelloni's eyes were on fire, glaring at her husband.

"Why don't you sit at our table?" she asked.

"Thank you, Mrs. Angelloni, but we don't want to impose," I said.

"Well, then, you come to my house so we can talk, OK?"

"Is tomorrow OK? Saturday too?"

"Yes, yes. Marco will be at his office." Directing her attention at him, she asked, "What time you will leave for work, dear?"

"Let's dance, honey," he replied.

The two got up hand in hand. Miss Harris was very upset. I was observing the drama unfold.

Ruth Angelloni was a very attractive woman, elegant and distinguished. She looked impeccable. Angelloni looked drab next to her.

"They make a beautiful couple," I said, observing Miss Harris from the corner of my eye.

She frowned. "I think she is too old."

"Your boss is older."

"She dresses old."

"I think she looks classy."

"Who wears pearls anymore except for Mrs. Bush?"

"Pearls are elegant."

"Seems that they are arguing."

"Did she tell you something when you went to the lady's room?"

"Yes, that she will have me fired."

"Then she knows that you and Marco are screwing around."

"Bitch!" She got up and said she needed to go outside for a smoke.

I offered to go with her. Marco followed us with his eyes from the dance floor. "So tell me, why do you put up with this?" I asked Elsa.

"I love Marco."

"Really? I didn't see love when I walked in on you this morning."

She finished her cigarette, and we returned to our table. I smoothed my clothes and, with my hanky, wiped my lips.

Angelloni was fuming.

Miss Harris ordered another martini. "Don't you have to work tomorrow, sweetie?" I asked her.

She was tipsy already. "I'm pretty sure my 'boss' won't mind if I get in a little bit late." She let that sink in and then added, "Right, Marco? I mean, Mr. Angelloni."

This time Mrs. Angelloni was the one getting angry.

"Marco, are you going to tell her what we were discussing?" Miss Harris said.

She was shit-faced by this time. She started a belly laugh that made everybody turn in our direction.

"Mr. Angelloni, have you told your wife what we were discussing at the office this morning?" Miss Harris said.

It was as if she had dropped a grenade. I carefully watched everybody's reaction. Then, looking at me, she added, "Sam, did you tell Mrs. Angelloni of your visit to the office this morning?"

"Let's go." Mr. Angelloni said to his wife and got up.

"Honey, our orders should be here any minute. I'm hungry!"

I grabbed Miss Harris by the arm and went back to the dance floor.

She stumbled. She was too drunk and had become incoherent. Too drunk to dance.

I sat down and enjoyed my New York strip. I couldn't tell what I like the best, the steak or the triangle.

I ordered coffee after our dinners; I needed her to sober up. I didn't know where she lived.

Before we took off, I went to the Angellonis' table to thank Mrs. Angelloni for the invite for the next day. "What time should I come over?"

"Eleven. We will have lunch together."

"Mr. Angelloni, do you think that you'll get me the information I need tomorrow before eleven?"

He muttered something under his breath.

"If you don't mind, I'll drive Miss Harris to her place."

On the way, I had to stop my car to let her down to puke while I found her address in her purse. When we arrived at her place, I had to carry her in. I helped undress and tuck her into bed. I set her alarm for six thirty; she was going to have a shitty day. She was a mess.

I made a mental note to get in touch with her tomorrow to find out how had gone went for her. I was getting ready to leave when I heard dangling keys being inserted into the front-door lock.

Angelloni looked threatening when he appeared at the bedroom door. Angrily, he launched at me. "Son of a bitch!" he sputtered like a venomous serpent.

"Did you bring Mrs. Angelloni with you?" I asked cynically.

When I had set out to meet Angelloni early that morning, my intention was to keep a friendly front. It was too late for that; I had antagonized him beyond repair.

"If you know what's best for you, don't come to my house tomorrow," he said.

"Are you threatening me, motherfucker?"

"You heard me!" He spoke ever so slowly, making sure I caught his menacing inflection.

"I just want the information on my aunt," I said, grabbing him by the lapels of his overcoat.

"What will you give me for the information?"

Now we were talking—better yet, negotiating. "I won't see your wife."

"What about the map?" he cautiously asked.

"What's in it for me?"

He became silent.

"Anyway, what kind of map is it? A treasure map?" I asked ingenuously.

He had fallen silent and wasn't making any sound.

"Did you know Max and Clem?"

He nodded—at a snail's pace.

"Was my aunt fencing stolen goods?"

He looked at me fixedly for a long moment that felt like an eternity. "She was a businesswoman," he mumbled coarsely.

"Who killed her?" I asked him sharply. "*Who killed her, God damn it?*"

He said he wasn't sure, that he was trying to find out. She had been his business associate, and his funds were running short without her.

"Do you think Miller killed her?"

"No, not at all."

"Do you know who was she working for?"

"Look, you don't want to get involved. Your aunt asked me to keep you away."

"Victor said he saw three men."

Shit! I opened my mouth too much, too soon. I still couldn't bring myself to trust this guy; my gut was telling me to keep my guard up. It was too late.

His face lit up. "Where is Victor?" he asked.

"I don't know," I said curtly.

"When did he tell you that he saw three men?"

Now what? How was I going to get out of this one? I thought awhile about what to say to him.

"Well?" he pressed.

"The night the cabin was on fire." I was soon to find out how gullible he was.

"When was the last time you saw him?"

"I haven't seen him since."

Why was he so interested in Victor? I felt that the truth was staring at me, but I couldn't understand it. There was only one body and many suspects. Would I ever get to the root of it all?

38

It had been an energizing day. However, I felt I was getting close to the same destiny as my aunt's. Should I follow Angelloni's advice and keep out of it? I had gone too far to hit the "escape" button. I had to continue. I made a commitment to myself to find the killers.

I was parking my Jeep in the driveway when my cell beeped with a new voice message. This time it hadn't rung. Finally, after all the directives for how to access the voice mail, I got to the message.

"Sam? This is Andrew. Give me a call when you have a chance."

I felt a rush of excitement. My heart started to race as I dialed Andrew's number. Shit, I'd have to leave a message. "Andrew, I'm sorry I missed your call. Call me when you hear this message. Thanks."

It was still early, only six o'clock in the evening. I thought about examining the documents in Jacob's room, but I didn't know what to look for. I didn't want to end my delightful day frustrated. I would wait until Steve came back. That would give me an excuse to see Sophia once more.

My thoughts went back to Angelloni. I had a hunch that he knew who murdered Millie—and also knew the reason. I just couldn't believe he was upset about his funds running short. His knowledge of the map really surprised me. Where had I put it? I needed to find out the details of that hand-drawn crappy piece of paper. How important could it be? It was drawn on a legal pad sheet! Where was the shitty thing?

The rain kept falling. It pounded against the windowpanes, giving me chills. It sounded so ghostly and foreboding, I was beginning to feel terror-stricken when the phone rang.

"Hello?"

"Sam, this is Andrew."

"Hi, Andrew, what do you have for me?"

"This fucking guy is weird," he said. "Are you sure this is not a woman?"

I figured he was referring to Victor. "You tell me."

Andrew's voice sounded garbled. I couldn't make sense of what he was saying—fucking phones!

"Andrew, you are not coming through!" I felt like throwing the fucking device against the wall.

"Sam, are you still there?"

"Andrew! Andrew!" The phone went dead. I dialed his number; "failed call" showed on the fucking piece-of-shit screen. I felt my arterial tension rising and started to feel the locomotive moving inside my head. A "tension headache," they called it. It should be called a "fucking cell-phone headache."

I tried to call Andrew once more; this time it went directly to his voice mail. "Call me" was the message I left for him.

When I pushed the off button, my phone started beeping. I had a message. I needed to get a better phone, I thought as I went through the contortions to get my message.

"Sam, call me," was the message left by Andrew.

The phone rang again. "Andrew?" I said anxiously.

"Who is Andrew?" was the response.

"Who is this?" I asked impatiently.

"It's me!"

Someone fucking with me, I thought.

"*Who in the fuck are you?*" I yelled, my patience gone.

"Calm down…it's Jacob."

"What in the *hell* do you want?"

"Chill, man, chill," he said. "Did you get my message I left for you the other night?"

"Yes, that you are coming back on the second?"

"I might be there sooner than that. Am I still welcome at your house?"

"How soon?"

"Maybe on the thirty-first."

Shit! I was not ready to see him. It felt good having the house all to myself, and the idea of having him back mortified me. I didn't know what to say, so I didn't say anything.

"Sam? Are you still there?"

I didn't respond.

"Shit! I lost the call!" I could hear him bitching about his cell.

I just pushed the "end" button.

Immediately, the phone started ringing again. This time I checked the caller ID. It was Jacob. I didn't take the call. It went directly to my voice mail. I didn't bother to retrieve the message either.

I had to decide whether to let him come back to my house. I guess I needed to talk to him before I did that. My only advantage of accepting him was that I wouldn't be alone and wouldn't have to fear the creepy noises in the house. I realized the events in the basement had really fucked me up.

I decided to call Jacob later.

I stirred around the house, waiting for Andrew to call me back. *Wait! What if he is waiting for me to call him back?* I was on pins-and-needles. Just my luck!

I needed to calm down. I fixed a cup of coffee, which showed how irrational I was. Who calms down by drinking coffee? The alternative was a shot of booze.

Finally, the phone rang. I jolted to grab it.

"Sam? Can you hear me now?" It was Andrew.

"Yes, yes!" I said with enthusiasm.

"As I was saying…who is this weird guy?"

"He was my aunt's butler."

"He is a loner. I have tailed him. Nothing big: the store, the video store…you know, that kind of shit."

"Any other activity that is dubious?"

"Yes, last night he was visited by three seedy characters."

"Did you see these guys?"

"I got pictures, and I'm running them through a database to see who they are."

"How long will it take?"

"Usually about a week."

"How long were they at his place?"

"Quite a while—'bout five hours." Andrew was speaking fast. "He left with them, and I followed them. They went to the Mercantile Bank."

"Are you sure?"

"Yes, I took pictures." He paused for a moment. "Want me to send them to you?"

Then I could hear nothing but static. We had lost the connection again.

Had Victor erased my aunt? He said he saw three guys the night of the murder. My head was spinning.

The phone rang again. "Continue, Andrew."

"I'll go tomorrow to the bank and see if I can find someone to give me any information on him."

"Thanks, Andrew," I said, feeling better. "Have you find anything on Louisa Malone, is she related to Victor?" Have you heard from Steve and Sophie?

"No, they rarely call when they travel."

"Thanks again," I said. "Say hello for me if they call, OK?"

"Sure. Hey, Sam…do you still feel the same about Steve?"

"I don't know…I have enough problems. You seem to trust him, right?"

"I'll call you tomorrow with new info. If I don't call you, it's be—" The call was lost once more.

The house was still and quiet all over again. The rain kept falling. Shadows danced on the windows and walls of the old house. I decided to retire. Maybe I would have a better night—no terror, no spooky feelings.

~

I slept through the night—no strange sounds, no feelings of terror, and no dreams. I was void of sensory emotion. I got up around eight thirty and plodded along, marking time before my visit with Mrs. Angelloni.

I had time to look for the map. I checked in my room but couldn't find it. When had I last seen it? I couldn't remember. I checked my suitcase—perhaps I took it with me—but it wasn't there. I was working myself into a frenzy, checking all possible places for it. It was futile. Did I put it in the safe-deposit box? I would take a trip to the Riverdale bank after calling on Mrs. Angelloni.

The shower was hot and comforting. I let the hot, steamy water run over my body for a long time. The tension in my muscles dissipated. There's nothing like a hot shower, I thought as I indulged. I had to look extrameticulous today; my hair was a bit long but looked stylish and windblown. I combed it back, leaving my earlobes exposed. I didn't shave. I had the new rough look. I would wear a black turtleneck shirt, trousers, and a gray short jacket. The final touch was a dab of Obsession.

I waited for Mr. Angelloni to call, as I had told him to do, but his call never came. I got in my Jeep and took off.

~

I arrived at the Angelloni's promptly at eleven. A young maid opened the door and told me the lady was waiting for me in the solarium. She guided me to the room.

Mrs. Angelloni looked beautiful except for her red eyes—she'd apparently been crying. I tried to be cheerful. "Good day, beautiful lady!"

"Hi, handsome," she said in a jovial voice.

"What do you have scheduled for us today?" I asked, feeling like a child about to get candy.

"I want you to meet some of my friends," she said. She was making an effort to sound joyful. She ordered the maid to bring me a cup of coffee and asked if I wanted strawberry crepes. I nodded.

"What was the deal with you and that slut?" she suddenly asked.

"Let's see, I went to look for your husband to discuss my aunt's estate, and after our encounter, he was in a hurry to leave. I offered Miss Harris lunch and a ride home."

"She had been crying, right?"

"I don't know."

"I had asked Marco to fire her," she said sternly.

"Why? I thought she was an efficient secretary."

"Too efficient."

"Wherever I see Mr. Angelloni, she is with him," I said in an inno-cent-sounding voice.

"If he doesn't fire her, I'll divorce him," she said harshly.

I didn't say a thing. I stood in silence wondering what the best approach would be. She seemed resolute in her decision. I just low-ered my head and finished my crepe.

"I imagine you would like to be alone," I said softly.

She shook her head. "No, I would appreciate if you stay and finish our meeting."

I nodded. " And meet your lady friends some other time?"

"Sam, why are you here?" she said. "What did the son of a bitch do to you?"

I was embarrassed. I felt like she was taking my clothes off, one by one. I tugged at my collar and cleared my throat. The words didn't want to come out my mouth.

"Sam, I need to know. I can help you!" she implored. I felt like it was my time to be caught with my pants down; she was insightful.

"As you know, my aunt got murdered over two months ago." I couldn't look at her eyes. "And I don't know anything about it. I don't even have a death certificate to specify her cause of death."

"I'm sorry, dear."

"I know that your husband was her attorney, but he refuses to cooperate with me."

"He is such an arrogant bastard, and I'm about to pull the rug from under him."

"What if he doesn't fire Miss Harris?"

"He will do what he has to do, and I will do what I have to do—it's that simple."

I apologized to her for wanting to use her, for wanting to extort her husband.

"That's the kind of games he likes to play," she said emphatically.

She offered another cup of coffee, and I eagerly accepted.

She explained that she had married Angelloni eleven years ago when he arrived in Mapletown from New York City, driving his economy sedan. "Now the son of a bitch drives a Mercedes, top of the line."

"I thought you and he have a son."

"No, he is from his first marriage."

"Did you know my aunt?"

She shook her head and said, "I heard about her, but I never got involved with my husband's clients. You know…conflict of interest."

"I don't know much about her," I said. "I stopped visiting her when I was a teenager."

"I also heard that she was a shrewd businesswoman," Mrs. Angelloni said.

The maid appeared with hot coffee and freshly made pastries. As soon as she left, I decided to ask about her husband being connected.

She laughed. "Connected to what? The mob?" She stopped laughing and said, "He is connected to me. The poor devil didn't have anything when he arrived."

Her eyes sparkled with rancor and disdain. I could only guess the pain and frustration she was experiencing because of her husband's infidelity.

I was relieved that I didn't have to carry on with my threat to Angelloni. Come to think of it, I couldn't have done such a thing to this stoic woman. I glanced at my watch and said, "Three o'clock!"

"Time really flies," she said as she got up. She looked tired and worn out, but elegant. I tried to guess her age, maybe fortysomething. She had a svelte figure, and her face had fine soft features. Any man would be happy with her.

She apologized for keeping me, then moved close to me and gave me a gentle kiss on my lips.

~

It was four days until New Year's Eve, and people in town were getting ready for the grand bash, making last-minute resolutions for the New Year.

When had I stopped making resolutions myself? I couldn't remember. But I was ready to make the most important resolution in my life, and this time, I was sticking to it.

I stopped at the liquor store to buy an expensive bottle of champagne to celebrate by myself. I was absorbed in making my selection when I heard a familiar voice.

"Hello, Mr. Stone." I turned around. Miss Harris was standing beside me. She seemed to be a different person than she was yesterday. Her eye makeup was in place, not running. She looked happy.

"Oh, hello, Miss Harris," I said, surprised to see her there.

"Cut the crap! You can call me by my first name."

"I don't think Mr. Angelloni would like that."

She thought it over and nodded. "Yeah, he is possessive…but it's worth it." She showed me her left hand and pointed to a huge diamond ring. She wasn't fired, I guessed.

"How did it go at the office for you?"

"Well, Marco asked me to leave the office for a while."

"Did he fire you?"

"Hell no!" she said quickly. "It's just while he deals with his stupid wife."

"And what are you doing here?"

"Picking up champagne for Marco and me, to celebrate New Year's."

"By the way nice ring—engagement?"

She grinned and rubbed her ring against her coat. "My Christmas present."

I paid for my bottle and said good-bye to Miss Harris.

"What are you doing for New Year's Eve?" she asked.

"Nothing in particular."

"Why don't we celebrate together?"

"I thought that you and Marco—"

"He is going to a party with his soon-to-be ex-wife to keep up appearances."

Mr. Angelloni was a clever asshole. He would try to keep both women on a string as long as he could. I really wasn't interested in continuing the game anymore.

"What did Mrs. Angelloni have to say?" she asked in a perverse way.

"If you promise not to smoke and puke, I might consider telling you."

She gave me her cell number. I wouldn't give her mine but said I would call her.

39

Maybe it wasn't such a crazy idea to get together with Miss Harris for the New Year's Eve celebration. I was curious about what Angelloni was planning, and she could provide me with the information, so what the heck!

I hurried back to my place to see if I could locate the map. It was strange to find the front door ajar. I gasped when I walked inside. The place been ransacked.

Drawers emptied, and their contents lay on the floor. Broken glass, silverware, and books strewn all over the place. What could possibly have happened here? It looked like a tornado had hit the house. I went upstairs to check the extent of the damage.

It was the same. My clothes thrown on the floor; the mattress had been cut open. Personal accessories were broken. I checked Jacob's quarters; they were in the same condition, except that my aunt's documents were missing. Angelloni!

I got in my car and drove to his office. I was livid. I forgot about the fucking speed limit in this damn town. It was too late; a cop tailed me with his lights on, and I had to stop.

He asked for the required documents driver's license and insurance. I reached to get the insurance form out of the glove box, and the map fell out. I had forgotten that the map had been there all this time. I couldn't help but smile.

After the policeman issued my citation, I drove the couple of blocks to Angelloni's building.

I went straight to his office. He was on the telephone, so I yanked it from his ear and hung it up. He didn't seem surprised to see me.

"Did you have a nice time with my wife?" he asked nonchalantly.

"To think I almost felt sorry for you!" I said with a sneer.

I reached over his desk and punched him squarely on the lips. The surprise knocked him off his ergonomic chair; the impact of his teeth sent a sharp pain to my fingers and wrist. Miss Harris ran into the room and stopped me from kicking the shit out of him.

"*Call the cops!*" he yelled at Miss Harris.

"Yes, call them," I said. "He broke into my place and stole important documents."

"You can't prove that," he snapped back.

I waved a monitoring device in front of his face. "I got you on video, asshole."

Miss Harris was applying a cold, wet towel to his lips to stop the swelling.

I dialed the police. "I want to report a robbery," I said with no emotion.

I walked toward the exit and heard him yelling, "*You'll pay for this!*"

"I got the map in a safe place," I said back to him and left.

~

The cops arrived at my house at the same time I did. They took pictures of the disheveled place and asked if I was missing anything. Then they asked me to come down to the station to fill out a report.

The police station was quiet when I arrived. They put me in a report room to wait for a detective to talk to me.

Sergeant Miller appeared at the door. "Well, well, Mr. Stone." He wasn't friendly at all. I felt intimidated. "I understand that someone broke into your residence, is that correct?"

"Yes, and I have a video of the thieves." I showed him the video.

"Anybody I might know?"

"Your friend, Angelloni," I said.

He leaned over and paid attention. For once, he looked serious and interested in what I had to say.

Then he said, "Mr. Stone, we have been following a ring of thieves, and we believe that your aunt and Angelloni were involved."

"But I thought—"

"That I was involved?" He interrupted me, saying exactly what I'd had in mind.

I nodded and said, "The night that I was arrested, remember? I was forced to sign some documents, and you didn't do a thing to stop the abuse. Why?"

"I wanted to make Angelloni feel at ease and see if I could get closer."

I didn't know whether to believe him. "Do you know who killed my aunt?"

"No, we think that Victor Parker has that information, but he has disappeared."

I looked at him attentively, not knowing what to say. I tried to hide from his gaze; he was a detective and could probably guess by my body language that I was nervous.

"Has he tried to contact you?" Miller asked audaciously.

I shook my head and dared to ask, "Why would he contact me?"

"They were also involved in counterfeiting, and Victor was your aunt's right-hand man." He stopped for a moment and stared at me. He was reading me.

I panicked and became defensive, saying, "I don't care about any of that—I need to have the stolen documents back."

He became silent and looked at a pad of paper he was holding, then started to write. The silence was heavy and uncomfortable. I remembered someone saying to me once, "Whoever speaks first, loses." I got up and started for the door.

Sergeant Miller stopped what he was doing and asked, "Are you leaving?"

I nodded and kept walking.

"Wait a moment, please!"

I turned around and told him, "This better be good."

"Sit down and listen." He gave the order as if I were a soldier.

I wanted to hear what he had to say, so I said, "If I feel you're jerking me around, I'll leave."

He sat across from where I was sitting and looked me square in the eyes. He shot out a question unexpectedly: "Who was the woman you saw in San Francisco?"

"How do you know I went to San Francisco?"

"The feds have started to keep an eye on you in case you are approached by your aunt's associates."

"How come you don't follow Angelloni instead?"

Another detective who came into the room interrupted us. He whispered something to Miller. They both excused themselves and left the room. Through the blinds on the glass window, I could see them talking outside the door. Sergeant Miller returned to the room. "Who was the woman you saw in San Francisco?"

They had followed me to San Francisco. He was serious about staking me. "What woman? My ex-wife?" They had better not bring Sophia into this.

"Ugly woman, your ex-wife, eh?" He pulled a photo from a folder he got from the other detective. It was Victor!

Shit, now what? If I said she was not my ex-wife, then who? I was not going to tell them about Victor until I knew for sure that they weren't involved with Angelloni. "After several beers, all women are pretty." That was all I could think to say.

Sergeant Miller snickered. "We also got the name of the PI you saw. May I ask why?"

"Sure. Since I don't see the police doing their job, I thought a PI would come in handy."

"Had you found any documents at your place that could be important to this investigation?" Miller asked.

I thought awhile, then shook my head no.

"What are the documents that were stolen from your house?"

"My aunt's last and will and testament."

"And you think Angelloni did it? Was he supposed to have them?"

"See for yourself." I waved the video at him.

He took it from my hand and asked me to follow him to another room with video equipment. He inserted the video and pushed the play button. Immediately, three guys came on the screen, with a fourth guy in charge. My blood was boiling, again, as I watched the demolition. One of the three guys gave a handful of papers to the fourth man. He examined them and said, "The map is not here." They continued searching. The fourth man checked his watch and called off the search, and they left.

"How do you know that's Angelloni?" Miller asked.

"C'mon! You can tell it was him!"

"Would you leave the video to have our experts clean it?"

"Make a copy," I said. I just couldn't bring myself to trust him yet; I still wasn't sure that he wasn't on Angelloni's payroll. He seemed to be picking my brain to see what I knew; maybe he wanted the map, too.

"What map were they talking about?" he asked.

"I don't know," I flat-out lied, and without more ado looked away so he wouldn't know I'd lied. He called a video tech and told him to make a copy. We went back to the report room we were in before. Miller offered coffee; I declined.

"What are you going to do about it?" I asked him.

"The feds are handling the case."

"Why then am I wasting my time talking to you?" I said, hot headed.

"We are cooperating with them."

"I need to talk to the person in charge then."

He stepped out of the room. When he returned, the video tech was with him. He handed me the tape.

"I need to see what's in it," I said.

"Trusting soul, aren't you?"

"How do I know whether you switched my copy and I got a tape of *The Three Stooges* instead? These days, I do not trust anyone."

We went back to the room with the video equipment.

40

As I left the miserable town's police department, I felt miserable too.

My aunt wasn't the sweet woman I remembered; the idea that she had been a hard-core criminal sent a chill all through me. My gut feeling made me turn around and check whether a shadow was following me. I couldn't detect anyone; several people were on the street at that time. I got in my Jeep and took off. I drove around but saw no tail.

It was seven when my phone started to ring. *Could they intercept my calls?* I didn't answer. The call went to my voice mail; I would get a message in about...one...two...now. My cell beeped to let me know I had a new message in my voice mail. Remarkable technology, I thought.

The message was so garbled I couldn't understand any of it. I checked to see if I could recognize the phone number. "Private number" was displayed.

A cold rain was falling intermittently. The headlights of the vehicle behind mine glared brightly on my mirror, blinding me momentarily, as the driver switched from low beams to high beams. The vehicle stopped at the curbside, then instantly took off again, and the same thing with the lights was repeated.

Morse code, I thought. It had to be the spooks.

~

The city was empty. The sky was dark and menacing, the rain quite heavy. I could see lightning stretching across the horizon. The thunder was getting closer and louder; a storm had been predicted.

I went home, exasperated to know that I was being watched—my every move. The storm was already hitting us. I prepared candles, matches, and flashlights just in case we had a power outage. I also swept the debris that the crooks had left in a pile—did homeowner's insurance cover this? I got big garbage bags to start throwing the broken stuff away. My body ached when I finally decided to take a break.

I looked out the window to see if the cops were staking the house. A black van was parked outside. At least I would be able to sleep, knowing that I was protected by the feds.

Finally, at eleven, I decided to go to bed.

As I lay awake looking at the ceiling, the map came to mind. Aunt Millie didn't mention the map at all in the letter she had left for me. How did I know she was the one who left that letter? It could have been Victor or Angelloni. I didn't know my aunt's handwriting looked. I needed to find some of her journals with her writing to compare… with what? I had burned the letter she left me! I was sure I would find notebooks, old letters, and diaries. Now Angelloni had everything, but I still had the list of names at the bank. What was in that map that Angelloni wanted? I needed to decipher the map myself. I knew it was the map of the Mapletown cemetery. I needed to have a clear day without rain to go and explore the memorial park.

I thought the fortune been hidden in the basement storage; obviously, I was wrong. The fortune be hidden in the town's graveyard. It had to do with money—I was sure of it.

I couldn't fall asleep. I needed my magic sleeping elixir. I went to the liquor cabinet and poured a scotch. I was beginning to worry about scotch becoming my sleeping aid. I didn't want to get another addiction—I had just kicked the gambling problem. I was prone to addictions, I sudden realized. *What the fuck? I don't have anybody to explain myself to.*

~

I awakened at seven the next morning by the obnoxious ring of my cellular. I grabbed the fucking device and answered.

When no one responded, I was about to disconnect the call. Then I heard, "Hi, Sam, this is Andrew. I'm sorry I didn't identify myself right away."

"That's OK," I said in a sleepy voice.

"I thought that your phone was being monitored," he said.

"Can they monitor a cell phone?" I asked.

"Nowadays, nothing surprises me," he said. "Since nine-eleven, everything is possible, and Big Brother has all the experts."

"Do you know what time it is?"

"Yeah, I just wanted to update you," he answered. "Want me to call you later?"

Hoping that he would catch my drift, I said, "Do you have news on my 'ugly ex-wife' in San Fran?"

"I just wanted you to know that everything is quiet. She stepped out, and I put surveillance in her apartment." I was relieved that he had understood.

"Any news on her bank account?"

"Call me back. I have another call."

I'd better find another way to communicate with him.

~

It was nine when I left the house. I went out the back door, jumped the neighbor's fence and several more fences, until I was about a block away from my house. Nobody was following me.

I went to a Radio Shack on Main Street. I'd once heard that pre-paid cell phones were untraceable. I bought one and paid cash for it.

I immediately called Andrew.

He picked up the call on the first ring. "This is Andrew."

"Hi, Andrew, this is Sam. I just got this prepaid phone to call you."

"Is someone bugging your calls?"

"I don't know."

"I thought so, the way you were asking about your 'ugly ex-wife.'"

"I'm glad you caught it, man," I said. "I'll call you back from my regular phone so they don't suspect, OK?"

Then he told me how Victor had received a large amount of money at the beginning of December. "Did your aunt leave him anything in her will?" he asked.

"Yes. If I remember correctly fifty big ones."

"I'm still checking to see if I can find where this money came from."

"OK. Hey, Andrew, I'll refer to him as my ex-wife whenever we talk about him."

"Do you know who is following you?"

"Not for sure. Sergeant Miller told me the feds were tagging me."

"Have you checked the newspaper when your aunt was murdered? Sometimes there are clues," he suggested.

I returned home the same way: jumping fences.

~

As soon as I arrived home, I got in my Jeep and drove away. This time I was going to the *Mapletown Gazette* office; maybe I'd be lucky enough to find information back to October. I didn't remember exactly when my aunt had died; I didn't have the death certificate with me. It had to be sometime in October—that's when I got the call.

The archives of the *Gazette* were where I needed to start. I spent a couple of hours before I came to an article in the October 20 edition: "Local Woman Murdered in Her Home." I couldn't read the rest of the report. I was dizzy and nauseated; I felt like I couldn't breathe. I went to the men's room, splashed cold water on my face, and tried to regain composure.

When I returned to the archives room, I asked if I could get a copy. I needed a strong drink to muster the courage to read it and finally know what had happened to my aunt.

I needed to be objective to read this article. I decided to put the copy away for a couple of days; I had to calm my mind and make my best effort to find the clues that would lead me.

I was trembling when I arrived home. I ran to the restroom and emptied my stomach. I needed to talk to someone; I needed to hear that everything was going to be OK. The one who came to mind was Andrew.

41

I let Andrew's phone ring several times; he didn't answer. I checked to see if I had dialed the right number—yes, it was his number I had called. Something was wrong. Usually, his voice mail would record the call, but not this time. I had to wait and see if he would return the call. It was one o'clock; I would wait until two to try again.

I was so jumpy that my phone startled me when it rang. *Shit, I forgot to use my new cell.*

"Hello?" I said.

"Sam?" It was Andrew.

I didn't want to talk to him on my regular phone. "Listen, I cannot hear you. Let me call you back."

I switched phones and made the call.

"Andrew?" There was silence at the other end.

"Sam?" he asked. Andrew wanted to make sure he got the right person on the right phone this time.

"Yes, this is Sam," I answered.

"What's going on?" he asked, sounding alarmed.

"I just wanted to talk to someone." I sounded like such a sissy.

"OK. What can I do for you?"

I told to him about the article in the *Gazette.*

"Sam, if you want, I can check it for you," he said.

"Are you coming here to do that?"

"I have a computer, you know."

I felt like such an incompetent idiot.

"You could also fax me the info."

Yes, go ahead and kick me when I'm down, I thought.

"What is the name of the paper again?"

"The *Mapletown Gazette,*" I said. "October nineteen is the date of the crime."

He said he would call me as soon as he had the chance. He would try to get to the article by tomorrow.

I thanked him, and we disconnected.

~

I felt blue the rest of the day. I needed to entertain myself to keep the terror of the night of my aunt's assassination out of my mind. Did she know she was going to die? Did she beg for her life? How terrified she must have felt knowing that the killers were the last people she would look at: unfriendly faces, cold, full of hatred. Worst of all, she knew her assailants—the people she was associated with were her killers.

What did she do to deserve such fate? I had to stop; I was making myself sick. Her story had even made it to the *Gazette*'s front page; it was on page 1. My mind wouldn't stop; it kept going and going, torturing me relentlessly.

I tried to recall what I had done that day. My mind was blank; I couldn't remember. Probably I was hiding from the loan sharks in Frisco the day she was murdered. I was fighting my own battles with my gambling addiction. *Sam, you have to stop this mental masturbation,* I told myself.

I couldn't take it anymore. I drove to a local hangout on the outskirts of town. I needed to be around people. The bar was close to the cemetery, and as I drove by, I made a mental note to pay a visit to my aunt's gravesite, maybe tomorrow. I would bring the map and examine it at the location indicated; I needed to do so inconspicuously. I looked back in the mirror, and, yes, I was followed. I would be courteous and offer them a drink.

Fog started to blanket the road ahead of me. Everything looked ethereal: the gnawed tree branches and the winding road. *Steven King would love to be here tonight and write a horror thriller.* I played with the idea.

By sheer will, I forced myself to think of more pleasant memories. I thought of happy times with my aunt: at a Fourth of July parade down Main Street, when she took me to the movies for an afternoon flick, going to the ice cream parlor for our favorite sundaes—she liked chocolate fudge and I liked strawberries, nuts, and whipped cream. I started to feel better.

I sat in my Jeep awhile, listening to music. When my followers stopped their car's engine, I approached them and offered to buy them a drink.

"Thanks, but we don't drink when we are on duty," one of them said.

"Thanks anyway," said the other.

"By the way, who is watching my house when you guys are here?" I was curious.

They looked at each other and shrugged. "Our orders are to watch you."

"Don't you get bored?" I asked. "To entertain yourselves, do you play with each other?"

They both shot me dirty looks.

~

The Living Dead Bar was vibrant with wall-to-wall people. The music was loud; it drowned out the animated conversation of the patrons. I sat at the bar and ordered a beer. I was hungry and asked the bartender if they served snacks. He motioned with his head to a tray of cold meats, cheese, and bread at a table. "Happy hour is about to finish, but maybe there's some leftover food."

I grabbed a plate with the usual: Buffalo wings, Swedish meatballs, and veggies. That would be enough for now.

The music and the noise of the place stopped my nagging thoughts about my aunt's last, tragic night.

The bartender made small talk. "Are you coming for the New Year's Eve celebration?" he asked.

"Is there a charge?" I asked back.

"Fifty per person. We are serving steak, champagne, and party favorites. Bring your significant other for a good time."

"I don't have a significant, or for that matter, insignificant other," I said joking.

"Come anyways. You'll meet someone here."

I looked at him, amused at the idea of meeting someone in a place like this. I looked around to see what kind of women gathered at a place like this.

"I met my wife here," the bartender said.

All I could think of was meeting a bum or a radical chick. It would be an amusing way to start the New Year. Besides, I didn't have anything better to do. Then I remembered. Shit! Jacob said he was coming back on the thirty-first. I didn't want to see the son of a bitch. Would Eva be coming back with him? I guessed I would soon find out.

I was engrossed thinking about the imaginary women in that bar when a woman sat down next to me, startling me.

"Would you like to buy me a drink?" the suggestive voice asked.

I turned around to reply; to my surprise, it was Miss Harris. She was wearing a black, low-cut blouse and jeans, making her look provocative and cheap.

"Hi. Is Angelloni with you?" I tried to sound friendly.

"No, the wimp is with wifey," she said bitterly.

"I'm sorry." Not really.

She ordered a martini. The bartender couldn't take his eyes from her cleavage. She looked pleased that he'd noticed her. She put a cigarette in her mouth with a wanton hint. "Are we going to celebrate New Year's together?" she asked.

The bartender winked at me and nodded approvingly.

"I don't think so," I said. "I want to make it to next year."

This time, the bartender looked at me as if I had lost my marbles and shook his head disapprovingly.

"Are you afraid of Angelloni?" Miss Harris said.

I didn't say a word. She continued, "He doesn't do anything if the missus doesn't tell him."

Was Miss Harris suggesting that Mr. Angelloni took orders from Mrs. Angelloni? What man didn't take orders from his wife? We had to be told how to dress, how to talk, even how to eat. Even Mr. Angelloni The super attorney followed orders. He wasn't the big shot he pretended to be Maybe it wasn't such a bad idea to celebrate with her after all. I had considered the idea before, but I wasn't interested in her company. I had a couple of days to make up my mind.

The bartender bamboozled looking at the two of us.

"I was expecting an invitation from Mrs. Angelloni," I said.

Miss Harris laughed until she had tears. "Watch out—she may ask for your head on a silver platter."

All of a sudden, it started to make sense to me: the day of the break-in, I was with Mrs. Angelloni—had she kept me there so her husband had time to look for the map?

"Does Mrs. Angelloni work for her husband?" I asked Miss Harris.

"No. It's the other way around," she said.

I remembered how, during my visit with Mrs. Angelloni, she had mentioned that she was the one with the power; her husband came empty-handed.

My suspicions were rising faster than flour with yeast. "Did Mrs. Angelloni know my aunt?" I asked her.

"Ha! Did she know her? Your aunt would jump every time Madam Angelloni called her."

I was speechless…dumbfounded!

42

It was ten when I left the Living Dead Bar, after I'd made plans to spend New Year's Eve with Miss Harris. She could provide valuable information about my aunt and the Angellonis. I felt optimistic. The troublesome thoughts had dissipated for now.

The fog was denser. I looked back, and the car with the cops was still behind me. The car's headlights looked like a couple of matchsticks dimly burning in the distance. I was tired, but I was glad I had gone out tonight.

I went straight to bed when I got home.

Miss Harris had stayed at the bar, flirting with the bartender.

~

When I woke up, I was drenched in sweat, but I couldn't remember any nightmares or night terrors. I looked out the window; the day was wet and dreary. The surveillance car was parked by the curb across the street.

I did my customary morning ritual: two cups of black coffee. I sipped unhurriedly; it was only nine in the morning.

I jumped into the shower and stood under the water, letting the hot water run down my body. The steam reminded me of the fog from the night before.

I decided to give a casual call to Mrs. Angelloni to wish her a prosperous and happy new year. The old-maid answered. I waited for Mrs. Angelloni to come to the telephone.

"Sam! Darling! what a pleasant surprise." She sounded fresh and amiable. "How are you?"

I wondered if I should say something nasty like, "Your fucking husband ransacked my place, you fucking bitch!" Instead, I was as polite as could be. "Fine, thank you. I just called to wish—"

She cut me off. "We are having a small get-together—are you coming?"

"When?" I asked.

The thirty-first at eight." Shit! I had made plans with Miss Harris. But I was curious to see who would be at the Angellonis.

"Yes, I'm delighted. Is it casual?"

"No, black tie," she said.

~

I realized I had to buy the proper attire. The men's store was packed. At last, I made my selection of a tuxedo. The store clerk said it needed a little alteration but there wasn't enough time to do it. He suggested I rent one instead.

I had to cancel with Miss Harris…unless I brought her with me. Why not? I contemplated the scene in vivid colors: I would walk into their house, Miss Harris hanging from my arm, looking cheap and sluttish. I chuckled when I imagined their astonished faces: Mr. Angelloni green with jealousy; Mrs. Angelloni offended in front of her friends to have her husband's mistress at her house.

Would Miss Harris play along? I needed to let her know.

I phoned Angelloni's office looking for her. "Law office. May I help you?" she answered.

"Miss Harris? This is Sam." I felt uncomfortable. "New Year's plans have changed."

"How so?" She sounded disappointed and let down.

I told her about Mrs. Angelloni's invitation. And that I was asked to bring a guest. *Liar*, I thought with disgust. Would she like to come with me?

I waited for her to answer. It seemed like an eternity, but finally she said, "Are you crazy?"

"C'mon! We'll have fun," I said enthusiastically.

"You really don't know the inner workings of criminal minds!" She sounded terrified.

At first I didn't answer. I couldn't say much; I couldn't force the words out of my mouth. Finally, I mustered the courage and said, "I'll pick you up at seven thirty." I tried to keep cool and act indifferent to her words, but my stomach was in knots. She sure was afraid of "Dragon Lady" and her drone. "By the way, it's a black-tie dinner."

Thoughts and questions came as avalanches, and I couldn't keep up with them. Like cotton candy, my mind being spun. I needed to suppress my apprehension and tension. I held my breath and continued to arrange for the "show."

~

I couldn't stop thinking about Miss Harris's reaction to my inviting her to the Angellonis'. What did she know that made her horrified? What did she mean by "criminal minds"? I hoped she'd come with me, even though I was embarrassed for using her. I felt sorry about that, but I needed to get to the bottom and explore every possibility to find my aunt's killers. I wasn't turning back.

I stopped at Maggie's Diner for a cup of coffee. The air was frigid, and I wanted to warm up. The smell of freshly baked apple pie was inviting, and I invited myself to a piece. I was so busy enjoying my pie that I didn't notice someone standing in front of me. I looked up.

"Happy New Year, Sam," Sergeant Miller said.

"Thanks." I couldn't bring myself to return the same greeting. I continued eating the still-warm piece of pie and drinking my cup of Juan Valdez coffee.

"I heard you are going to the Angellonis' party."

I nodded. Then I asked, "How's the investigation going?"

"We are moving ahead," he said, not convincingly.

"It's already a cold case, isn't it?"

He motioned to a table and said, "Got to go—my wife is waiting for me over there."

I was thankful for Mrs. Miller. I waved at her. She waved back.

~

After finishing my pie, I sat for a moment and looked out the window. People bundled up, walking swiftly against the icy wind. I thought of the many holidays I came to spend with my aunt. She would bundle me up, and we would stroll into town. We would stop at the diner for hot cocoa and pie. We would laugh and kid each other with a warm camaraderie.

I'd never had a relationship like that with anybody. I was afraid people would know that I was a bastard product of an rape. I never told Sophia my dark secret, either. I lied and told her my parents had divorced when I was too little to understand. With Aunt Millie I didn't have to put on a performance; she accepted me as I was. Yeah, I owed her to find the killers.

I remembered the mental note I'd made night before, to visit her gravesite. It had to wait for a better day with no rain. For now, the sky was black, with fat, heavy clouds hanging low and menacing, ready to let loose at any time.

I waited awhile at the diner before I left. By now, it was raining torrentially, and my umbrella was in my Jeep. *Great. Asshole!*

I was sitting drenched in the Jeep trying to shake the rain from my face when my new phone started to ring. "Hello," I answered, knowing it was Andrew; nobody else had my new number.

"Hi, Sam. Two things," he said. The thunder was so loud I couldn't hear what he was saying.

"Andrew, let me call you back in about twenty minutes."

"Is everything OK?" I managed to hear him say.

"So far. It's raining, and I can't hear you; I'll call you when I get home."

The short commute to my house was ever so slow. It was raining so hard that the streets were flooding quickly. The wipers on my Jeep were at high, and I still had trouble seeing. I turned my blinkers on for precaution. I wondered what kind of weather we would have tomorrow for our celebration. I couldn't see whether the detectives were still following me.

At last I walked into my house. I changed into dry clothes and fixed a cup of green tea. I took it upstairs and settled in to call Andrew.

"This is Andrew," he identified himself.

"Finally, I'm home. What a storm, man."

"Yeah, like I was telling you, I have two things to talk to you about," he said. "First, I had the chance to read the article on your aunt in the *Gazette.*"

I held my breath and became detached. I pretended that Andrew was talking to someone else.

Andrew went on, conveying what he got out of the article. She had been bludgeoned to death with a heavy, blunt object. There were no eyewitnesses; no one came forward with information. It was a bloody slaughter. No sign of robbery, and no sign of forced entry.

"According to the ME, your aunt died at nine." He paused for a moment.

I was horrified, and after the shock, the guilt hit hard. Guilt, that I had never made any effort to stay in touch with her after I got married. Guilt that she had died without knowing what she meant to me, that I had never thanked her.

"I'll go over it once more to get the missing pieces of the puzzle," Andrew said.

I excused myself and told him I'd call him back.

I needed time to weep and time to feel sorry for Aunt Millie, to feel sorry for me. I realized I had been ill equipped to handle the details of her death.

By sheer will, I forced myself to call Andrew again to hear about item number two.

"Sorry about that," I told him.

"I understand."

"What's number two?" I asked almost in a whisper.

"Your 'ex-wife' is coming to town," he said.

I didn't understand who he was talking about. Was Sophia on her way back?

"What's going on in Mapletown?" he asked.

Shit! He was talking about Victor. "Nothing that I know of."

"Is 'she' coming to visit you?" he asked with concern.

"No."

"I heard that 'she' got an invite for a New Year's party."

"When?" I managed to ask.

"Tomorrow."

"Who invited her?"

"A woman named Elsa. Do you know her?"

"No."

"That's strange. She said you would be there."

"Yes."

"I could come too. After all, you're paying for the service."

We agreed for him to come to Mapletown. He would stay at the Mayflower. I was to contact him only by phone.

~

I tried and tried some more to remember Miss Harris's first name. Was she the one who had contacted Victor? Was her name Elsa? *Shit! Shit! Shit!*

I was drained. I cursed myself for the soft tissue I had for memory, and for derailing my life. Maybe something good would come out of my aunt's death. Maybe I would become less self-centered, thinking that everything was about me.

At some time after three, the ringing of a telephone jolted me from a guilty and somber contemplation. I answered the goddamned thing.

"Sam…it's Jacob," he said hesitantly.

I didn't need him right now—or ever, for that matter. "Hello… hello?" I pretended I had a bad connection.

"Sam…can you hear me?"

I cussed a little more about the "dropped call" and then disconnected.

The phone rang again; this time I didn't answer. He left a message saying he would be back home tomorrow morning. I didn't care. I would deal with him tomorrow.

The phone rang one more time. This time it was the new phone. It was Andrew.

"Yes, Andrew, did we forget anything?" I asked.

"Just being curious," he said. "Your 'ex-wife' and this Elsa are talking about a map."

"Thanks, Andrew," I simply said.

"What about the map, Sam? They said that you have it."

"I don't know...Are they talking about Mapletown's map?"

"I was hoping you could tell me."

"What phone is this Elsa calling from—can you tell?"

"It's a blocked number."

"OK, thanks."

"Sam, do you have a gun?" he asked, "You see, with the feds tailing you and these people talking about you...well, seems like it's something big."

"I just want to get to the killers!" I said.

"Be careful."

The famous map—all of a sudden, everybody wanted the map. What did Victor have to do with all this mess? He'd never worked for my aunt; he really worked for Angelloni. He and Elsa knew about the map; Maybe Andrew was right that I needed to consider getting a gun.

I gave conscientious thought to attending the "Dragon Lady's" New Year's bash. I just couldn't expose Miss Harris—what was her fucking first name? I had twenty-four hours to decide.

Meanwhile, I had time to consider Jacob Sinclair's return.

43

I thought I'd seen a Bible on one of the bookshelves in the house. I decided to put the map between its pages when I went to visit Aunt Millie's grave. Nobody should see that map in my possession.

I dressed in layers to keep warm and then drove to the cemetery. The day was cloudy and dark. The weatherman had forecast precipitation. This time I carried my umbrella with me; it could also serve as cover from curious eyes.

I located Millie's headstone in the family plot—what family? It had fresh flowers; someone had deposited the bouquet recently. I looked around but didn't see anybody. I shivered when I read, "Mildred Emily C. Wilmot 1945–2005 Beloved Daughter, Sister and Aunt." Instinctively I touched the stone; it was cold and wet. I shuddered violently. I offered a prayer and asked to be forgiven. Then I opened the Bible to the page where I had placed the map.

I couldn't make much of the map. I wasn't even sure that it was of the cemetery, as I had thought before. I stared at it, trying to figure out the coordinates.

In the family plot next to Aunt Millie's grave was another headstone inscribed "Augustus C. Wilmot 1943–1999 Beloved Son, Brother and Uncle." I didn't remember an uncle at all. I always assumed that the Wilmot children consisted of only my mother and Aunt Millie.

I scanned the map again and looked at the area. I was getting frustrated; the car with the feds parked a few feet away. I checked my watch; it was still early. I had time to go the cemetery's office to get a map from there to compare with the coveted map in my possession.

~

A plump woman was sitting behind a desk doing computer work. She lifted her head up when she heard me entering her office.

"Can I help you?" she asked in a calm voice.

"Yes, please, do you have a map of the cemetery?"

She got up, walked to a back office, came back with a map in her hand, and gave it to me. I took it eagerly.

"Thank you," I whispered.

She went back to her desk and continued her work.

I asked if I could use the restroom; she nodded. I needed to put the maps side by side and compare the coordinates of the area.

It was the same map. I was astonished. My aunt's map had an X where the headstone of Augustus C. Wilmot stood. What did it mean? I put the two maps aside and took off.

~

Back at home, I frantically started to look for evidence of Augustus's existence. I pulled out the family album and turned the pages, looking for him. I found nothing.

I felt a ghost-like presence in the room; it was only my mind racing. Did Victor know about Augustus? Since he was coming to town, I could ask him then.

My mind went ahead to the party tonight. If I didn't go to the Angellonis' party, I would regret it the rest of my life. But if I went, how long would my life be? I was panic-stricken. I felt like I was going to walk inside the lions' cage on my own. *Not a very bright idea, dude.*

I decided to go to the basement to look in the boxes neatly piled at the bottom of the stairs. Maybe I could find something about Augustus there. At the top of the stairs, the strong smell of astringent hurt my nostrils, and I started to choke. I was paralyzed, looking down into the darkness of the cellar.

Willpower urged me to take a deep breath and conquer my terror. I slowly descended the wobbly, steep stairs. I could see Toothless Max looking at me with loathing. *Don't think about Max, don't think about Max.* The more I repeated that mantra, the more I thought about Max.

I needed to do something about the astringent smell; with Jacob coming back, I didn't want him to ask questions. I cracked open the only window in the cellar, figuring the cold air would neutralize the smells.

Frantically, I looked in a couple of dozen boxes. I found nothing confirming Augustus's existence.

I glanced at my watch and thought to pay a visit to the City Hall records department. They would have a copy of his birth certificate. I deemed it necessary to check out the probabilities. Where these people born here or in New York? I will soon find out, I hope.

I had to make it fast; it took me fifteen minutes to arrive at City Hall. I went directly to the records department. A clerk said they would be closing in twenty minutes.

I asked how to get a copy of a birth certificate. Coldly, she said she could help. She asked if the copy was mine or someone else's.

I gave her the information I was looking for.

"Eleven dollars and an ID," she said.

I apologized for coming at the last minute; she seemed to ease off a bit.

"Your dad?" she asked.

"No. My uncle." I nodded.

She typed the information into her database and waited. Then she reentered the information. A message on her computer screen displayed "No Matches Found."

"Sorry, there's no matches," she said, shaking her head.

I thought for a little while and asked, "What about a death certificate? Would it be much trouble for you to look up?"

"Same name?" she asked.

I nodded.

The computer screen again displayed "No Matches Found."

"Sorry," she said.

"One last name, please?" I begged.

She nodded and I gave her Aunt Millie's information.

"You want a copy?" she asked.

I nodded and thanked her again gave her the fees the copies will arrive via USPS and wished her a prosperous new year.

~

I got in my Jeep and drove away, followed by the surveillance team. I just couldn't think any more of what-ifs about the map, or about Aunt Millie and Augustus. I felt I was teetering on the edge of a cliff; one false move and I would end up at the bottom.

I needed to think outside the box. I needed to see the big picture from another perspective. I needed to find the missing pieces for this damned puzzle. I needed to stop thinking about it and let my mind come up with the answer.

I would have the chance to do that tonight at the Angellonis'. I would get shit-faced and act irresponsible. I would dance, eat, and flirt with Mrs. Angelloni.

If Elsa didn't want to go, I would go by myself. *Elsa? Elsa?* At last, I remembered Miss Harris's name! Elsa. Elsa. Elsa. Elsa. Who was the Elsa Andrew had talked about, then? Oh well, I would not worry about that.

~

The clock chimed four when I walked into my place. The house was dim. I didn't notice a pair of eyes staring at me, but I could sense someone's presence. I adjusted my eyes to the dimness of the sitting room, and I could make out the silhouette of a person sitting on the sofa. *Jacob!*

I turned on the light switch and was surprised to see Victor in his drag costume.

"How did you get in?" I asked, bothered by it.

"I kept a set of keys," he said without emotion.

He was motionless. His deep-set eyes were unperturbed watching me. He looked sinister and menacing. I struggled to maintain my cool under his fierce gaze.

My phone jolted me when it started to ring. It was my new phone.

"Sam, I need to see you before you go anywhere tonight." Andrew sounded out of breath.

"I have company right now," I said.

"I know. Victor is there with you."

"Yeah," I muttered.

"Get rid of him and meet me at Maggie's."

"OK. I know the place. I'll see you in thirty minutes."

Turning my attention to Victor, I asked, "What are you doing here?" I tried to sound convivial. I wondered if the watch boys noticed him going into the house. How could they have missed seeing him? They were shadowing me.

Victor didn't answer; he just kept on staring.

"I thought you said you were not coming back to Mapletown," I prodded.

"I think Mildred left something for me." He sounded grave.

"Yeah, she left some property and cash. You have to see her attorney," I said.

I watched him closely. The man looked dead. I couldn't read him at all; he must have been a poker player. I was determined to shake him a little.

"Who sent you? Elsa?"

He shifted in his seat and blinked several times. "I don't want any trouble," he said.

"Am I giving you trouble?" I asked, raising my voice.

"I want the map," he said without beating around the bush.

"Oh yeah? Well, Victor, I want to know who killed my aunt," I said sardonically.

His eyes glared with evil.

"And you refused to tell me."

"Just give me the map, and I'll get out of here!" he threatened.

"What is with this fucking map that everybody wants?" I said. "What makes you think I have it?" I didn't say another word. I waited to see what his response would be. I had the advantage; I had the map, I thought.

He still didn't respond.

"Victor, let's make a deal: you give me the killers, and I give you the map. What do you think?"

I told him that I knew he knew who the killers were. I told him that I believed in my gut that he had sold Millie up the river, that he was never the loyal employee she had bragged about, but was corrupted and evil.

"Besides, the map is not here. It is safe, and without me, nobody can get it." My body covered with cold sweat and I was trembling—did he notice? "Please go and tell Elsa to fuck herself." I glanced at my watch and said, "I have to leave."

The man didn't move.

"Get out of my house! You know the way."

He got up and wobbled toward the door as if his knees were made of rubber.

I ran to peek out the front window. A black car picked him up and drove away.

I was still shaking and perspiring profusely.

44

I was running out of time. Andrew had to make it short and to the point. I just couldn't imagine what his urgency was about. Besides, I was upset with him—he should have warned me about Victor's visit. I would listen to what he had to say for himself.

He was already waiting for me at the diner. "I'm glad you could make it," he said as I sat down.

"It's five fifteen. I only have till six," I said sternly.

"I tried to call you to tell you that Victor was on his way to your house," he said, "but your phone was busy."

I accepted his explanation by nodding. "What's the urgency?" I asked with interest.

"I was able to obtain a statement of Victor's bank account." He looked at my eyes fixedly as he was speaking. I paid close attention without interrupting.

"The day after your aunt died, he made a large deposit in his account."

"Do you know where the money came from?"

"Not quite sure. Maybe you recognize the name?"

"How much did he deposit?"

"A hundred grand!"

"That's quite a large amount!"

"Did your aunt leave him anything?"

"Yeah, a piece of property, and fifty thousand dollars."

Andrew pulled out a copy of the statement and handed it to me. I didn't recognize the information.

I told Andrew that Victor had asked for the map. Andrew said he'd heard about the map from the electronic bug he'd placed at Victor's place.

I also told him that I suspected Victor's involvement in my aunt's murder. The deposit to his account proved that he had received that amount for turning her in. "Don't you think?" I said.

Andrew agreed with me. "What about the map?" he asked.

"It is safe," I told him, "but I don't know what it's about."

I confided in him about Augustus and the lack of information at the records department, that there was no evidence of his birth or death, and that there was a gravesite with his name inscribed on the headstone, which was marked with an X on the map.

He thought awhile, and then a big smile showed on his face. "Something is buried there besides a body," he slowly muttered.

We looked at each other in silence. We were unable to make a sound. I speculated on the possibilities. Money? Gold? What could be buried there? I could feel Andrew's wheels spinning in his mind.

Finally, I broke the silence by saying, "I got to go."

"Where are you going to be?" he asked.

"I'm going to my aunt's attorney's New Year's celebration."

"Who? Angelloni's?"

"Yeah. I think they are involved in my aunt's death."

"Who are 'they'?"

"Mr. and Mrs. Angelloni."

"What is Mrs. Angelloni's name?" he asked.

I couldn't remember her name.

"I'll bet it's Elsa," he said, gloating. He gave me a wireless tap. "Wear it in your tux. I'm pretty sure that Victor will be there, and I will be just outside the place."

I'm in deep shit! I thought as I took the electronic device and inspected it. It looked innocent enough to wear as a cufflink or on a boutonniere. I asked him, "What about Victor? You lost his trail."

"I don't think so; I know where he is staying."

I paid for the tab and walked toward the exit.

Outside, a light drizzle had started to fall. The temperature was in the fifties, but I still felt a chill. I checked my watch to see how I was doing. Not bad, not bad at all.

I made up my mind to go to the Angellonis' get-together. If something were to happen, I had the advantage of the map. I felt like a secret agent.

My phone rang as I was driving away. "It's not a game. It is very serious business with dangerous people," Andrew advised in a very stern tone. The phone went dead.

~

I took a brisk shower, towel-dried my hair, and applied a glaze for shine. I left the hair looking tussled, and I didn't shave; I wanted the rugged look. I was deliberate in every move I made.

Finally, I was ready to go pick up Miss Harris—Elsa. I look at the mirror once more for a last-minute check; I liked the reflection in the mirror looking back at me. It was amazing how having money could turn people around to the point where they could feel fashionable.

I got in my Jeep and drove away. I was thrilled. The idea of toying with the Angellonis gave me a rush.

~

I arrived at Elsa's place at seven. She looked flushed when she answered the door. Her eyes were swollen. Had she been crying? She was wearing a tight, long, purple dress with a revealing low cut. She looked statuesque. The slinky, stretchy material accentuated every curve in her body. Her hair was up in a French knot, showing her delicate-looking neck.

"You look stunning!" I said admiringly.

"Thanks," she replied in a sad tone.

"Are you OK?" I asked, concerned.

"He was here," she said. Her eyes brimmed with tears.

"Angelloni?"

She nodded quietly. I could see the terror on her face. She was trembling. "My life is in danger," she uttered in a low, guttural tone.

"How are you involved?"

"He forced me to call your aunt's butler and tell him you had a map."

I couldn't find words to reply. The words just couldn't form. I was speechless.

"I am to get the map from you, or I'm dead by tomorrow." Her lips were quivering. A lonely tear rolled down her cheek, leaving a track on her perfectly made-up face. She looked completely terrorized. What an actress. My self-confidence knocked down in an instant.

"What do you know about the map?" I asked.

"Nothing." She looked at me with her big, sad eyes, shaking her head.

"Do you know who else is going to their party?" I asked again.

Again, she shook her head.

"Do you want to go?" I prodded.

"Let's go for a drink first," she said. *Make it two strong drinks*, I thought.

~

We drove to a local bar downtown. It was more of a hangout for husbands and wives playing the field. Out of the corner of my eye, I saw the feds parking. I approached them.

"Have you seen anything worth reporting to your special agent?" I asked.

They didn't answer.

"I need to speak with the field agent in charge of this operation."

The morons thought I was joking and ignored me completely. I thought of Sergeant Miller. He really was concerned last time I saw him; maybe he could help.

We went inside the bar. We ordered dry martinis, and I dialed the police station while we waited for our drinks. A detective took the call. I told him it was urgent that I speak with Miller; he took my number and said he would call him right away.

I grew impatient and dialed the police again. I was put on hold—how much I hated being on hold.

"Hello, this is Sergeant Miller."

I hesitated for an instant; I didn't know how to start.

"S-sergeant? Th-this is Sam. Can I see you?" I was stammering. I was mortified and very nervous. The rush I had felt earlier was gone, and I still wasn't positive about him. But he was the best bet for now.

"Sam, what is this about? I was told this was an urgent matter." I couldn't tell whether he was annoyed or impatient.

"I have important information," I blurted out.

"Can this wait for tomorrow?" he asked.

"Might be too late for tomorrow," I said with finality.

"I'm going to a New Year's party. Where are you?"

"I'm at the Playing Field Bar."

"The one on Main and Maple?" he asked.

He said he'd be there in thirty minutes and hung up.

Then I called Andrew. He answered promptly. "Hello, Sam?"

For some reason, his voice comforted me. I felt that he was watching over me. "Andrew, where are you?"

"I followed Victor to a mansion on the hill," he said.

"The Angellonis' place!" I said.

"Are you supposed to be here, too?" he asked.

"Yeah, but I'm downtown in a bar. I want you here."

"How far is it from where I am?"

"Maybe twenty minutes?"

I gave him the name of the bar and directions on how to get there.

~

Elsa started to relax with her second martini. I asked how she'd gotten involved with Marco. It was always the same story: she was lonesome after her failed marriage. She had married right after high school; he had turned into a wife beater, she left. Her parents helped with her divorce. She found a job with Angelloni and had work with him until now. After her divorce, she moved to this small town, looking for tranquility and thinking it would be easier to start her new life in Mapletown. She admitted that she had never been afraid of Angelloni, but he had slapped and threatened her earlier tonight, and she didn't want any involvement with him anymore. Her ex-husband had been violent and abusive.

Nervously, I glanced at my watch; I forgot how many times I had done that in the last twenty minutes. I looked toward the bar entrance—Andrew should be here anytime now, I thought. Said and done, Andrew walked in.

I introduced him to Miss Harris and offered him a drink.

He ordered a beer. "Are you supposed to be at the party?" he asked.

"Yeah, we are deciding on that," I answered. "Things got complicated."

Andrew looked at Miss Harris and then at me. "I don't understand," he said.

"She is Mr. Angelloni's secretary, Miss Elsa Harris."

He looked puzzled and couldn't make the connection. "I still don't understand," he said, intrigued.

I didn't know how to say that the only reason I'd invited Miss Harris to go with me to the party was to screw Angelloni. I was embarrassed to say that I was using her to get to Angelloni. Again, the words wouldn't form, and nothing came out of my mouth.

"Did you tell your boss that you were attending his party with Sam?" Andrew asked Miss Harris. "Elsa?" Andrew said her name lightly, looking at me.

I nodded faintly at Andrew.

~

Sergeant Miller made his appearance before Elsa answered Andrew's question. I introduced him to Andrew, and he began asking questions.

"What's going on, Sam?" He looked stylish in his tuxedo.

"Miss Harris has received a death threat," I said blatantly.

Andrew and Miller turned toward Elsa.

She took a deep breath and said, "I was ordered by Mr. Angelloni to get a map from Sam." She stopped to take a swallow of her almost-empty martini.

"That doesn't sound like a threat to me," Sergeant Miller said.

"If I didn't get the map, I'd be dead the following day," Elsa finished.

Miller turned to Andrew and asked, "Who are you, and what is your involvement?"

"He is Andrew Daniels, a PI I hired," I said. I realized that he hadn't asked me.

He looked at me and snapped, "I asked him."

"I'm Andrew Daniels. Sam hired my services to find his aunt's butler."

"Victor?" Sergeant Miller asked.

"I followed him here to Mapletown; he is right now at the Angellonis' party."

"What in the hell is he doing at the Angellonis'?" he asked as he finally sat down. "Are you Miss Harris, Mr. Angelloni's secretary?"

Miss Harris timidly nodded her head.

"Can somebody explain to me what's going on?" he asked with exasperation.

I offered him a drink.

He ordered a shot of whisky and said, "You got half an hour to explain."

Andrew and Elsa looked at me. I cleared my throat and started to tell Sergeant Miller about the day I found a map. I hadn't made anything of it and put it away. All of a sudden, everybody started to have an interest in the map: Marco Angelloni broke into my house looking for it, Victor was sent to threaten me to get it, and now Miss Harris was threatened by Angelloni to get the map from me, or die if she didn't. I reminded him that he had also inquired about the map himself. I then told him I thought the map was of the cemetery.

He patiently listened to my conjectures. When I paused for a second to collect my thoughts, the sergeant asked, "Where is the map now?"

"I have it in a safe place," I replied.

"Is that it? Is that the end of your story?" he asked.

I shook my head no.

He glanced at his watch and said, "Continue."

I held my breath and sipped my drink. *I hope I'm not losing my mind,* I thought. Then I told him how I had gone to the cemetery to see if I could make any sense of the map and found Augustus C. Wilmot's grave on the family plot. I told him I didn't recall an uncle by that name and that his name was not recorded in any of the family albums or in City Hall's records department. Here or in New York.

"What do you want me to do about it?" he asked.

We all fell silent. The moment was loaded with tension. I still doubted whether I had made the right choice in confiding in him. He could be working for the Angellonis, as well. My aunt had warned me of that in her letter.

"Mrs. Angelloni invited me to her New Year's dinner party," I said, breaking the dense silence.

"Really? That's where I and my wife have to be, too," Sergeant Miller said.

"I need protection," I said.

"I'm the one that needs protection!" Miss Harris said indignantly.

"How are you and you involved in this?" he asked pointing to Elsa and me.

We looked at each other without saying a word. We were quiet for a moment. Elsa waited for me to say something.

"We are not," I said at last. "I invited her to the celebration—that's all."

"How did Angelloni find out that she could get the map out of you?" Sergeant Miller inquired.

"I told him I was coming to their party with him," Elsa said. She was upset that he hadn't invited her. She only wanted to make him jealous.

"You better not go tonight," Sergeant Miller told her.

I didn't feel so bad after all; she was using me as well.

Sergeant Miller got up to leave. He motioned to a woman waiting for him at a table close to the exit.

"My wife," he said. On his way out, he said, "I will see you at the party, and whatever you do, act casual." And he disappeared into the night.

Sergeant Miller had suggested that Andrew accompany me to the dinner and be introduced just as a friend from out of town. He also said he would keep an eye on us at all times. I called a cab to take Miss Harris home. Andrew parked his car at my place, and we drove together to the Angellonis'.

~

It was almost nine when we arrived at the party. Miller was already there. I felt Victor's eyes glaring at me. Angelloni's face looked relieved when he saw me without Miss Harris.

I looked for Mrs. Angelloni. When I found her, I tried to hide the disgust I was feeling for her. She approached me and gave me a light peck on the lips. "I'm glad you could make it," she said, sounding genuinely pleased. She looked like she always did: proper and elegant.

"Mrs. Angelloni, this is my friend Andrew Daniels," I said, observing her closely.

She extended her perfectly manicured hand to shake Andrew's. "You two can call me Ruth."

I furtively looked around, trying to locate Sergeant Miller. I saw him talking with Mr. Angelloni and looking in our direction.

I whispered in Andrew's ear to check them out and to tell me what he could make of Miller and Angelloni.

Andrew suggested separating and mingling; we had to pay attention to the other guests to see what we could catch from their conversations. He mentioned that he had a pistol with him. That certainly made me feel better. I told him I was wearing the device he'd given me earlier.

~

I didn't know most of the guests. I could make out Judge O'Hara among the people. I approached the group and introduced myself. O'Hara asked if I was Mildred's nephew. I nodded.

Mrs. Miller was among the group. I offered to get her a glass of wine, and she walked with me toward the bar. We made small talk. After a while, she turned serious. "I'm worried about Hiram," she said. "These are very greedy people."

She was constantly scanning the place for Sergeant Miller and would make a sigh of relief whenever he came into her focus.

"We have lived in Mapletown all of our lives, and we have never been guests of Mr. and Mrs. Angelloni before." I looked at her and could sense her distrust of the situation. "For several years my husband has been trying to find out about their clandestine operations."

I wondered why she was telling me this.

I saw Andrew across the room talking to a group of people close to where Miller and Angelloni were talking. "From here it seems that your husband and Mr. Angelloni are good friends," I said to Mrs. Miller.

She nodded and said he had been nervous since he'd met with us at the Playing Field Bar.

I thought Mrs. Miller was very well informed about her husband's business. I felt sorry for her; I could see her anguish.

The party went smoothly; the Angellonis graciously attended to their guests. Andrew was checking for suspicious-looking individuals.

Close to midnight, an entourage of several individuals entered. Mrs. Angelloni stopped dead in her tracks and moved swiftly to greet the new guests. I glanced at Mr. Angelloni. A sudden change had come over him. He was panicky and jumpy.

Mrs. Angelloni motioned him to come to where she was with the "important" guests. Reluctantly, Marco headed toward the group.

I scanned the place to locate Andrew; he was paying keen attention and studying the situation.

The group looked very menacing and unfriendly. They went to a studio and closed the door behind them.

Sergeant Miller observed them do so, then told his wife to take the car and leave. She argued with him but left, nevertheless.

I saw Miller walking toward me, and I just stood looking at him. "Sam, you have to get out of here," he ordered.

I stared at him. "What's going on?" I asked. "Who are those guys?"

"I think this guy is his son," he said, "and I don't think they are on a friendly visit."

"What were you discussing with Angelloni?" I asked him.

"I was telling him about the incriminating video of the break-in at your place," he answered. He said he'd wanted to catch him with his guard down.

I caught Andrew's attention and motioned to him that we were leaving.

"Sam, bring the map to the station tomorrow," Miller said as I started to leave.

I felt Victor's angry stare. I ignored him and politely waved good-bye.

45

We didn't say a word on the way home. I checked my watch; it was twelve thirty. People were happily out on the streets, hugging and kissing to welcome the new year.

"Happy new year, Andrew," I said bitterly.

"Happy new year, Sam," he responded in a like manner. We both started laughing.

"Let's go for a drink and compare notes about the party," I said.

Andrew thought for a moment. "It's not a bad idea. Where to?"

"The Living Dead Bar," I said and started to drive toward the cemetery.

The night was clear but very cold. The heater was blasting on high. Andrew pointed out that a car was tailing us. I told him that the feds had been on my tail since a week ago.

"Is that the cemetery in the coveted map?" Andrew asked as we passed the graveyard.

"Yep," I answered. There wasn't much to elaborate about it.

Andrew rubbernecked at the burial ground and asked, "Will you let me take a look at the map?" He immediately turned to look at me and see my reaction.

I thought for a moment. "Why, sure," I said. Maybe with his keen eye, he could see more than I could. "Anyways, Miller asked me to bring it to the station."

He didn't say anything about Miller at the moment, but later asked, "Why does Miller want to see the map?"

I shrugged. "I don't know. What do you think of him? I always thought that he was involved with Angelloni." I couldn't remember if

I'd told him about my arrest and the beating I received at the detention center. And that I was forced to sign some sensitive papers.

After thinking awhile, he said in a low voice, "I don't think he is involved. He and Mrs. Miller seem to live on a fixed income. She wasn't wearing fur, and no big rock on her fingers." He observed that her clothing was maybe from JC Penney and his was a rented tuxedo. "I wondered what they were doing at the Angellonis'."

~

I was still thinking about Andrew's observations on the Millers when we arrived at the bar. With deliberate slowness, I exited my Jeep and walked toward the entrance. I noticed that our stalkers were parking within a few feet of us.

As we entered the place, two women were slapping each other. A guy was trying to separate them. From the looks of it, he had been caught cheating. A brawl was imminent.

Said and done—one started in full force. It was dreadful how humans treated each other in this place. Or in any other place, for that matter. My aunt Millie's murder was an example of humans' cruelty.

We took a booth on the farthest side of the pub and ordered beers. We drank while we watched engrossed as the fight escalated. We were amused at the disorderly conduct.

Then Andrew said, looking directly at my eyes, "Sam, I overheard the assholes in the studio conspiring to get to the map. You need to get away from your home, at least for tonight."

Who said that a new year brought new hope? All it meant was that I would have made it through the night without confrontations.

"Why did you tell the sergeant that you had the map?" Andrew asked.

"Very simple. I cannot go to the cemetery and start digging in Augustus's gravesite; Miller can exercise his authority and have it done," I said matter-of-factly.

Andrew lifted his bottle. "I'll drink to that," he said with a broad smile. Then he nudged me and pointed. "Look, is that Miss Harris over there?"

I turned my head in the direction he was pointing and saw Elsa coming our way.

"Shit!" I said. She was tipsy and had to hold on to tables and the wall to walk in a straight line. Nevertheless, she made it to our booth. She was a mess.

"W-what happened at the Angellonis'?" she asked. Her speech was slurred. Her earlier perfect makeup was a runny disaster.

"She's wasted," Andrew said.

I nodded in agreement. She sat next to me. The stench of old tobacco and liquor was too strong to be ignored. I ordered coffee for her. "Please make it strong," I told the waiter.

She was so wasted that she was oblivious to the brawl.

"I-if I'm going to die tonight, I want to be drunk so I won't feel the p-pain," she slurred. She rested her head on the table and fell asleep.

"Do you think that they could kill her?" Andrew asked with compassion.

I nodded affirmatively. "These people have no respect for human life, and once people become an obstacle, they have no problem removing them," I said, feeling sick to my stomach.

"What are we going to do with her?" Andrew asked next.

"When are you going back to San Francisco?" It was my turn to ask him. He knew where I was going.

"No way, man," he said.

"I will give you money. Take her with you and place her out of danger."

We both turned to look at her; she was a mess all right.

We left the bar, bringing Miss Harris with us, and decided to spend the night at a local motel.

~

We just had settled into our rooms at the seedy Sleeping Well Motel when my cellular started to ring. It was almost three in the morning of the brand new year. Who could be calling this late? In a bad mood, I answered. I could only hear static, though.

The phone rang again. I doubted whether I should answer, but I was curious to know who could be calling at this time of night. I took the call on the fifth ring; curiosity killed the cat.

"Sam? This is Jacob," he said before I could say hello.

I thought of hanging up. "Yes, Jacob," I said against my better judgment. Well, better sooner than later; besides, I needed to know if he made it back.

"Sorry to call you this late. I just made it back. What happened here?" he blurted without stopping. He sounded out of breath. The background static was growing louder. "Sam?"

"I'm still here. We had a break-in a few days ago," I said.

"Is there anything missing besides the documents in my room?" he inquired.

"Don't know for sure," I said.

"There's a car parked in the driveway."

"Don't worry about that. It belongs to a friend."

"Did you report the break-in to the authorities?" he asked.

"Yes, Miller is handling the case."

"Miller? I thought he worked homicide."

"He thinks this is related to my aunt's murder."

There was silence for a moment. "When are you coming home?" he asked.

"Go to sleep, Jacob, I'll be home before noon."

~

I called Andrew in the room next door. I kept my voice low. Miss Harris was sleeping in the bed next to mine. "Andrew, we need to pick up your car early in the morning," I said.

"Who called you? Is everything OK?" he asked.

"Yeah, it was Jacob," I replied.

"Sure, we can leave early. What about Miss Harris?"

"We let her sleep. You pick her up on your way out of this goddamn town."

"Try to get some sleep for now," he said.

I tried and tried. But sleep escaped me. I lay awake, listening for the smallest of noises. My heart raced and my temples throbbed at the idea that Angelloni's goons would find us—especially me, with his mistress passed out in the same room. That was no way to start the new year. I would have given everything I owned to not be in this situation.

The air was filled with fear. One careless move on my part, and I would be blown out of existence like Aunt Millie. *But not today.* I had to outthink, outsmart my adversaries, the Angellonis. I was so restless that I got out of bed and peered out the window.

Thick, charcoal-gray clouds hung low; the rain seemed imminent. My mother had always told me that even the sun didn't shine when I was born; I had been born on a rainy day. Why was I thinking about that? I'd never asked what she meant. Maybe when she first saw me, she felt like I was feeling right now, engulfed by dreariness and desolation, a very bleak sentiment indeed.

There were a few cars parked at the motel, which made it hard to tell if the feds were watching us. Then, in a car parked farthest from my room, I was able to make out a couple of people smoking inside. The amber light of their cigarettes gave them away.

I got in bed again and stared at the four bare walls of this dank room. I caught a wink or two, but I was roused by sudden noises and moaning coming from the bed next to mine. At least she was breathing, I thought.

~

The time to get up came too fast. Andrew was knocking at the door. Miss Harris stirred, changed positions, and continued sleeping. I wrote her a note in case she woke up and found herself in this bare room.

We drove swiftly. In my rear-view mirror, I could see the feds' cruiser trying to keep up with me. We decided to stop for coffee, but every place was closed because it was New Year's Day.

We arrived at my place around seven thirty. Jacob was already up. I introduced him to Andrew just to see what his first impression of Jacob was.

"Andrew, this is a house guest," I said, carefully avoiding saying that he was my attorney. I also wanted to know if Jacob would catch not being introduced as my attorney.

"Nice to meet you," Jacob politely said. "Sam never mentioned you before."

"He never mentioned you either," Andrew said casually.

Jacob had already prepared coffee, and I asked if Andrew could have a cup for the road.

He nodded. "You're leaving?" he asked Andrew.

Andrew nodded while he carefully sipped his hot cup of brew. Outside, my surveillance team sat on their asses.

"Yep, I have to make it to San Fran by four," Andrew said heedlessly.

"Yeah, I'll follow you to the ATM," I said as casually as I could. I didn't want Jacob to know that I needed to talk to Elsa. I had to give her particulars about the plans for her to go away for a short time while things settled down.

"Where did you and Sam meet?" Jacob asked unexpectedly.

"In college," Andrew answered without hesitation. Jacob's grimace relaxed a bit. He *had* caught the attorney thing from earlier.

"Yeah, Sophia, my ex-wife introduced us." I confirmed Andrew's response.

"Sam, we really have to leave," Andrew said.

~

Andrew and I were of the same build, with the same hair color and height. We decided to switch cars; I would drive Andrew's, and he, mine. It wasn't for any reason—we just wanted to check the tailing cops and see if we could lose them.

We got in the respective cars and drove away. We had to meet at the Sleeping Well Motel, but for now, we had to take different routes. We drove away in different directions. I looked through the rear-view mirror; nobody was following. The tail had gone after the Jeep. My smile faded quickly, though, when I remembered this wasn't a game.

I made it to the motel and parked Andrew's car a few doors away from where Elsa was. I looked around to see if it was safe to leave the car. The parking lot was empty.

~

Elsa was in the shower when I entered the dark room. She came out of the shower in her birthday suit. She screamed when she saw me, blushed, and quickly ran to grab a towel. I just stood there admiring her voluptuous body.

"I didn't hear you come in," she said. She was still blushing and embarrassed.

"Did you read the note I left?" I asked, trying to sound normal. I was totally taken by her. She looked well rested and radiant. No heavy makeup or perfumes. I had picked up a gray sweat suit at home and gave it to her now. She disappeared again into the restroom and came out with the sweat suit on. She looked lovely. She sat on the bed Indian-style.

"Yes, I read the note," she said, drying her hair with a towel. "What happened at the party?"

"I think that you need to go away for a while," I told her sternly. I also told her about the events the night before at the Angellonis'.

"Where will I go? I don't have any family!" She was stressing out.

"You will go with Andrew to San Francisco," I said matter-of-factly.

"I don't know anybody in San Francisco." Panic was making her voice shrill. She looked like a lost little girl. I wanted to embrace her and tell her that everything would be OK. But I refrained.

"Andrew will make sure you are OK. You will have whatever you need."

Tears were rolling down her face. "What about my job?" she asked with desperation.

I couldn't believe my ears. Her boss had threatened to kill her, and she was worried about losing her job? I could only push so much. I didn't say another word. I just sat looking at her and waiting for her decision.

"Can I pick up some personal things from my place?"

I shook my head no. "You will buy whatever you need."

"I don't have any money."

"I will provide what you need while we resolve this mess," I said firmly.

"Where is Andrew, and when do we leave?" Her facial expression was as if she was experiencing the worst kind of imaginable torture.

"Just for a short time, I promise. Remember that time brings balance."

46

I decided to give her some time alone. I would sit in the car to wait for Andrew. I was sure he was nearby.

"Sam?" she said in a small voice. I stopped by the door and turned around.

"Yes?"

"I'm hungry!"

"As soon as Andrew gets here, we will take off," I said. I turned the doorknob and stepped out.

Walking briskly, I crossed the wet parking lot. A chill shook me from the top of my head all the way down my back; it was unseasonably cold. I was getting comfortable in the car when out of the corner of my eye, I saw the Jeep fast approaching the entrance to the parking lot; he had no tail.

Andrew jumped out of the Jeep calling, "I lost them!" He was proud of himself. "You wouldn't believe their faces when they saw me."

He proceeded to ask how it went with Miss Harris. I told him she was scared to go.

"Is she coming with me?" he asked.

"She is ready. She is hungry, too," I said. I pulled an envelope from my jacket pocket and gave it to him. "Make sure she gets what she needs."

"I'll save the receipts," he said, and I nodded.

~

I got Elsa, and she rode with me in Andrew's car; Andrew followed us in my Jeep.

We stopped at a small café outside of town and ordered eggs and ham for breakfast. Elsa wolfed hers down as fast as she could.

"How long am I going to be in San Francisco?" she asked, her mouth stuffed with toast. Andrew looked at me for an answer.

"Until further notice," I said. "And please, no phone calls to Angelloni."

She excused herself and went to the restroom.

Andrew was extremely silent. "You don't expect me to babysit her, do you?" he said, fixing his eyes on me.

"I don't think she needs a babysitter," I said, "but I would appreciate if you check on her."

He nodded in agreement.

"She will need to have cash on hand. Give her a thousand dollars."

When Elsa returned from the restroom, we went over a few details. She would get a pay-as-you-go cellular. She was not to give its number to anybody except Andrew and me. She was not to call me. I would call her when I deemed necessary. Andrew was not to babysit her; therefore, she needed to depend on herself. Andrew was to check on her three times per week. For emergencies, she was to call Andrew.

"I will let you know when it is safe to come back to Mapletown," I pointed out.

She paid close attention to the details. "Maybe if you give him the map, I wouldn't have to do this," she said hopefully.

I shook my head. "Not unless he tells me who killed my aunt. Do you know who did?"

She shook her head.

"It's hard to fight an enemy without knowing who he is. And it seems like this is an army!" I said with a tinge of desperation.

"I could find out if I were to stay," she offered.

"Don't you care? Your life is at stake!" I almost yelled. Then, "It's up to you." I raised my arms in a gesture of giving up. I glanced at my watch. "It's time to go."

"What will it be?" Andrew asked Elsa. She got up and walked toward Andrew's car.

Turning my attention to Andrew, I asked him "Did you ever get anything more from the *Gazette's* article?"

Andrew didn't answer.

I watched the car until it disappeared over the horizon. I got in my Jeep and drove toward home, thinking of Sergeant Miller and that I was supposed to bring the map to the station for him to examine.

I wasn't sure yet if that was the right thing to do. If I gave the map up, I wouldn't have any advantage. But I was anxious to find out what had happened at the Angellonis' after we left.

First, I would go home and face Jacob. I drove slowly. I was not in any hurry to get home anyway.

I drove near the cemetery and decided to stop awhile. I went directly to section two, plot sixty-one.

I don't know how long I contemplated Augustus's sepulcher. From time to time, I would turn to Aunt Millie's grave, and a question would form in my mind: *What should I do? Where? Please tell me, Aunt Millie.* But I could hear only the cold wind's lugubrious blowing. I was so absorbed in my depressed thoughts that I didn't feel the rain falling until I was drenched.

Feeling down in the dumps and incompetent, I went home.

~

Jacob was waiting for me when I arrived. He had a scowl of disgust all over his face. I would attempt to be cordial, but I was not going to take any shit from him. Who did he think he was? I had quite a few questions for him, too.

It was still early in the morning for a shot of strong liquor, but I was wet and cold and in an uncomfortable situation.

He watched my every move. With suspicious eyes, he looked at me up and down. I went to the kitchen for a cup of hot coffee; his eyes followed.

I went to my room, took off my wet clothes, and put on a warn sweat suit similar to the one I had given Elsa. When I came back to the kitchen, Jacob resumed watching me. He made a disdainful gesture toward me; I completely ignored him.

It felt like we were playing cat and mouse. But I didn't want to play. I decided to let him be the one to speak first. I was deliberate and patient.

He shifted a little. His expression suggested concern for his position. His body language said he was also tense and anxious. I wondered what he was reading in my body language. The same vibrations, perhaps? I just had to wait and see. Finally, he broke the heavy silence.

"Who is Andrew?" he demanded. He sounded like a jealous wife.

I was not going to answer such a ridiculous question. I had already introduced Andrew. "I'm fine, Jacob. And you?" I replied sardonically.

He caught my drift. He shifted again. "What really happened here?"

"As I told you, we had a break-in."

"Do you know what the intruders were looking for?"

"They took several documents."

"What's the smell in the basement?" he asked. "The house was cold when I got here. There was a draft of cold air coming from the basement; the windows were open." I could hear the nervousness in his voice; he was speaking too fast.

I tried to stay calm, hoping there was no evidence of the struggle that he could notice in the cellar. I shuddered when I remembered Toothless Max's and Louisa Malone's deaths. How about Clem? Did he make it OK? I looked away so Jacob wouldn't detect my uneasiness.

I felt like telling him that if he didn't have anything to say, he should shut up, but instead I continued making small talk. I very much wanted to go take a nap.

He looked profoundly into my eyes. "Let's talk seriously about business," he ventured. "Whether you will need my services…" He trailed off.

I waited for him to finish his reckoning. I just kept quiet for a few moments more.

"Or not," he said and started to pace back and forth.

"If you have nothing else to say—" I began, when he interrupted me in the middle of my observation.

"Sam, in the past few weeks since I met you," he started to say. It felt like he was preparing the opening statement of his dissertation in front of the jury. "I have examined the opportunity before us to solve a crime that was committed against a human being, a member of this community, Mildred C. Wilmot, your aunt. She was brutally assassinated."

Shit! Was he serious? I thought I was going to barf. "Jacob, you are not in front of a jury," I said. "Could you be less ceremonious and get to the point?"

"Sam, what I'm trying to do here is to prove that I'm a darn good attorney," he said defensively. "If I don't help solve this case, you don't have to pay me."

"Jacob, once you lose your trust in someone, it is hard to repair the relationship."

"I know I fucked up. Give me another chance—you won't regret it," he said vehemently.

"All right then, what were you doing with Eva?" That had been burning me since I saw them boarding the bus. "I think you're two-faced. You kept telling me to keep away from her."

I stopped for a moment to hear myself. Now it was me sounding pathetic. Just a minute! This was about his actions that made him untrustworthy, not about him being with her.

"Remember? And all this time you were involved with her. How come you didn't tell me about your relationship with her?" I stopped again. My breathing became labored, and I felt a train rolling through my head. I became sullen, bothered that this conversation was upsetting me. It had nothing to do with this argument, I reasoned; I'd had a tough night with no sleep and too much drinking.

Jacob just sat there—thank God he'd stopped pacing—and he looked as upset as I was. At times he stared at the ceiling and then back at me. I took a swallow from my now-cold coffee.

"What else have you hidden from me?" I asked.

"Sam, I'm sorry about Rita Malone—" he started to say.

I quickly interrupted him. "Jacob, how well did you know Rita Malone? Let's start there." Now I was confrontational.

"Rita was the court clerk and—" he said.

I interrupted him again. "Jacob, did you know she was not Rita Malone?" This time I fixed my eyes on him.

"No, I didn't know. I know there was a Rita Malone at the courthouse."

"Yes, there is. But not the one that sent you, supposedly, to me."

He looked embarrassed. He didn't say a word and motioned me to continue.

I paused for a moment, thinking that we were getting agitated. I went to the kitchen to warm my coffee; I needed to catch my breath. He had a drink in his hands when I returned.

"Her name was Louisa Malone," I said with a throaty voice. Her memory came back to haunt me. I could see her all over again: the feel of her rigid body, the pallor of death on her once-pretty face. I went to the door and opened it. I needed a gasp of fresh, cold air to clear my head.

Jacob's gaze on me was deep. He had a puzzled look.

Closing the door, I said, "Jacob, we need to leave this conversation for later. I'm feeling dizzy."

"I think we should finish. I would like to know where I'm standing."

"No! I really need to take a break. And I tell you what. I think we should take a ride to the courthouse so you can point out Rita Malone."

"The courthouse is closed today; it's New Year's Day," he said. "But I would be happy to go tomorrow."

"OK. We will get back together to discuss the rest of our disagreement in a couple of hours," I said. "I think we both need a break."

Jacob glanced at his watch. "Around one o'clock, then." Then he looked up at me and said, "Thanks, Sam."

I nodded as I hurried to my room.

47

At exactly one o'clock, Jacob knocked softly at my door. I didn't answer, hoping he would go away. He knocked harder and called my name. I just couldn't keep ignoring the sudden commotion coming from the hallway. I went to the door.

In a low monotone, he said, "It's one o'clock."

We exchanged momentary and cold glances. "I'll be down in ten," I said in the same tone.

I went to wash the sleep from my face. I caught a glimpse of a tired, unshaven face looking at me. There was a look of frustration in the hazel eyes. The graying hair was rippled from the pillow. I didn't recognize the stranger in the mirror. The face in the mirror looked disturbing and grotesque.

I ran my fingers through my hair but didn't bother to shave. At last, I went downstairs.

Jacob was impatiently waiting for me. I sat down and looked at him, a loud rolling thunder announcing the storm that started to beat down on us.

"Where were we?" he asked.

I pointed out that we would continue with "Rita" later.

"Oh yeah, tell me about Eva," I said. I patiently waited for his answer.

"When I found out about her," he began, "I wanted to get closer to see what she knew about Angelloni."

I slowly shook my head. He didn't trust me. He didn't have the decency to tell me his plan. That was going to be hard to swallow.

"Jacob, I don't think that even you believe that bull." I looked directly at him. "You really think I'm that naïve?"

"I-I didn't want to involve you," he said sheepishly.

"How could you not involve me, for heaven's sake? It's my case. I'm involved!" I said angrily. If I had been closer to him, I would have punched him squarely in the mouth.

"Let me tell you what I believe, since you don't have the decency to tell me, Jacob. You're involved with the Angellonis. And you were working me from a different angle. The 'good-cop,' 'bad-cop' shit with Miller."

I glared at him with repulsion. I got a shot of the hard liquor I had become accustomed to drink to calm myself. This time he was shaking his head no.

The liquor started to give me the desired effect, and I felt calmer.

"Jacob, I will give you till tomorrow to come up with the truth and level with me. If you persist in insulting my intelligence, there's no need to talk any further."

I got up and went to the kitchen to look for something to eat. I opened the fridge, but it was empty. I didn't notice that Jacob had followed me to the kitchen. I opened the cupboards to see if I could find something.

"Sam, let's bury the hatchet and let me buy you lunch," he offered amiably.

"Today is the first of the fucking new year, and every place in this damn town is closed," I said.

"There's a place about half an hour from here," he said.

I knew that if I accepted, I would have to put up with his argument. Or I could eat saltine crackers for lunch and dinner. I looked out the front window; the stakeout car wasn't parked by the curb across the street where I had become accustomed to seeing it every time I peeked out the window. The thunderstorm had ceased, while the noises in my stomach were getting louder. I put my pride away and, like Esau, I sold myself for food.

"I'll be ready in ten minutes," I told Jacob as I went upstairs to grab a long coat to put over my sweats.

We rode in silence to the restaurant. It was as he said a half hour away. Maybe he was capable of telling the truth after all, I thought. But I wouldn't hold my breath.

Jacob pulled out a cigarette and asked, "Is it OK to smoke?"

I shook my head no.

He put the cigarette between his lips without lighting it.

"Jacob, we are almost there; then you can smoke," I said. He looked tense and irritable. I decided not to say much. I would let him do the talking.

"There's a goddamn law that bans smoking in public places, you know?"

~

The Roadside Café was deserted. Only a waitress and a cook were tending the occasional patrons who ventured in. The place was a dive, but the food would still be better than saltine crackers.

The server took our orders and disappeared behind the counter. We could hear the banging of the pans as the cook started preparing our food. She reappeared with our drinks.

Jacob got up and went to smoke a cigarette outside. I could see him pacing, billowing smoke. He had a look of determination when he returned.

"Sam, I think I can help find who killed your aunt," he blurted out.

"Do you have an idea who did it?" I asked.

He saw that he had gotten my attention. "I might have a couple of clues that I got from Eva." He was closely observing my body language.

To hide my emotions from him, I took a swig from my cola; but he knew he'd struck a raw nerve. I couldn't speak; the words wouldn't come out.

The waitress came with our food. "A bowl of chili," she said, "and meatloaf with gravy." She set our food in front of us. "Do you need anything else?"

"Yes, I'll have a hamburger to go, please," I said. That would be dinner later on, I figured.

"I'll have the same," Jacob said. "That will carry us until tomorrow."

We ate in silence for the most part.

"Victor told me he saw three men beating my aunt," I said without looking up. I became very emotional every time I remembered the vile manner in which she had met her demise.

I could feel Jacob's eyes staring at me.

"Jacob, what makes you think that Eva knows anything about my aunt's murder?"

"She has to. She was married to Angelloni's kid."

"Why would she tell you anything?"

"I know where to push," he said with a grin.

"Where is she?"

"Hiding, in Los Angeles."

I reminded Jacob that unless he told me the truth, I didn't want to hear anything he had to say. I didn't want hearsay; I wanted facts. I wanted corroborating evidence as well. "Do you have any?" I asked.

He thought awhile, apparently about what he would tell me next. The way his eyes were darting from side to side told me that he was coming up empty.

The waitress came to clear our table and offered a piece of apple pie with coffee. Jacob was paying—why not? I thought.

"Jacob, do you know that I never got a police report and that her death certificate is inconclusive as of now?" I said, my voice raspy with sentiment. "Angelloni never read her testament either," I concluded with a lump in my throat.

I took a swig of coffee to wash the lump away. I excused myself and went to the men's room. I splashed cold water on my face. My eyes were red and looked irritated.

When I returned to the table, Jacob was outside smoking a cigarette and talking on the phone. He seemed very upset, talking as if something had gone wrong. The rain didn't seem to bother him at all. I wondered if he would be able to kill a person.

I was ready to leave as soon as the waitress handed me the two bags with the hamburgers. "Your friend already paid," she said.

I gathered my coat, stepped outside, and walked toward my Jeep. As soon as Jacob saw me, he threw his cigarette away.

"Bad news, Jacob?" I asked.

He didn't answer. He buckled up, and we drove away.

The rain was heavy. The windshield wipers were on high. The ride back home was in silence.

"Do you still want to go to City Hall tomorrow?" I asked.

He gave me a cold stare and shrugged his shoulders. "If we must," he said without emotion.

~

We arrived home at two. I put the food in the fridge. Jacob still looked disgusted and in a bad mood. Who had called to put him into such an irate state? I was not going to make things difficult for either of us; I was tired and wanted to rest. No more useless chitchat for now.

A strange noise distracted me when I entered my room. It sounded like a bumblebee. I looked around, trying to pinpoint the source of the weird buzz. There on my night table, my new cellular phone was vibrating. Yeah, now I remembered—I had set it to vibrate; with Jacob here, I didn't want him to know I had two phones.

The new phone had a voice-mail message. I had been thinking about Andrew and Elsa, wondering how they'd managed their trip. I was about to know.

"Sam, call me as soon as you hear this. Thanks." That was all.

I cracked open my room's door to make sure Jacob wasn't eavesdropping. I dialed Andrew's number.

He answered at the first ring. "Hello, this is Andrew," he said politely.

"Hi, Andrew. How did it go?" I asked anxiously.

"The trip went fine. She settled in a nice place. I also took her shopping."

"Thanks, Andrew," I said with sincerity. "Where is she staying?"

"It's better that you don't know for now," he said.

I immediately understood his reasoning.

"Sam, I just read again the article on your aunt's murder in the *Gazette,* and I don't know for sure, but I think I found a few clues."

"Tell me, tell me," I said.

"Not now. Please, I need you to read the article and see what do you see, and then we'll compare." He was very serious. He wasn't asking, he was ordering.

The idea made me ill to my stomach. I would try my best to get out of this grim task. "Andrew, why don't you just tell me?" I asked earnestly.

"You need to do it, Sam!" he barked.

"The idea makes me sick. You don't understand," I cried.

"Call me when you do!" he said and hung up.

~

Where did I put the copy of the article? Shit! This was not the way to start the new year, I thought again.

I could hear Jacob pacing in his room, talking on the phone. His voice sounded muffled, and I couldn't make out what he was saying, but it didn't sound nice. *Forget about Jacob and his problems—I have mine to contend with.* For example, why was I blocking where I had put the article? I knew exactly where I had left it. *Stop being a sissy boy get cajónes, and start,* I told myself.

I went downstairs to the liquor cabinet and got a bottle of vodka and a short glass. *This ought to give me some cajónes.* I gulped down a shot of the hard liquor and went to the drawer where the article was waiting for me to read. My hands shook as I opened the envelope.

Woman, 62, brutally bludgeoned.
Found at her house by her butler.

MAPLETOWN—A 62-year-old woman was found dead at her home on October 19. Mildred C. Wilmot's body found by, Victor Parker when he returned to work. The police found no signs of forced entry or robbery. She died of blunt-force trauma to her head and torso. Her throat, had been slit, from side to side, by a left-handed perpetrator.

The police held Victor Parker for questioning. He was released. Victor Parker saw three men at the scene. No suspects have been identified. According to the medical examiner, she was dead since the night before. She knew her assailants.

I read the article a couple of times. The only things I thought odd were Victor been questioned with no results and my aunt knowing her murderers. What else was I missing?

A heavy train stationed in my head. Its engine sounded monotonous and weighty, echoing through my brain. My temples throbbed; I could feel my heart pounding in my chest. I felt a panic attack coming. I got another shot of vodka and drank it slowly this time.

I heard Jacob talking on his phone again. I started to calm down. I laid down, stared at the ceiling, and gently closed my eyes. Ghostly images came to me: Toothless Max, Louisa Malone, and my aunt, all suffering grotesque deaths.

I saw the three men, soaked in blood, beating and stabbing my aunt, laughing and dancing around her in a demonic way. My aunt's moaning was distorted by pain. Louisa and Max were standing looking at the butchery. The backs of the three men were toward me, and I couldn't see who they were.

I opened my eyes. I was sweating profusely. I was upset because I hadn't been there when she died and didn't see into her eyes as she was dying. Would I ever forgive myself?

My dark moment was interrupted by the ringing of my new phone. It must be Andrew.

In a daze, I reached for it and answered, "Hello, Andrew?"

"Did you read the article?" he asked, holding his breath.

"Yes," I answered. I didn't recognize my own voice. It sounded gloomy.

"Did you read both articles?"

"No. I only have the one on the twentieth."

"There was another in the next day's edition," he said. "On page six. It was the results of the autopsy."

I started to gag and to feel faint. I immediately sat down to avoid falling.

"What did you make out of the article?' he asked.

"Not much. Victor was questioned and my aunt knew her assailants," I said sheepishly. "And you?"

"The same as you, plus one of her assailants was left-handed. Are you sitting?"

"As a matter of fact, yes, I'm sitting."

"When you introduced me to Jacob, I noticed that he is left-handed." His voice was a low monotone. I really felt like a moron. The man had lived here for the nearly three months, and I'd never noticed.

"Sam, are you still there?"

"Yes, I'm here. To be honest with you, I have never paid attention."

"Please be careful. And remember: once a person kills for the first time, the act stays with that person for the rest of his life. Killing a second time gets easier, becomes automatic." He let that sink in.

I was dismayed.

"Sam, get a room for tonight. I'll see you tomorrow."

"What did the other article say?" I managed to ask.

"Her head was crushed beyond recognition. A left-handed individual administered most of her injuries, her house was completely ransacked. They were looking for something." He paused for a moment. "I bet they were looking for the map, Sam."

"I'll take the map to Sergeant Miller tomorrow!" I said, very agitated.

"No! Wait for me."

"Jacob is left-handed too," I slurred.

48

In haste, I threw a change of clothes and some essential toiletries into a duffel bag. My heart was pounding so hard I was afraid Jacob would hear it. As quietly as I could, I opened my door and went downstairs. Walking briskly, I reached the front door and opened it without looking back.

Jacob must have heard me; he called my name as I closed the door behind me. Without looking back, I got in my Jeep and drove away. He stood by the curb yelling, "Sam! Sam! Wait! Goddamn it!" I didn't look back.

When I was out of his sight, I looked back to make sure nobody was following me. I checked in at the Sleeping Well Motel. I was out of breath. I got room eleven, the same room I had shared with Elsa. I doubted that they had changed the bed linens.

I called Andrew as soon as I settled in. His phone rang several times. I left a message in his mailbox: "I'm at the Sleeping Well Motel. Call me."

I paced as I waited for his call.

The phone rang. I held my breath and grabbed it. I didn't notice it was my old phone until I answered.

"Sam, where in the hell are you?" It was Jacob. Shit!

"I'm with a friend," I answered dryly.

"Why didn't you stop? I called you."

"I didn't see you. And my radio was on. I didn't hear you either."

"I need to see you right away. Where are you so that we can come over?"

I caught the "we" but chose to ignore it. Seeing him was not at the top of my priorities at that moment.

"Not now, Jacob. I'm with a 'friend,' if you know what I mean," I said, trailing off.

"Sam, listen to me. This is more important than the bitch you are with," he said, sounding very irritated.

"C'mon, Jacob, what can be more important than getting laid."

"I don't know what's going on, but Angelloni is looking for you," he said, sounding concerned. "Also, Miller called me looking for you. He said it was very important. I gave him your number."

"Do you know what they want?" I asked.

"Yes. The two of them are looking for a map that's in your possession."

"Jacob! Jacob! Shit, I'm losing you! Fucking phones." I wondered if all people did that when they didn't want to continue talking. It worked all the time. I could hear Jacob bitching on the other side.

The phone rang again. I didn't answer this time; it was the old phone anyway. I was so restless; I felt the four bare walls closing in on me. I turned on the TV for noise and distraction. *C'mon, Andrew, call.*

I flipped through stations, looking for the news. I stopped at Channel 8. The news was about to start. Politics were at the forefront of the news and some new scandal. Who cared?

"Earlier today," the anchorwoman began, "a truck was found in a ravine outside Los Angeles. Two decomposed bodies were found: a man and a woman wrapped in plastic bags. They have not been identified yet."

Max and Louisa, I thought. I felt my heart skip several beats. I became sick with worry that somehow they would connect them to me.

"Here are the drawings that forensic artists have recreated," she continued. "If anybody recognizes them, please call the police. Both victims were shot at close range."

I turned the television off and ran to the bathroom to toss my cookies. Afterward, I dialed Andrew's phone again, and again it went to his fucking voice mail. I noticed my voice was shaky when I left him a new message: "*Call me!*"

~

I couldn't stand being in the cold room anymore, I got in my Jeep and drove away to find a liquor store. I needed some strong liquor to calm me down. I ended up at the Living Dead Bar, and lucky me, the place was open. The bartender recognized me and asked what was new. I shook my head.

"I just called the Los Angeles cops," he said very excited.

"Oh yeah, why?" I tried to sound detached.

"I just saw in the news a couple that was found dead." He was going sixty. "I recognized them, and I called the cops as they asked."

"They are in Los Angeles. You are in Mapletown," I said dispassionately.

"They were here before Christmas," he said.

"Together?"

"No. First the guy. He was toothless, and he was with a younger man. And then the woman," he said as he washed glasses under the counter.

"That doesn't make any sense," I said. "What were they doing here?"

"They asked if I knew where they could rent a truck," he said. "I asked them what happened to the place where they had rented before; they said it went out of business."

"You saw them before?" I asked, sounding curious.

"Yeah. They came a few times a year," he said.

"They had relatives here?"

"No. They were movers and had a route here," he said. "Excuse me. Lemme take care of that guy over there." He grabbed a bottle of Charlie Daniels.

My mind was racing. The cops would have no trouble tracing them back to Mapletown, to me. I had to talk to someone. I would continue to pick the bartender's brain when he came back, I thought. Guys like him would give anything to have their fifteen minutes of fame and wouldn't stop talking.

He came back and offered another shot of the scotch I was drinking. "What was I saying?" he asked.

"You were talking about the movers," I said.

"Oh, yes. They were moving stuff for the lady that got whacked in October, they said."

"If she was dead, did they mention anybody else?"

"Lemme see." He thought awhile.

I didn't say another word; I didn't want to break his train of thought.

"I don't remember if they said the woman's attorney or the police."

My temples were throbbing violently. I took a swig of my drink and asked for another.

"Hey, what happened to the sexy babe you were with?" he suddenly asked.

"I haven't seen her."

"Come to think of it, there were a couple of guys looking for her a couple of nights ago," he said. "I told them that she was shit-faced last time I saw her and that she left with a couple of guys."

I didn't say a thing. I waited for him to finish his babbling—useful babbling though it was. "Did you have a threesome?" he asked with a wink.

I shook my head. "We were too drunk." I kept quiet for a moment, then asked him, "Who were the bozos looking for her?"

"I didn't ask. You know, I have to be discreet in my profession," he said.

Yeah, unless you're paid for the info, asshole.

"Maybe a jealous boyfriend or an angry husband," he said with a silly grin on his face.

With that, I paid for the drinks, got up, and left.

When I got in my Jeep, I noticed I had a missed call on my new phone. Andrew had left a message. "Sorry I couldn't call you earlier. I'll explain. Call me."

I returned to the bar and asked the bartender if he had a car. He nodded. It was a battered Ford Focus. I told him about my decent-looking Jeep and offered to trade vehicles with him. He looked at me as if I had lost my marbles. He came out to check the Jeep, softly purring. "Even exchange?" he asked.

I nodded.

I signed my title, and he signed his. We proceeded to exchange plates. "Is this legal?" he asked.

You have to be kidding me, I thought.

"Afraid of the angry husband, huh?"

I nodded again.

I drove away. I felt better that I was driving the battered Focus. Angelloni, Jacob, and Miller knew I drove a Jeep; if they wanted to get me, they only had to find the Jeep. I had to outsmart them all.

~

There was fog on the road again. I decided I'd call Andrew when I got to the motel; it would be dangerous to take my eyes off the road now.

I drove into the motel's parking lot. A suspicious-looking car was parked just outside the door of room eleven. Three guys were smoking inside the car; I could see the light of their smokes. I decided not to stop. I was glad about the car exchange.

I had to find another motel. I had seen a couple outside of town. I drove south on local roads, and after twenty minutes of driving, I saw the neon light of Silver Dollar Motel off of exit 72. I registered under the name on the title of the Focus, Martin Evans. I gave a bogus address in San Francisco. When the clerk asked for an ID, I told him I'd lost my wallet and showed him the title. He noticed the different address from the one I'd given him. "Yeah," I said, "I moved a couple of months ago. You know, I had to get away from the ex."

He nodded in agreement. "Yeah, can't live with them, can't live without them—you know the cliché," he said.

~

Once I settled in, I called Andrew.

"Hello, Sam," he answered promptly.

"Andrew, where in the hell have you been?" I was angry but at the same time relieved. I was out of breath. "I called you twice."

"Elsa is in the hospital." He sounded concerned.

"What happened? Did Angelloni find her?"

"No. She took over-the-counter sleeping pills. She is OK."

He said she had cried all the way to San Francisco after they left Mapletown. Andrew thought she would get over it as soon as they arrived. But she called him late last night, still crying and sounding drunk. She told him she was very depressed and didn't have anybody, and maybe it was better for her to be dead.

He paused for a moment. I could tell that he was still shook up.

"I came to take her for breakfast..." His voice trailed off.

"What hospital is she in?" I asked.

"Sam, you cannot come. You can't expose yourself," he said. "I assure you she is OK." He stopped for a moment. "I'll see you tomorrow as agreed."

"What about Elsa? You can't bring her. Things are *hot* here."

"No. I have a friend who will watch her."

"A friend?" I asked him doubtfully.

"My girlfriend. She helps me research cases."

"I'm not at the Sleeping Well anymore. I'm at the Silver Dollar, exit seventy-two on local roads."

"I'll see you early in the morning," he said. "Get some rest."

~

I couldn't sleep at all. My head was spinning with all the events since I'd first set foot in Mapletown after my aunt's death. Was this a conspiracy? Or was it just a ruthless murder motivated by greed and hatred? I tossed and turned all night long.

My childhood ghosts visited and exposed my deepest memories, long blocked away within my consciousness. The image of my mother's beloved cat came to mind. It made me shudder with terror.

Driven by jealousy and anger, I had killed the defenseless cat. I put the dead animal in a box and left it at the door for my mother to find. I had felt immense pleasure in causing her pain. She was feeling the same pain that she had caused me—payback time, mommy dearest.

I felt vile for the longest time afterward and blamed her. The last time I saw her, I maliciously told her in detail how much I had enjoyed killing her cat, her precious golden-eyed cat. She had looked at me with horror.

When I met Sophia, I realized that I had not only hurt the cat and my mother but scarred my soul forever. I thought of confiding in her, but I remembered the horror in my mother's eyes and resisted. The idea of seeing Sophia's eyes looking at me like that had congealed the blood in my veins. I managed to put the memory into the darkest corner of my consciousness.

I had to live with the knowledge that once I killed, even in the name of revenge, that hideous act would stay with me the rest of my life.

I went to the bathroom to splash cold water on my clammy face. It was very important for me to vindicate my aunt's death; I would also be vindicating myself for the horrible act I did to Stripes, my mother's cat—I could only hope.

I directed my mind to more pleasant thoughts. Today was January 2; did Sophia say they were coming back on the second? I wondered if she was happy. And what kind of thoughts she had about me. Did she ever think about me? I really wanted to see her again and apologize for the pain I gave her.

But my stubborn thoughts returned to my mother. I would always regret the feeling of emptiness I had about her. I could have made other choices—for instance, asked her why she had such bad feelings toward me. I could have tried to love her instead of being scared of her. God only knows how much I'd longed to be held in her loving arms when I was feeling scared or lonely, to hear her comforting voice telling me that everything was going to be OK.

A lonely tear rolled down my face. Her cat had been the object of her love and her warmth. How could a young kid understand that? How could a grown-up man deal with that?

I drifted into a restless, terror-stricken sleep. I was covered in blood, stabbing Stripes over and over again. I saw my aunt dying the same way, stabbed and beaten repeatedly with a blunt instrument. Now my eyes were filled with horror, just as my mother's had been.

I felt Victor's sinister presence. He had a blunt object in his hands and brandished it at me. "Aunt Millie would never know that Victor is evil." She couldn't answer, she was choking on her blood, and I wasn't able to help her. I was running to escape from danger.

"Forgive me, please forgive me," I was saying when I woke up from my visit to hell.

I lay awake in the dark, too afraid to turn on the light and see the dead sitting in the room.

I was drenched in sweat, and so was the bed where I lay. I moved to the other side of the bed.

I thought about Elsa, and I felt sorry. Maybe she would have been OK if she had stayed in Mapletown. Trying to protect her, I had forced her to go away, and she almost died. Angelloni loved her, didn't he? He wasn't going to hurt her. He had been angry and jealous when he threatened her.

I ruined the people who came close to me.

I made a vow to turn my life around if I lived through this horrifying ordeal.

49

A rap on the door awakened me. I glanced at my watch on the night table: seven in the morning. It had to be Andrew. I peeked through the window; yeah, it was Andrew. I was beginning to like this guy; he was punctual and reliable.

I opened the door and let him in. He had two cups of coffee and breakfast rolls.

"Where is your Jeep?" he asked as I walked toward the restroom to freshen up.

"The bartender at the Living Dead, remember him?" I said. "I traded cars with him last night." I took a swig of the coffee; it was so hot it scalded my mouth.

"Be careful, the coffee is hot," he said, and then asked, "Why did you do such a stupid thing?"

"Angelloni, Jacob, and Miller know that I drive a Jeep," I said. "They were looking for me, according to Jacob."

"And why did you change motels?"

"When I came back from the bar, they were waiting for me at the Sleeping Well," I said. "If I had been in my Jeep…" I trailed off.

I suddenly remembered the news on the truck found in Los Angeles. "Andrew, I need to talk to you. Please hear me out."

My face must have looked serious. Andrew sat still and paid attention. "I'm all ears," he said.

I thought awhile, but the words snagged in my throat. I realized that once I started talking, there was no coming back.

I looked at him. His hands were folded in front, and he was staring hard at them.

I cleared my throat and confessed the two murders to him. His mouth dropped open in astonishment. It's not easy to tell someone you're an accomplice to murder.

He moved his lips, but no words came out. He cleared his throat, then looked fixedly at my eyes. "You need to go to the cops," he said in a grave voice, "before they come to get you."

"I have wanted to do that, but I feared for my life," I interjected.

"Do you know where Clem is?" he asked. "He may corroborate your story."

I shook my head no. I was apprehensive about going to the cops. I knew I was an accomplice because I hadn't reported the murders.

"Sam, you are really in a lot of trouble. If the cops don't believe your story, I would find this Clem guy."

"Thanks, Andrew." That's all I managed to say.

"Let's go to the cemetery before we go to the police station, OK?" he said. "Do you have the map?"

"Yes. We need to go get it at the bank."

"By the way, Sophia and Steve are back," he said.

That brought a smile to my face. Everything else looked ill-omened and menacing. The thought of going to jail sent distress through my whole being. I was quiet and remote.

"Are you OK? You seem pensive," he asked when he saw that my face was frozen by the weight of the decision I would have to make.

"Do you know what the punishment for not reporting a crime is?" I asked.

"I don't know for sure. It depends on your attorney."

"Is Steve a good attorney?"

"He is," he said. "But I think you would be better off with a local attorney."

"I got one! What about Angelloni?" I said sarcastically.

"Seriously, you will need one when you go to the police station."

"I need to get this entire ordeal over with."

~

When we arrived at the Riverdale bank, Andrew waited in the car while I went inside to get the map. Andrew was on the phone when I got back in the car.

"It was my girlfriend. Elsa will be released tomorrow."

I nodded and smiled lightly. I showed him the map. "Now what?" I said.

He took the map and examined it awhile. "Let's go back to the cemetery," he said.

"Should we go to the cops instead?" I asked. "We cannot do anything with the map."

He didn't say a thing. He became quiet, as if he was thinking things through.

"Maybe Miller can get an order to exhume the Augustus grave," I said. "What do you think is there?"

"Evidence," he said in a matter-of-fact tone of voice. "Nobody will ever suspect that other objects can be interred in a grave."

"Yeah, nobody will ever look there."

"Call Jacob. He can go to the police with you for now."

"Why Jacob?" I inquired.

"Because if he, has something to do with the killings, we'll get him there."

"You should come, too," I said. Then I thought of Elsa and grew concerned. "Elsa gets out tomorrow. Where will she go?"

"My girlfriend will stay with her until I get back," he said, giving me a reassuring pat on my shoulder.

I understood why I was so worried about Miss Harris. A few people who had been in contact with me had been hurt, and I had done nothing to help them; this time I was doing something to help her.

~

I decided not to call Jacob on the telephone. I would talk to him when we got home in another fifteen minutes. I felt uncomfortable asking him to accompany me to the police station, but I thought Andrew was right. He had wanted to talk to me last night with urgency, and I had ignored him; I hoped he would not turn me down and would come with me to see Miller.

It still bothered me that I'd never noticed he was left-handed. It also bothered me that I would have to look into his eyes and convey to him that everything was OK and that I was retaining him as an attorney. I doubted that I would be able to hide the true emotions I had about him.

Andrew sensed the apprehension I was feeling and gave me another pat on my arm for encouragement. My hands relaxed the grip I had on the driving wheel; my knuckles regained their normal color.

"We'll get through this one," he said in a reassuring tone.

I nodded. "When are you going back to Frisco?" I asked.

"As soon as you get through this mess."

"Thanks. Do you have other cases?"

"Yes. Right now, I have three cases and a continuous one that I call a 'Nut.'"

"A nut?"

"Yeah a nut case. You see I have to see my ex-wife when I pick up my kid, and she is a serious nut case," he said in a Sherlock Holmes-like tone of voice.

We both laughed. Laughter was such a good tension reliever.

I noticed more traffic than usual as I turned the corner to reach my place.

Andrew and I exchanged glances. There were police cars and TV trucks parked outside my house.

"They are here to arrest me." I parked the car across the street.

"Call Jacob," Andrew said.

~

I was shaking when I dialed Jacob's number. My voice snagged and wouldn't come out; Andrew took the phone away from me.

"Jacob? What's going on?" he asked.

I could hear Jacob's voice. "Who is this?" he asked.

"This is Andrew, Sam's friend. Remember?"

"Yes. From San Francisco, right?"

"Yes. Why are the cops and the news people here?"

"Where are you?" he asked.

"Here, outside."

"It's Sam. He is dead," he said. Andrew motioned me to keep silent by placing his index finger across his mouth.

I was feeling terrible, but I did not feel dead. I was puzzled.

"What do you mean? I just saw him."

"He was found dead in his Jeep early this morning," he said. "I tried to warn him last night, but he wouldn't listen."

"Jacob, listen to me—"

Jacob cut him off in the middle of his sentence. "Angelloni and Miller were looking for him about a fucking map," he said. "His head was bashed in just like his aunt."

"Is Sergeant Miller there?" Andrew asked Jacob.

"Yes. I'm a person of interest."

"Are you under arrest?"

"Not yet. I have to go to the station to give my statement."

"Jacob, I need to see you. I have something to show you," Andrew said. "Can you come?"

"Where?" Jacob asked.

"Do you know where the Silver Dollar Motel is?"

"Yes, the one on county road seventy-two?

"Yeah, come alone."

"I'll try to sneak out."

~

We drove back to the Silver Dollar. I was devastated.

The bartender was a victim of mistaken identity; it was supposed to be me dead. I felt like an assassin. I had killed him. Why in hell did I trade cars with him? He was another ghost to add to my nightmares.

The day was overcast, with fat, heavy, black clouds. Fear was in the air, and I was paralyzed by it. I couldn't move; I couldn't run. It was as if a wet, weighty blanket had been thrown on me. Andrew was quiet as well.

What in the hell had happened? Why in hell had they killed him? Why in hell had they wanted to kill me?

We stopped for coffee. We both needed to get back on track and not lose our heads. We needed to stay a step ahead.

"How are you doing, Sam?" Andrew asked. He pulled a flask from the glove compartment and poured some in my coffee.

"I'm feeling numb all over," I said.

"Sam, listen to me. It was not your fault."

I didn't know whether I believed that. The coffee felt good going down my throat. I extended the cup, and he poured some more.

"I wonder how this ordeal will end," I muttered in a low raspy voice. I took another a swig.

~

We arrived at the Silver Dollar, and Andrew went to check the room again. We turned on the TV to see if we could catch the news and learn more about my supposed death. Andrew's phone started to ring.

"Hello." He answered almost instinctively. I couldn't hear who he was talking to. "No. no, he is not dead. He is here with me," he said.

They were talking about me. I wondered who he was talking to.

"Sophia, calm down. I'm not lying," he said emphatically. "I understand how you feel, but here, talk to him." He passed his phone to me.

"Hello?" I quickly said.

It was Sophia, and she was having problems accepting that I was not dead.

"Mistaken identity," I said in a low, monotone voice ridden with guilt and shame.

She said she was watching the news to see what had happened while they were gone. When the newswoman talked about the murder at Mapletown, she had said the victim's name was Sam W. Stone. She had immediately called Andrew. She wanted me to give her details. Why did that man have his Jeep? Had it been stolen? Was it about his aunt's murder?

I didn't want to sound cruel by telling her that I had traded cars with the victim. "Sophia, I don't know anything about it. I'm as astounded as you," I said mildly.

I promised her I would call as soon as we had more information. I told her we were on our way to the police station to clear things up. We said our good-byes, and I passed the phone back to Andrew.

"Sophia, we will keep you posted," he said.

"Another call is coming," he said. "Hello?"

I tried to get to the news again. Stupid commercial, I thought gloomily. Then the young-looking field reporter was back again. Why did all these reporters have the same hairdo?

"We are here in Mapletown, a small town in Mendocino County, where families move in attracted by its tranquility. And yet another horrible murder has been committed, on another of its residents. Mrs. Mildred C. Wilmot was murdered in October of last year. That's when her nephew, Sam W. Stone, moved here—Wait, here is Sergeant Miller. Sergeant Miller, what can you tell us?" the inexperienced reporter asked.

Miller looked annoyed. "We don't have any information as of yet." *Police babble.*

"Do you have any suspects?" she asked.

"Jacob Sinclair is a potential person of interest, but he is nowhere to be found."

"Is this linked to Mildred C. Wilmot's murder?"

"Like I said, we don't have any links."

"Mr. Stone was the heir to Mrs. Wilmot, was he not?"

"We still don't know the cause of this tragedy, but we will get the perpetrator or perpetrators. And that's all I have for now,"

"That was Sergeant Miller from the Mapletown Police Department. This is Allyson Craig reporting to you live from Mapletown. We will keep you updated." She signed off with her big white smile. *They really look alike.*

Andrew was done with his phone conversation by now. "That was my girlfriend and Elsa on the phone," he said. "Elsa was hysterical when she heard the news about your death."

We heard a car parking outside. Andrew peeked out; a taxi was dropping Jacob off.

Andrew opened the door and waved him in. I just sat on the bed.

Jacob's eyes were as big as saucers when he saw me.

"Relax, Jacob, you are not seeing a ghost," I said dryly.

"I-I don't understand," he said. "I ID's your body at the medical examiner's this morning."

"Sorry to disappoint you," I said cynically.

"What in the hell happened?" he asked.

I repeated the story for the fourth time. The more I did, the less guilty I felt.

"Good. You should come with me to see Miller," he said.

Those are the plans, moron, I thought. "Exactly. That's why we called you," I said. Andrew and I exchanged glances.

"There's more," Andrew told Jacob.

Jacob sat down. From the look on our faces, he must have concluded it was going to be long. Andrew motioned for me to tell him about the basement murders.

Jacob looked astounded and burdened. His mouth was in a tight line, and his fingers were curled into fists. The rest of his body was tense. Jacob obviously hoped I'd see the potential threat, and he'd prepared himself for action. "You are over your head, Sam."

I nodded slowly and asked, "Who are 'we'?"

Jacob didn't respond.

"Are you a leftie?"

My unrelated question surprised him. He didn't answer immediately. "Are you referring to the article in the newspaper?" Jacob asked sharply. "Your aunt's murder? The cut on her throat?" He had a trace of annoyance in his voice. Then he fixed his eyes on mine and asked, "You think I killed your aunt?"

"That would help us," Andrew said. "We need to regroup."

Jacob and I ignored Andrew. "Yeah, Jacob, and that has been bothering me."

"Let me tell you about your aunt and me," he said softly.

I was dying to know how my aunt had been involved with this clown. "Is this going to be long?" I asked in a serious tone.

Jacob was sitting in the only chair in the dank room. Andrew sat down on the other end of the bed.

"Five years ago your aunt came to me. I was the district attorney." He was breathing heavily, and sweat was hanging from his brows. "She said she had retained Angelloni as her estate-planning attorney a year before." He paused for a moment to take a drink from his paper cup. His body language indicated he was on edge and fretful.

He continued with his narrative. Angelloni had been pressuring my aunt to lend him her house, since she lived in a huge house, to store stuff. She didn't want any part of associating with him other than as attorney and client.

Angelloni found out my aunt was related to the infamous Ciprianno family. He threatened to expose her relationship to the community if she continued to refuse. She had moved to Mapletown to put distance between herself and the family and had become a pillar in her new community. Angelloni pressed her so much that she ended up accepting his proposal.

She told Jacob that when she found out from Max, the driver, they were dealing with stolen goods; she became afraid that nobody would believe her because by that time her bank statements were showing large amounts of money deposited to her account. She had become Angelloni's associate—, which Angelloni used to keep blackmailing her.

Jacob instructed her to go along and to keep him posted about the activities developing at her house. Which she did. She suspected money laundering and counterfeiting. Jacob had to notify the feds. He was the liaison between my aunt and the feds.

"She was scared enough. Then somehow, it leaked out, and your aunt was brutally murdered, and I somehow ended up losing my job, and my career went down the drain. Your aunt couldn't find out who the main guy was. She didn't think it was Angelloni. He was getting his orders on his cell.

"I feel responsible for your aunt's death," he concluded with lot of emotion.

"What now?" Andrew asked.

Jacob glanced at the two of us for a moment and slowly shook his head. "I'm working with the feds now," he said, showing us his badge. "We still don't have any hard evidence to bring down this ring."

Then he fixed his eyes on me and shook his head. "I hate to ask you, Sam, but I think you could help us," he said and waited for my answer.

"You want to put me in harm's way like you did my aunt?" I asked. Now I waited for an answer.

He thought awhile, then lifted his eyes to meet mine. "Don't you want to catch your aunt's killers?" He knew my Achilles heel.

I guessed that I had gone too far down that road to go back. Jacob and Andrew waited for my answer.

"What do you want me to do?" I said quietly. I had resigned myself to the idea that I was a dead man anyway.

"Your aunt said she had hidden valuable evidence—"

He stopped when Andrew interrupted him. "The map."

I nodded.

Jacob smiled. "You got it?" he asked me.

I nodded. "I'll help you, but these are my conditions: charges in Max and Louisa's murders will be dropped against me, and I'll keep the monies and property in my aunt's accounts."

"I don't think that's a problem. Your aunt earned every penny, and as for the murders, you were a victim as well."

Andrew was a witness to our agreement.

"Does Sergeant Miller know you are with the feds?" I asked.

Jacob shook his head no.

We worked out the details of our plan. Jacob knew the corruption was at City Hall. He would go to the police station for questioning, as ordered by Miller. Pretending that we didn't know Jacob was there, Andrew and I would show up an hour later.

I was to stop at Angelloni's office before going to the police station to tell him I was turning the map over to Miller.

Andrew would wait in the car. If I didn't come out of Angelloni's office within ten minutes, he would go in looking for me.

~

Angelloni was on the telephone when I walked in. He looked at me as if I were a ghost and said, "Guess who just walked into my office?" I reached his desk at the moment he said, "Sam Stone, you moron!" Click.

I pushed the conversation off. I was cocky. "Your morons got the wrong guy, asshole. I just wanted to inform you that the game is over. I'm going to see Miller right now and give him the map." I turned around and left.

I could hear him speed-dial to make a phone call. Boy, he was a heavy breather. I slowed down to eavesdrop. It seemed like I waited an eternity.

"S-S-Sam is not dead." He sounded scared. "He is going to give the map to Miller." He was breathing heavily. "He just left."

There was a pause, then, "S-sorry, sir. OK, I'll see you at the police station." Angelloni had gotten his orders.

Andrew and I would sit in the car until we saw Angelloni drive away in his shining car toward the police department. I glanced at my watch; we were thirty minutes from making our entrance. Angelloni would have to sit and wait too.

Twenty minutes went by, then Angelloni came out of his office. He made a phone call. Even from a distance, we could see how restless he was; he was pacing.

As soon as he arrived at the police station, he went inside. We entered the station on Angelloni's heels. He looked agitated and sweaty.

I went straight to the speakerphone. "I would like to see Sergeant Miller."

The female voice said, "He is busy at the moment."

He was still interrogating Jacob. "Can you please tell him that Sam Stone is here?"

We didn't wait long. The door opened and there stood Sergeant Miller, looking at me, astonished. He held the door open and motioned for us to come in. "Shit. Who is the dead guy?" he asked, scratching his head.

"He is—was—the bartender at the Living Dead Bar," I said. "I'm here to give my declaration."

"Son of a bitch," he muttered. "I have someone here who will be happy to see you."

He led us to the interrogation room. Jacob was sitting with a recorder in front of him and a cup of black coffee. Miller motioned me to sit down; Andrew was asked to step out.

"Can you explain what's going on?" Miller asked me. A detective opened the door and told Miller he had an urgent phone call. He told the detective to take a message.

The detective motioned for him to take the call. Miller excused himself and stepped out.

He looked pissed off when he came back. "Do you have something to turn in?" he asked.

I looked at Jacob, indicating it was his turn to speak.

"Sergeant Miller, my client here has a piece of evidence to turn in, in exchange for his aunt's name to be absolved of any wrongdoings, the same as his."

"First tell me how this poor devil ended up in your Jeep," he said.

I told him about the trade we had made. He shook his head and laughed. I also told him about the two murders that took place in the basement.

"Now the map," he said, extending his hand.

I produced the map and put it in his hand. He took it and waved it in front of the double- sided mirror on the wall.

The door slowly opened, and Angelloni appeared. Miller gave him the map. Smiling, Angelloni took it and left.

"Sorry, I got orders to hand it over to him," Miller said.

"Do you know who gave the order?" Jacob asked.

Miller shook his head.

"You guys can leave," he said in a defeated voice. "I tried to find the corruption."

"Can you find out who gave the order? It is very important," I said. Jacob confirmed it.

"I think I can. Wait here." He got up and disappeared.

He came back after a while. "It came from one of the judges," he said.

"Judge O'Hara!" Jacob interjected.

"Here, your friend left a note for you." He handed me a neatly folded Post-it. "I went after Angelloni," said the note.

50

Miller, Jacob, and I ran toward Judge O'Hara's chambers. Andrew was talking with someone there. As we got closer, we could see it was the real Rita Malone.

Jacob pointed and said to me, "That's Rita Malone."

I nodded.

Andrew came to meet us. "Angelloni went inside the chambers of Judge O'Hara," he said, almost out of breath. Miller ordered Rita Malone to open the judge's chambers.

We busted in.

"What in hell?" O'Hara said. He still had the map in his hands. Angelloni held an order to exhume Augustus's grave, signed by O'Hara.

It became apparent who the boss was.

Jacob put out all the stops. "Judge O'Hara, you are under arrest." Jacob looked nervous. He had perspiration on his upper lip. I hoped he was right.

"Get the hell out of my chambers." Judge O'Hara's voice was like thunder.

Sergeant Miller approached the judge with his handcuffs ready.

"On what grounds?" the judge asked.

"What about conspiracy to murder, extortion, prostitution, stolen goods?" Jacob said.

"You have no proof," the judge said.

"Yes, I do," Jacob said, taking the order from Angelloni's hand and waving it in front of the judge's face.

Jacob gave the exhumation order to Miller. "We'll see you at the cemetery."

We scrambled to leave.

Miller handcuffed the judge and Angelloni, then recited the Miranda rights to them.

~

We were at Augustus's graveside, waiting for the casket to be disinterred. We all were silent and engrossed by the activity. The casket was finally disinterred and placed in the coroner's hearse to be taken to the medical examiner.

It was like a dream. A light drizzle was falling on the black open umbrellas of the witnesses. The afternoon was dark, but I knew that light was on the way. Andrew put his arm across my shoulders and whispered, "Your problems are about to be over."

I was overtaken by emotion; and shuddered from head to toe.

Jacob patted me on the back and said, "Good job, Sam."

We rode in silence to the coroner's office. I was allowed to see the coffin opened. We wore surgical masks and gowns just in case there were gases or spores of human remains. We stood in silence beside the gurney. The stillness of the place gave me goose bumps; the smell was very strong. *That's how death smells like,* I thought. That made me gag.

The casket seals were removed, and the top was carefully lifted. We all gasped at the sight.

Counterfeiting molds for different denominations of money and a large ledger with names and dated events that took place at my aunt's house were in the casket, as were disgusting pictures of minors performing vile acts with O'Hara and other important political figures at parties given at my aunt's house for important city officials.

Sergeant Miller issued an arrest warrant for Mrs. Angelloni.

Miller was radioed that Mrs. Angelloni had been found dead at her mansion. She had committed suicide. An officer at the scene told Sergeant Miller that the bullet had entered her left temple.

~

I didn't want to stay for the judge's and Angelloni's trial. I'd had enough. I just wanted to sit quietly and watch the fan in the living room spin. I don't know how long I sat.

My mind was calm and at peace.

I got up, grabbed a duffel bag, got in my new Jeep, and drove away. I stopped at the florist shop and got a bouquet of white roses. I drove to the cemetery to place the roses on Aunt Millie's tomb. "Thank you, Auntie," I said with a prayer-like reverence.

Silent tears rolled down my face as I left her last resting place.

~

I arrived in San Francisco at around five o'clock. I called Andrew. We agreed to meet at Fisherman's Wharf; Elsa was to come, too. I was nervous about breaking the news to her about Angelloni. The good news was that she could go back to Mapletown.

I thought about calling Sophia to wish her the best in her relationship with Steve.

I glanced at my watch—Aunt Millie's gift, I warmly thought. Then I looked up and saw Elsa walking briskly toward me with open arms. She embraced me and gave me a long kiss on the lips. *Wow!*

I told her the good and the bad news. She didn't seem to care.

"You can go back to Mapletown. It is safe," I said.

"No. We are staying here. San Francisco is a great city to fall in love in."

I saw how the sun's twilight golden glow reflected in the sea and looked magical. *I could fall in love in San Francisco again.* Nevertheless, I was happy to have survived Mapletown!

The End

www.ingramcontent.com/pod-product-compliance
Lightning Source LLC
Chambersburg PA
CBHW070854250626
47159CB00003B/1062